TIMEBANGERS VOL. 1

ONE DOES NOT SIMPLY WALK INTO TUDOR

IVERY KIRK
LUNA TEAGUE

RÊVE DE VIE PUBLISHERS
KANSAS CITY

TimeBangers, Vol. 1: One Does Not Simply Walk into Tudor
www.timebangers.com

Copyright © 2015 by Ivery Kirk & Luna Teague
www.iverykirk.com
www.lunateague.com

Rêve de Vie Publishers LLC, Kansas City, KS
www.revedeviepublishers.com

Cover illustration by Bryan Ward.
www.bryaneward.com

First publication: Jul 2015

10 9 8 7 6 5 4 3 2 1 15

ISBN-13: 978-1-942957-00-3
ISBN-10: 1-942957-00-9

TO LOVE AND FRIENDSHIP

WHICH MAKE US GREATER
THAN THE SUM OF OUR PARTS

ACKNOWLEDGMENTS

Thank you to every person who, when presented with our idea for a comedy adventure series about two women and their time traveling sexcapades, reacted with generous enthusiasm.

Thank you to author Sandra Moran, who gave us the advice and the impetus we needed to begin this adventure.

Thank you to our significant others, who did their best to answer our litany of questions on subjects such as what men think of pussy farts and cunnilingus, and who provided unflinching moral support for the duration of this project.

Thank you to the members of the DHS writing group, for their support of this idea during its infancy.

Thank you also to the makers of the Bota Box, whose affordable products were an integral part of our creative process.

Special thanks to Werner Herzog.

Time is of all losses the most irrecuperable, for it can never be redeemed for no manner price nor prayer.

— HENRY VIII OF ENGLAND

INDEX OF EROTIC SCENES

Because sometimes you feel like taking your time, settling in, and enjoying a story…

…and sometimes you want to skip right to the fun bits without having to guess where they're hidden!

DRAMATIS PERSONAE

BETH BIRD, divorcée and scholar of history. Blow job queen.

TAWNY COPENHAGEN, scientist and inventor of time travel. Omnisexual unicorn.

JULIET BIRD, daughter of Beth. Kindergartener. Pony slaver.

MRS. HYDE, a hag.

LANCE, a parent from school.

HIS MAJESTY KING HENRY TUDOR VIII, a man with a 52-inch chest circumference.

HIS GRACE HENRY FITZROY, DUKE OF RICHMOND AND SOMERSET, acknowledged bastard son of Henry VIII.

LORD CHANCELLOR OF THE EXCHEQUER THOMAS CROMWELL, chief advisor and dogsbody to Henry VIII, misogynist, destroyer of hats.

LADY CATHERINE WILLOUGHBY, a lady of gentle birth.

JANE SEYMOUR, future Queen of England.

HER MAJESTY QUEEN ANNE BOLEYN, current Queen of England.

SIR FRANCIS BRYAN, a man with a sexy eyepatch.

FIELD PROTOCOLS

ONE. Do not conduct research alone. Research participants should work in pairs and each participant should be aware of the other's location and physical safety at all times.

TWO. Use a prophylactic for all research endeavors. Conduct visual examination of subject's mucus membranes before commencing research procedures. Do not participate in research if there is any doubt as to whether subject might carry an infection.

THREE. Avoid use of intoxicants when working in the field. Researchers should not consume drugs or more than two alcoholic beverages during the research process, and should monitor each other for impairment. Researchers should maintain careful custody of beverages at all times, and preferably should use a drink container with a lid to prevent introduction of undesirable intoxicants. Before accepting drinks from a potential subject, request subject to taste the beverage. Do not continue research if subject refuses.

FOUR. Maintain confidentiality of subjects and of project at all times. When discussing research, refer to subjects by number to protect confidentiality. To prevent psychological harm to subjects, do not allow subject to believe that relations undertaken as part of research procedures indicate an exclusive emotional relationship between participant and subject.

PARTE THE FIRSTE

PROLOGUE

IN WHICH THE READER IS SHOWN
THINGS SHE DOESN'T YET UNDERSTAND
BUT SHOULD READ ANYWAY

THESE PEOPLE ARE SNAKES. SAME AS IN MY OWN TIME. JUST SNAKES.
Just. Snakes.

Tawny had repeated her mantra about a hundred times already as she stood outside the receiving area, but it wasn't helping. She was still too afraid to face the court.

Come on. You can do this. It's. Just. Fucking. Snakes. The image of a snake orgy popped into her mind at this, and she stifled a laugh. Fucking snakes, indeed.

She had been about to stride forth and reveal herself to the court of King Henry VIII in all her resplendent glory, but just as she approached the elaborate archway that led to the courtyard where the King received his royal visitors, she heard the voices outside and stopped dead in her tracks.

The accent was all wrong.

She couldn't make out any actual words in their conversation. Whatever they were saying, it came out in a bewildering jumble of Scottish brogue, pirate growl, and Southern drawl with a hint of French. She'd turned around and pressed herself face-first against the tapestried wall, and that was where she was now— eyes closed, fists clenched, every unbearably awkward social interaction she'd ever endured playing on repeat in her head.

Social anxiety could not be allowed to ruin this, her greatest hour of triumph.

Tawny took a deep breath, counted to four, then exhaled, counting down this time. All of her usual methods of relaxation—even her snakes mantra—had failed her now, just when she needed them most.

Originally, she'd thought the hard part would be just getting the damn machine going. Then she finished the data modeling and realized that the hard part would be working up the courage to step in and pull the handle, knowing she was the first human test subject.

Now that she was here, though, she understood that everything she'd assumed about time travel was wrong. She hadn't gotten to the actual hard part yet. The sixteenth century was just like the twenty-first century—people were the hard part. The people just through this doorway, even though they weren't speaking English in any form she understood, were just like everyone from her own time.

It wasn't fair. All along, while she'd congratulated herself on her bravery, the real test of her mettle had been yet to come.

Or, she wondered, was it more correct to say the real test had been over five hundred years ago?

Tawny shook her head, trying to focus on the task at hand, trying to regain her nerve.

They're just snakes.

The *just snakes* mantra had evolved from her first major *a-ha!* moment regarding human relations, which had come embarrassingly late in her adolescence, during a nature documentary she'd seen in high school titled *Reptiles Are Our Friends*. In this educational classic, a male narrator explained in a patient voice that snakes, no matter their scary appearance, primarily attacked out of fear. Her teenage brain, mired in a toxic brew of neurotic dread of—and hormonal longing for—human contact, had connected the *National Geographic* dots thusly: that in social situations, most people were like snakes—not because they were inherently treacherous, but because they were as afraid of you (or more!) as you were of them. Most of them were too preoccupied with their own snake stuff to even bother judging you. Treat them with respect and care, and they wouldn't strike.

This wasn't true all the time—people, unlike snakes, sometimes attacked for sport—but after that epiphany, repeating *just snakes* to herself helped to calm the raging seas of social anxiety that had surged within her all throughout her life.

And yet, here she was, tongue-tied and frozen in place like a bug in amber, as stiff and awkward as she'd ever been in high school.

Fear is the obliviator, she reminded herself. *Fear is the silent enemy that kills the soul.*

Now she was truly regressing. Tawny had found a copy of *Sand Lords* as a little girl, and, intrigued by its cover, secretly read the whole book under her covers over the course of a week. Impressed by the wisdom of its young heroine, Paula Treides, she had armored herself against the world in snippets of it and other science fiction ever since.

I will stand before my fear. I will let it wash over me like a stone within a rushing river.

And I will bang the everloving shit out of Henry, Eighth of his Name, by the Grace of God, King of England and France, Defender of the Faith, Lord of Ireland, and of the Church of England and of Ireland Supreme Head.

She could definitely handle the supreme head part.

ONE

IN WHICH BETH IS INTRODUCED AS A WOMAN OF DIMINISHED CIRCUMSTANCES

CONNOR STOOD IN THE OPEN DOOR, SILHOUETTED AGAINST THE BLAZING sunset. *His flaming golden-red locks blew gently in the evening breeze. Home at last from the war. The long struggle with the southern fairies had claimed many of the local McDobber clansmen, but her man had returned safely. Fiona said a silent prayer of thanks as she stood transfixed by the sight of him.*

He crossed to her in a single long-legged stride and folded her into a passionate embrace. "Mae cannie wee thing," he said with feeling. He twisted a lock of her shining raven black tresses in his fingers. "Hae I missed ye—"

His words cut off as she stood on tipped toes to kiss him, and he caught her in his strong arms, meeting her desire with his own as he intoxicated her with kisses. Words no longer semed important. She felt the familiar tingle surge through her body. It had been so long since she'd felt his touch.

"I canna—I canna wait long," Connor managed, his voice husky. "I must take ye now." She met his eyes for one long moment, her hunger matching his fire, and then his hands were everywhere, pulling at the strings on her bodice, skimming her straining nipples, sending pleasure shooting through her.

He pulled her to him then, and she felt his hard length against her, even through the fabric that separated them.

The bed was too far. They tumbled to the floor together, stripping layers of clothes away from each other, and he took her in another passionate kiss.

"Connor," she begged, looking into the depths of his brown eyes, "dinna make me wait any longer."

She felt him between her legs in another instant and cradled him there, savoring the feel of him against her velvety sex, and in another moment she gasped as he sheathed himself to the hilt.

"Is that what ye want?" he asked in a low, intense voice. "Me to ride ye?"

Fiona could only nod in reply, and he bent his head then, taking her again and again with long strokes that sent waves of pleasure washing through her until she could feel her need reach its breaking point. She—

"Moooooomm! Mommmmy! Are you awake?"

For a long moment, Beth froze, considering whether she could still salvage her chance at a "waves of pleasure" kind of morning, then sighed and set down the book. "Just a second, honey! Mommy's… getting dressed." She switched off the Magic Wand and stowed it out of sight under the bed.

She dressed in a hurry, and a few minutes later, opened the door and almost jumped out of her skin when Jules yelled, "Boo!" and leapt out from where she'd flattened herself against the wall outside Beth's room, lying in wait for her quarry. Some child at school had taught her daughter this gag a few weeks ago, and after thirty or forty iterations Jules still hadn't grasped the concept of declining returns.

Her daughter shrieked with joy and waved her off-brand Barbie doll at her before jumping into the air and landing heavily on both feet. "Mommy, put her pants on for me! Please," she added, favoring Beth with her most winning smile.

Beth took the doll in her hands, inwardly cursing whatever sadistic bastards at the toy companies had decided first to design a fashion doll with soft vinyl legs and second to sell tight ankle-length pants for said doll, which children would require parental help to put on. Every time. Multiple times a day. The doll's hair was sticky with something—who knew what—Beth's hair spray, apple juice, something worse, perhaps.

"Here you go." She handed it back.

Jules brandished the doll at her. "She's a knight! In King Arthur's court."

Well, actually, sweetie…

Beth stifled the urge to explain to her daughter that the history of female knighthood was a bit complicated.

And that there was significant dispute as to whether King Arthur even existed, or was simply a twelfth-century invention concocted by people who wanted England to have a historical tradition of courtly love.

And that if he was real, there was only limited evidence to suggest his women-at-arms wore neon pink and green spandex body suits.

"That sounds fun, honey," Beth said. She suspected that good mothers didn't "well-actually" their preschoolers, and while she might be underemployed, divorced, and a grad school dropout, she thought she might still do okay as a mom. After all, it was easier being a single mom to a five-year-old girl than a married one to a five-year-old girl plus a thirty-five-year-old man.

Their life was decent, even without Dan. She had food on the table, reliable—if not affordable—child care, and a daughter still young enough to think that "camping" in the living room every night was fun. Sometimes on weekend nights, they made a tent over the hide-a-bed with a sheet and crept under it with flashlights and a host of dolls and stuffed animals, telling each other stories until they fell asleep.

So while it got a little lonely on occasion, in some ways Beth didn't mind how things had worked out.

"Let's get you ready for school," she said. "You can tell me about King Arthur's court in the car."

"—SO I NEED YOU TO CALL FUCKING PaperPride AND TELL THEM WE aren't paying for this shit pile they're calling a paper shipment," Beth's boss said. "Tell these assholes that if they don't want a lawsuit on their hands they'd better come through with a replacement. Tell them—tell them I'll destroy their stupid asses if they fuck with me on this. I'm serious, I will punch fuck them into an early grave. Use those words exactly. We're not paying additional freight, either."

Beth nodded and wrote *Ted will punch fuck them* on her notepad, then glanced up at him.

Ted gave her a look that suggested he didn't think she'd taken down enough of his wisdom. *Into an early grave,* she added.

"I'm serious, Beth," he said. "Write that down word for word."

She thought for a second, then wrote, *Ted, noted pencil-dick, will write PaperPride an unfavorable Yelp review.*

"Good," he said. "Let me know what they say."

Back at her desk, Beth punched numbers on the phone keypad, skimming her notes as it rang the other end.

"PaperPride," a female voice answered.

"Melinda?"

"Yeah, hey, Beth. How are you?"

"Okay, except Ted is freaking out about the last three pallets we got at the warehouse."

"The ones you e-mailed me about? The condensation damage?"

"Yeah. I went down and checked—it looks like it's only the stuff on the outside that's damaged. Anything you guys can do? He practically had a seizure when receiving told him about it."

"Let me see if Mark is in. If he's not I might not have an answer until Monday. Do you have the purchase order handy?"

"Yeah, just a sec—" Beth shook the mouse to wake up her computer. "Let me get in the system and check real fast." Her cell phone buzzed violently on the desk. It was Mrs. Hyde from the preschool. "Oh, shit, sorry. I have to take this, it's my kid's daycare. Can I e-mail you the PO in a few?"

"Sure, no worries."

Beth hung up her desk phone and took a deep breath before answering the call. "Hello?" she whispered, hoping Ted wouldn't hear her taking a personal call. "Jules isn't sick, is she?"

Every time Jules got ill at school, Mrs. Hyde did her best to insinuate that Beth had intentionally smuggled a tiny Patient Zero in with the rest of her flock.

The woman sniffed, actually sniffed, like a sneering villain in a children's movie. "Not as such. It's a behavioral issue, I'm afraid."

Beth's heart sank. She couldn't afford to leave early again this pay period.

"Behavioral issue?" she repeated dumbly.

"It seems Juliet was involved in an altercation."

"What, like a fight? Jules—"

"It appears she bit another child," Mrs. Hyde cut her off. "You're well aware, I'm sure, that this school has a strict anti-violence policy."

"She bit somebody? What happened?"

"I will explain when you are here. Your daughter needs to be collected immediately."

Beth held the line in silence, trying to calm herself enough to use a courteous tone, even though what she really wanted was to punch fuck Mrs. Hyde into an early grave.

Little People's Academy was the one daycare option she could afford, and it had been hard to get a spot there in the first place—it was a special favor from her former mother-in-law, who knew someone at the school and pulled a few strings to get Beth a reduced rate. Mrs. Hyde loved to remind her that Jules only attended the school because of someone else's charity.

"Perhaps Juliet's father could come get her this time," Mrs. Hyde suggested after a short pause.

Beth took another deep breath. At least she only had to put up with this a few more months. In the fall Jules would start Kindergarten, which she hoped would be both cheaper and less likely to provoke her to felony assault.

"He's not available," she said through gritted teeth, resigning herself to leaving work early again. "I'm surprised you don't remember that," she continued in a fake polite tone. "It seems to come up every time we talk. Perhaps you should make a note of it in her student file."

Mrs. Hyde was silent. Apparently Beth's remarks didn't dignify a response. Or perhaps, Beth thought, she was too busy stirring her cauldron and grooming her wart hairs.

"All right, I'm leaving now," Beth told her, tapping out a quick e-mail to Melinda with the information she'd requested. She wheeled backward in her chair and peeked into Ted's office, but he'd already gone to lunch. "Uh, Lynn," she said to her nearest neighbor. "When Ted's back can you tell him I had to leave, but I'm taking care of the PaperPride thing? There's a problem at Jules's daycare."

"Sure," Lynn said. "Anything you want me to add? He'll be pissed."

"I know," Beth said helplessly. "But I don't have anybody else who can go pick her up."

"Don't worry," Lynn said. "I'll run interference here. Ted will cool down about it by next week. Well, as much as Ted ever cools down about things. Don't let this spoil your special weekend, 'kay?"

Beth gave her a grateful nod and hiked her purse up over her shoulder.

The humid warmth of late May closed in around her as she hurried to her car, phone in hand. She wrenched open the driver's door to her old Toyota, leaning back to avoid the trapped heat that rushed forth. The air conditioning sputtered when she turned it on and she heard a strange knocking sound from the engine compartment that stopped when she turned it off. Well… windows down it was. It would cool off as she drove.

BETH UNLOCKED THE DOOR TO THEIR APARTMENT AND THREW IT OPEN a lot harder than she intended, but made sure to face away from Jules. She'd spent the entire wait at the doctor's office, as well as the drive home, fighting tears of indignant rage. By now she must have full-on crazy eyes.

"Oops!" she exclaimed in a cheerful voice as the door crashed against its bumper and shuddered with the impact. "Come on, honey. Let's have another look at your head."

Jules had in fact bitten another girl named Nicky… after Nicky clobbered her in the face with a huge toy dump truck. When she arrived at the school, she was stunned at the sight of the huge goose-egg on her daughter's forehead.

Nicky had already been picked up, so she didn't know the extent to which Jules had injured her vanquished foe, but Beth kind of hoped Jules had taken a good chunk out of the vicious little brat. She had to stand there, seething, and listen to Mrs.

Hyde's shitty, reproving speech about how biting was a public health hazard, blah-blah-blah, and how violence could not be tolerated.

As much as it smarted, Beth had little choice but to stand there and take it. She'd lost her patience once with Mrs. Hyde's ongoing attitude of condescension and muttered something sarcastic. A week later she received a letter from the "school administration"—which really meant Mrs. Hyde and her long-suffering daycare minions—explaining that for her daughter to remain an "assisted" student there, she as a parent would have to be civil with the teachers at all times. It had been difficult to resist the temptation to write them a reply that began, *Dear motherfuckers, I was a Fulbright scholar. Eat shit.*

"So you're teaching children to react passively to physical attack?" Beth had asked, in as neutral a tone as she could manage.

"We're teaching children to follow correct procedure," came the answer. "They are to tell a teacher, not take matters into their own hands."

Hag.

Beth inhaled slowly through her nose, willing herself to get her shit together, and steered Jules to the kitchen area. Only three more months, and she'd be free of Mrs. Hyde forever. Beth wet a paper towel and dabbed at Jules's head. "Does it hurt?" she asked. The urgent care had sent them home with a few free samples of mild pain medication and while the doctor had assured her Jules's injury wasn't serious, her head still looked terrible.

"A little," Jules said. "Am I in trouble?"

"Uh, no," Beth said. "You're not."

"Mrs. Hyde said I was."

"Yeah, well, Mrs. Hyde isn't in charge of whether you're in trouble at our house."

"But it was wrong to bite Nicky."

"Maybe it was kind of wrong to bite her. But it wasn't wrong to defend yourself."

"Do I have to go back?"

A miserable lump rose in Beth's throat. "I don't know, honey. We'll figure something out later. Right now, I have to call Chris and tell her not to come over tonight."

Jules shrieked in outrage. "What? Why! Chris and me were going to do girl time! You said!"

"The doctor told me to keep an eye on you in case you have a concussion. I can't leave now."

"But you said Chris would stay with me while you went to your party. You *said*. She planned the whole thing. We were going to make cookies and play Princess Spies!"

"I know, honey, but I don't think it's a good idea anymore," Beth said, wondering what the hell Princess Spies was.

"I *am* in trouble, then!"

"No, this is different. I'm taking care of you because you got hurt when Nicky hit you."

"Just spank me instead. Then let Chris come over."

"You aren't being punished," Beth protested. "This is for your own good."

Jules collapsed in dramatic anguish on the IKEA couch that doubled as her bed most nights. "You hate me," she wept.

"Yeah, thanks for understanding," Beth muttered. "You know, this isn't how I wanted it, either." She wanted to cry too. She'd set aside money for three months for the trip and to pay their babysitter Chris to stay an entire weekend with Jules.

But… what would a good mother do—stay with her injured kid, or sashay off to her college reunion? She had a feeling it was the former.

Jules stopped her theatrical sobbing, having noticed Beth's failure to react, and changed tack. "Mom," she said, hauling herself to her feet. "Here's the deal. You *said* Chris and I would have a sleepover. That's a promise. Promises are *the law.*"

Beth's phone buzzed again inside her purse. She pulled it out and looked at the screen for a moment before declining Ted's call. He must be back from lunch.

"Mom!" Jules whined, pulling at Beth's arm. "Mom-mom-mom-mom-mom!"

"Stop," Beth ordered her, and stood there watching her phone until the voicemail notification pinged through. Ted's message was a minute long, and according to her visual message preview, he'd said "fog" three times in the first sentence. He was definitely pissed.

What if she ran into someone at the reunion who would help her network into a new job? What if the irresponsible move was *not* going? She'd already paid for most of it, anyway—it would be a huge waste not to go now.

"Tell you what," she said to Jules. "I'll talk to Chris and see what she thinks. But you have to stop pestering me about it now or the answer is no, period."

Jules clapped her mouth shut and stood ramrod straight in the posture Beth recognized as her I'm-being-a-very-good-girl stance.

"Yeah, yeah," Beth said. "I get it."

"Oh, no, check out your battle wound!" Chris exclaimed as Jules answered the door. "I'd hate to see the other kid!"

"I bit the other kid!" Jules announced gleefully.

"Jules," Beth objected. "Try not to be so proud of that, huh?"

"And I'm not in trouble, either," Jules bragged.

"Yeah, keep a lid on it," Chris said. "Nobody likes a sore winner."

Jules laughed uproariously. "Yes!" she cried, pointing at the bump on her head. "I'm a very sore winner!"

"Sure you are," Chris agreed, dropping her bags by the couch and smoothly ushering Jules to a seat in front of the television. "I bet you can't wait to get out of here," she said to Beth, grinning, as she turned on the set and slapped it on the side to banish the buzzing sound that issued forth.

"Are you sure this is a good idea?" Beth asked as Chris joined her in the kitchen.

"Totally," Chris said. "My little brothers hit their heads all the time growing up. I know what to look out for and what to do if anything goes wrong—which I seriously doubt it will."

"All right," Beth said, feeling guilty nonetheless. "Well… there's money in here, for pizza or whatever you girls want to eat." She stuck an envelope to the fridge with a magnet. "I guess I should get going if I want time for a shower before the party."

"Sounds great," Chris said. "And listen, we'll be fine. But call any time you want. And have a good time."

"I'm sure I will," Beth said, picking up her weekend bag. "Bye, honey," she called to Jules.

BETH SPENT MOST OF THE DRIVE THINKING ABOUT HOW WEIRD IT WAS that she'd finished undergrad more than ten years ago, and how while these people were her whole life at one time, she hadn't seen or talked to any of them in ages. The Psi Phi Epsilon sorority held a smaller event each year, and larger functions like this one every five years, but after she and Dan married and moved away, she hadn't made it back for any of them. After getting pregnant unexpectedly, she never reached a point where she felt like putting her life on display for people who had known her in a much different context, and who remembered her as a much different person than the one she'd become. Not that she was ashamed, but it just seemed like a lot to explain.

It was hard to know what to expect at the reunion. She was regretting having dropped off the face of the social media earth a few years ago. She had no idea what most of the sisters had been doing since then, and likewise they must know little about her.

But there was one sister in particular Beth was hoping to run into. During undergrad, Tawny was her best friend, more or less. But then grad school happened, and they were separated by distance, and eventually by the gulf created by Beth's marriage and motherhood. They'd talked, weekly at first, then monthly, and then not at all by the time she and Dan were together. Beth had Googled Tawny a few times, and thought half-heartedly of calling or e-mailing, but ultimately didn't have the nerve. What was she supposed to say to someone she hadn't called in five years, and who hadn't called her?

It might be nice to catch up with Tawny, though. They'd made the silly promise to each other as undergrads, to forever be friends, to abstain from marriage and family, devoting their lives to academics and science. Obviously Beth hadn't stayed the course herself. She was curious what path Tawny's life might have taken.

At the hotel, Beth slipped her keycard through the magnetic strip guarding her room and pushed the door open to the clean scent of linen and air-conditioned bliss. She wondered if any of the fraternities might be hosting a reunion event the same weekend as the Psi Phi Epsilons. It occurred to her after being interrupted that morning that she couldn't be the only thirty-something around whose marriage hadn't worked out. And these five-year parties were really something to look forward to—a banquet hosted by the current house sisters for the alumni, preceded by a fancy cocktail party at which the sisters met for conversation and networking. If she got the networking part out of the way and made a few promising connections, she could put her efforts into finding somebody else who missed physical contact as much as she did. Maybe even somebody she'd known in college.

Beth stepped out of the shower a while later and toweled her hair dry, admiring her naked form in the mirror. She'd always been comfortable in her own skin—not skinny by any means, but trim and proportionate, with ample curves bestowed by her pregnancy. Turning, she studied her silhouette. She was a little wider in the hips than she'd been in college. But her tits were bigger now. Overall, she judged herself vastly fuckable.

In the room, she laid out the clothes she'd chosen for the party, taking her time to get all the details right. Beth had built an ensemble of tastefully understated black lingerie, a slinky little black dress, and matching chain belt and statement necklace to go with the setup. She finished fastening herself into the black bustier, then carefully applied makeup, making sure to get her bright red lipstick perfect.

She still had it, all right.

The dress slipped on easily over her head, and she smoothed the silky material over her undergarments, wondering whether someone might undress her later, and if so, who that someone might be. Anticipating the eventual who of a night like this was half the excitement. She tidied up the hotel room, in case she brought someone back, and pulled the door closed behind her.

TWO

IN WHICH BETH LEARNS
THAT BITCHES BE CRAY-CRAY

AT THE CHAPTER HOUSE, A HOST OF YOUNG SISTERS SHE DIDN'T RECOG-
nize, presumably the current house residents, were greeting the
alumni. They looked like high-schoolers. Somewhere in the
house she could hear a chorus of female voices chanting, "Psi-
Phi-Ep! We bring the pep!" Beth grinned.

A perky young brunette wearing a ΨΦE pin on her shoulder checked Beth's purse, exchanging it for a name tag, before
leading her into the large formal living room, which had been
cleared for the occasion. As the girl withdrew, Beth scanned the
room for people she recognized. She quickly picked out a small
woman with a blonde pageboy haircut, dressed in what looked
like current season Kate Spade. Good grief, that wasn't cheap.

"Um—hey, Sarah Ann!" she called.

Sarah Ann had been two years ahead of her. She waved Beth
over. "Oh, Beth, how are you! It's been forever!"

"I'm good," Beth said. "And you?"

"Amazing," Sarah Ann gushed. "Jim's just made partner—
that's him over there, I'll have to introduce you—and Chelsea
is in honors Kindergarten, what a relief, Lana is just getting
into preschool now, and"—she patted her abdomen with both
hands—"we're expecting our third in three months!"

"Wow, congratulations," Beth said. "That's wonderful!" Apart from the bump, Sarah Ann barely looked pregnant. At six months Beth had frequently, and at length, made the unhappy comparison between herself and a baby elephant. "You look great!" she said.

"So where's your husband?" Sarah Ann asked, smiling. "Dan, isn't it?"

"We're not together anymore."

"Oh," Sarah Ann said. "That's too bad… it's, well, that's too bad. I guess not everything is meant to be." There was a short pause while Sarah Ann appeared to cast about for a new topic. "So how's everything else? You kind of disappeared a few years ago. Are you in academics?"

"I haven't finished my doctorate yet," Beth said, "but I'm hoping to go back soon. Speaking of which, I was planning to do a little networking tonight. I'm looking for a new professional challenge."

"Oh, sure, yeah," Sarah Ann said. "I haven't been in the workforce for a long time, of course," she patted her belly again, "been too busy with these little guys, but if I bump into anybody who sounds like they could help you, I'll be sure to send them your way. Anything you're particularly looking for?"

A boss who doesn't use the word "fuck" as a comma? "I've been working as an assistant to the VP of sales for a small printing company. But I'd like to get back to something more academic-spectrum if I could."

"Ah. Yeah, that shouldn't be too hard. I might know a couple people. If they show up I'll send them your way."

"Thanks!" Maybe finding a new job would be easier than she'd thought.

"So let me reacquaint you with Kim and Jess," Sarah Ann suggested, touching Beth lightly on the arm. "They're here stag too."

"Sure."

Sarah Ann dropped her off with Kimberly and Jessica, two of the women with whom she'd pledged. "God, Beth, have you had any of these lobster canapés?" Kim enthused. "They are *incredible*. Here." She thrust her little party plate toward Beth, who took one and tasted it.

"You're right," she agreed, helping herself to another. "So, how have you guys been? I sort of haven't been online much the last few years, so I have a lot of catching up to do."

"We're great," Jessica said. "Kim just got a VP promotion, and her husband's a director at his company so he's not far behind. And of course their kids are both little geniuses too."

"That's terrific," Beth said. "Congratulations!"

"It's not a big deal," Kim scoffed. "Anyway, Jess owns her own company! She has, like, a hundred employees!"

"Wow. That's so cool."

"Yeah, and she was the Milwaukee Small Businesswoman of the Year in 2013. I mean, it helps that she doesn't have any rug rats."

"Shut up," Jessica said, laughing. "Anyway, Beth, I'm so glad you made it this year! How's life treating you?"

"I'm good. I haven't finished my doctorate yet. I took a break to have my daughter and spent some time at home with her. Right now I'm working with a small printing company, but the plan is to get back to academics soon."

"That's terrific," Jessica said. "How old is your daughter?"

"Five. She's starting Kindergarten in the fall, thank goodness…"

Kim laughed. "I have a six-year-old. I know *exactly* what you mean, and it's way better once they're in school. I mean, part of me was like, oh no, my baby's growing up, and part of me was like, hell yeah, no more daycare! How's your husband?"

"We're not together anymore," Beth explained.

"Oh, sorry," Kim said. "I didn't mean to dredge anything up."

"No biggie," Beth said. "I've had time to get over it. People get divorced all the time."

"Yeah, unfortunately true," Jessica said. "Anyway, you'll do great. My mom raised my brother and me with hardly any help from Dad. And, I mean, I went on to be recognized by the City of Milwaukee." She made an exaggerated gesture in Beth's direction and pretended to look her up and down. "You're probably about as good as my mom. Maybe *your* kid will get Sioux Falls." Jessica giggled.

"She'd better *not* end up in the Dakotas," Beth said, taking another canapé from Kim's plate. "I refuse to have Christmas north of Des Moines."

"No kidding," Kim agreed, presenting her hand for a high five. "What are we, Swedes?"

"Right?" Beth said, slapping Kim's hand. "I raised her better than that."

Another woman joined them, wobbling slightly as she held a tray of drinks. "Hey, guys!"

"Hi, Lisa!" they greeted her.

"Check it. I stole this whole tray of white wine spritzers. Want some of my ill-gotten goods? I gotta dispose of the evidence!"

Everyone laughed and took a glass.

"So, I don't want to brag,"—Lisa paused and set the tray on a nearby table, her eyes twinkling—"but you *must* see the adorable little convertible my husband and I just got. You have to come take a quick spin with me later! I mean, it messes your hair all up, but it's still awesome. I swear I can't shut up about this stupid car. I think I love it more than I love my mom."

"I don't know," Beth protested, grinning, "how many of these spritzers have you had already?"

Lisa laughed. "Not… that many. Like you have any room to talk, though, you party girl!"

"I have a five-year-old now! Pretty sure my party days are behind me." Beth had never been the type to drink herself stupid, but she'd still loved going out.

"Whatever! Party days behind you... attitudes like that are how you get old! Anyway, partying is the whole point of being here! Days of yore and all that." Lisa downed the rest of her glass and immediately replaced it with another from the tray. "Wait till you get a few more drinks in you! Where's your girl Tawny, by the way?"

"I don't know," Beth said. "I haven't talked to her in ages. We just sort of... fell out of touch. You know how you get to that point where it's been so long and you still haven't called and then it would be weird, and the longer you go the weirder it feels? I was kind of hoping she'd be here tonight, but I haven't seen her yet."

"Oh my God, that's so sad!" Lisa said. "I totally thought you guys would end up living next door to each other and having kids who grew up to be best friends and everything and then going to the nursing home together. If she doesn't show up this weekend, you *have* to make the first move and call her. You remember how awkward Tawny was. She was always on Sarah Ann's bad side."

"She wasn't *that* awkward. At least, not once you got to know her." Kim made a disdainful little hand motion. "Sarah Ann's just kind of a bitch, frankly. Being chapter president for a year completely went to her head."

"I know," Jessica said, "remember how after rush, Sarah Ann was pissed because she couldn't understand how somebody so good looking could be that shy? Tawny was so willowy and pretty, with that shiny blonde hair of hers... she could have been a model. Sarah Ann voted her in because she was hot, and then spent the next three years punishing her for not being a social butterfly. Ugh. We were lucky not to have a house full of Sarah Anns."

"Shut up, she'll hear you," Lisa laughed. "Anyway, point being, it doesn't matter how many years it was. Get back in touch. You don't just abandon a friendship like that. I was always jealous of you guys. You were like sisters."

"I didn't think about the shyness thing," Beth said, frowning. "But you're right. I never thought about how much harder it might be for her."

"And who knows," Lisa pointed out, "maybe she'll show up tonight."

"Um, hey, I just saw Xiao over there," Beth excused herself. "I'm going to go say hi." Suddenly she wanted out of the conversation. It was sad talking about how great her friendships *had* been. These women had stayed in touch over the years, even if they didn't see each other often. Why hadn't she made more of an effort to do the same?

Before Beth could make it over to where her sophomore year roommate Xiaowen stood across the room, talking animatedly to a group of other women, a tall, dark-haired man intercepted her. "Beth! Hey! Sarah Ann told me you were here."

"Hey, Brendan!" she greeted him. "How have you been? It's been ages!" She'd had a brief thing with him for a couple of weeks near the end of her freshman year. She felt a tingle at the memory of one of their late night assignations at the Chancellor's fountain, but put it out of her mind. If he was here, it was because he was married to one of the sisters.

"I'm great," he said. "I'm married now, of course." He pointed across the room at Jen, a sister who had been a couple of years behind Beth.

"Oh, that's terrific, I always liked Jen," Beth said. "Any kids?"

"Yep, our daughter's eight and our son's six next month."

"That's wonderful," Beth said. "I'm so happy for you both!"

"So the reason I stopped you," Brendan said, "was I heard from Sarah Ann you were looking to change it up professionally. Is that true?"

"It is, yes," she said. "I'm with a small printing company, but I'm wanting to get back into academics at some point. Why, do you know somebody who's looking for administrative talent?"

"Well, when I heard what Sarah Ann had to say, it sounded almost too good to be true. I'm with a small academic press and our office manager gave notice this afternoon. We could use somebody with industry experience."

"Oh, wow," Beth said. "Where are you located?"

"Well, that's the thing. Are you open to moving to Saint Louis? Sarah Ann said you and your husband split. Sorry to hear that… but maybe you're free to pull up stakes now? If you want it, the job's yours."

Beth looked at him, astonished. "Just like that? You're not serious."

"No, I am," he assured her. "Here's my information." He handed her a business card. "Call me Monday and we'll discuss the details and see if you're even interested. I mean, we'll have to go through the formalities with HR, so you'll have to interview, but I have a hard time imagining it won't work out."

"Oh my God, thank you! This is amazing!"

"I'm glad you're interested," he said warmly. "We're going to be in a world of hurt if we don't fill the position fast. Well, I'd better get back," he said, nodding his head toward his wife.

"Thanks again," Beth said. "And tell Jen hi for me!"

"Sure." He moved in for a hug. It surprised her a little, but the man had just offered her a job. She owed him a friendly hug, at least.

Then she felt his warm breath on her ear. "I'd love to be inside you again," he whispered.

Beth froze for a moment, certain she'd heard him wrong. "What?" she asked, breaking the embrace.

"Jen takes a sleeping pill every night at ten. If you're up for some fun, I'll meet you by the fountain at eleven. If you take the job maybe we can make it a more long-term arrangement." He grinned, looking pleased with himself.

"I—*what?*" she repeated. "You're—are you propositioning me for *sex?*"

He drew back in apparent surprise at her confusion. "What the hell else?"

"What the fuck is wrong with you?" Beth hissed, feeling her face flush with embarrassment. "You're *married!*"

"Wrong with *me? You* were the one giving me all those signals!"

"What signals!"

"You know," he gestured vaguely, "with the—with that dress. And your tits up to your chin. You're… obviously looking to get lucky tonight. I thought—"

"You thought I wanted to get with a married man?"

"Not exactly," he defended himself, "but we have history. And everybody knew you, well, got around back in college. It's not like that's why I offered you the job, but I didn't think it would hurt anything if you were grateful for the offer and open to messing around a little."

"I don't think I've ever been that grateful for *anything*," Beth told him, tearing his business card in half and dropping it on the carpet.

"You don't have to be such a stuck-up bitch about it," he shot back as she turned to go. "You used to be fun."

Beth stiffened and walked away without looking back, her face flaming. She joined the outer fringe of Xiaowen's conversation a few moments later, but couldn't seem to bring herself to join in.

"Beth, are you okay?" someone asked her. She realized she was shaking—from nerves or rage, she wasn't sure.

"Yeah," she said, forcing a smile. "It's just a little warm in here. I'm feeling kind of claustrophobic. I think I'm going to go splash some cool water on my face."

Beth walked away, trying not to look in the direction Brendan had gone, and made her grateful escape to the restroom, going into the single stall and closing the lid before sitting down and drawing her knees up to her chest. She just needed a few minutes to collect herself. Then she'd go find Kim and the rest of them again and stick with them all night. The networking thing was a bust—she was too rattled now to put herself out there with anybody else. That was all right. She could start her job search next week, and she'd changed her mind about wanting to take somebody back to the hotel with her. It might not be turning out like she'd hoped, but the weekend was still salvageable.

The restroom door burst open then and she heard a voice raised in anger. "I can't believe that fucking whore," a woman said.

"Look, nothing happened, and I think she already left," another woman said. "I'm sure she won't be here next year. You're not even going to see her again for ages. Besides, he told her off, I doubt she'll try anything else."

"I just can't believe she would proposition Brendan that way, here, with me like twenty feet away the whole time. It's so gross!"

It was Jen, Beth realized in horror. She squeezed her eyes shut and hugged her knees, hoping neither of them would decide they wanted to use her stall.

"Yeah, well," the other voice said. "You remember how she was. She and that half-autistic beanpole friend of hers used to screw anything with two legs and a dick. And judging by some of those crunchy chicks they used to hang with, the dick was optional. At least Brendan came right to you and told you what happened. Not every husband would do that. You guys are solid. So cool off. Don't let her ruin your weekend."

Brendan must have gone right to Jen and told her everything, making it all sound like Beth's idea. He was probably trying to cover his ass in case anybody had seen them together. Her throat tightened. Jen had been a huge gossip in college. It would take her all of two minutes to spread the news to everyone at the party about what a husband-prowling skank Beth was.

She heard a funny little squeaking sound.

"What was that?" Jen said. "Is there somebody in here?"

Beth realized too late that the squeaking sound was coming from her. She clapped a hand over her mouth, but Jen was already yanking on the stall door.

"Go away," she said.

The door stopped rattling. "Beth?" Jen asked. "If that's you, you have a lot of nerve sticking around this party after what you tried."

Suddenly, her shakiness disappeared, replaced with white-hot anger at all the bullshit she'd been through over the last couple of years. Why hide? What did she have to be ashamed about, anyway?

Nothing. That's what.

She'd had some sex in college. All of it with unattached people like herself.

So fucking what?

Beth tore the door open, revealing Jen's startled face. "For what it's worth, I came in here to get myself together because I was so unnerved after my encounter with your creep husband. He offered me a job, which seemed great at first, until I realized he thought his generosity meant he'd get to fuck me. I declined. Emphatically, I might add."

"Are you calling my husband a liar?"

"Obviously. I have to assume, if he's enough of a pig to pull shit like this with you just across the room, I'm not his first. So maybe you should ask yourself if you *really deep down* believe what he told you, or if you just need to convince yourself that you didn't marry an asshole."

"Of course that's what you would say," Jen said in an accusing tone, "after you got caught red-handed."

"How else would I have learned that you take a sleeping pill at ten every night?"

Jen flinched visibly at her words.

"Take it from me," Beth said. "Divorced life isn't that bad." She stood there for a moment, but Jen didn't move out of the way. "Excuse me," she added. "I have somewhere better to be."

Jen stepped aside, staring after her. The other woman was a sister Beth hadn't known well. She stood by the sink, speechless and wide-eyed at the scene she'd just witnessed.

"Jackie," Beth acknowledged with supreme dignity, then left.

THREE

IN WHICH TAWNY MEETS AN OLD FRIEND
NOT AN ELDERLY FRIEND
SOMEBODY FROM HER PAST

Tawny hit the gas and sped backward through time at seventy miles an hour. She didn't even bother converting her miles to metric—that was how great a mood she was in. She could almost physically feel the years peeling away from her, sloughing off the leaden remnants of the last near-decade of disappointment and loneliness. By the time she got to campus and the Psi Phi house, she'd be floating out of her seat, especially if things went her way tonight.

Of course, she couldn't allow herself to get carried away with emotion. Tawny had a lead foot wired directly to her amygdala, but she had to be careful these days. No taking chances with even a speeding ticket anymore, not since she quit contracting with DARPA. She missed her sporty MacLaren F1, but it, along with the Victorian manor she'd been converting into a kind of Batcave, and all her social media accounts, had been sacrificed on the altar of anonymity once she made that first discovery with the virtual photons. Avoiding attention from the government was a top priority now—she'd almost canceled her plans for this reunion at the last minute, then thought better of it. Secrecy was *a* top priority, not *the* top priority. This reunion might be her last good chance to reconnect with Beth. And if the NSA already had informants at her old sorority house, the game was pretty much over anyway.

She'd expected to be more nervous, that the drive would be an hour and a half of snake-mantra chanting and deep breathing so she could relax enough to socialize. But as she got closer to her destination, happy memories trickled in—nights with the sisters spent drinking beer and gossiping about boys (and girls), writing skits for the Campus Revue, a kindhearted senior showing her how to apply bronzer for the first time. Memories of her and ten other girls piled onto a couch in their goofy PJs, screaming in delight at bad horror movies. And, of course, all her time spent on certain other extracurricular activities. By the time she pulled into the parking lot she was actually singing.

"Snake, snake, snake, Senora... snakes are made of lines. Snake, snake, snake, Senora... snake-it all the time." She laughed at the way "snake-it" sounded like "naked." This was the best she'd felt in ages.

Tawny parked her grey Acura, checked her lipstick in the rearview mirror, and walked up to the Psi Phi Ep house. On her way in, she passed Beth's car. She'd never seen it in person, but the make and model were the same as what she'd found in the DMV database, and while the tags were filmed over with dust, there weren't any other rickety old Toyotas in the lot.

Standing in the entryway, she scanned the room for anything resembling social unpleasantness—she had always visualized interactional gatherings like the Predator did, with imaginary heat signatures. So far, so good—everything was in the blue, maybe a hint of green—wait, over in the corner, an unmistakable patch of red bloomed where a group of women were arguing about something. They weren't talking loudly enough for her to make out their words. Thankfully, none of them appeared to be Beth, so it should be easy to just avoid them.

Tawny grabbed the weirdest-looking appetizer from one tray and a champagne flute from another and dived into the crowd. This would be the quickest way to find Beth. She had dressed for it—anyone could easily spot Tawny in her fire-engine-red dress and sparkly gold sandals. If she didn't find Beth right away, her strategy was to locate mutual friends. Somebody would know Beth's whereabouts. She spotted a woman they'd pledged with.

"Jackie, hi! How are you?"

Jackie startled. "Hey. Um… it's great to see you, but I… really have to run to the restroom, so, uh, catch you at the next reunion!" Jackie walked out the room, nervously looking back over her shoulder several times.

That was odd. Tawny doubled back to the full-length mirror hanging on the wall just past the foyer and examined herself. Nothing looked off to her—in fact, she didn't think her appearance was that different compared to college. She had the same long blonde hair, the same slightly upturned nose, and the same hazel eyes.

To be fair, Tawny was unusually tall. Maybe she hadn't made enough noise on her approach, and Jackie had just been unnerved and then embarrassed about it. Or maybe she'd simply forgotten Tawny's name and was afraid to admit it. Other people were so hard to read sometimes, even with her Predator heat-map.

She made sure to firmly heel-toe her way towards the next group of women.

"Hello, friends!" she said as loudly as possible. "I am now here!" Everyone jumped. Shit. The last few months of isolation had not improved her social instincts one bit. No point in backing away now, though. "Has anyone seen Beth tonight?"

Things went from blue to orange in a hurry. All of the sisters began to comment on how late it was getting, or how it was warm in here and they were heading outside to get some air, or how they also had to visit the restroom.

Okay, that was genuinely weird.

The last woman to leave the group, Xiaowen, narrowed her eyes at Tawny as she finished chewing her lobster canapé and wiped her fingers elaborately on a napkin before tossing it into a wastebasket with barely restrained fury. She pivoted on one Louboutin heel and stalked away without saying a word.

Tawny stood there, wondering if there was some kind of food poisoning in the hors d'oeuvres that was giving everyone fevers and explosive diarrhea. Then she realized—these people didn't have to go to the bathroom at all! They were deliberately avoiding her. That stung. What the fuck was going on?

All around, people were staring at her, but no one would make direct eye contact. Her Predator vision had turned almost completely red.

Finally, she sighted someone who would have information, even if it wasn't someone she liked very much. Sarah Ann, who had been the Queen B (not just in the apiarian sense) saw her coming and tried to edge away, but Tawny was swift and merciless. She interposed herself between Sarah Ann and the threshold to the dining room.

"Sarah Ann, hey!"

"Oh, hi, Tawny... it's so... interesting to see you after all these years."

"Yeah, let's cut the crap." She let her burst of shock and anger power her straight into a confrontation, which she never would have done under normal circumstances. "Why is everybody here treating me like I ran over their dog?"

"Are they? I hadn't noticed. I'm sure it's nothing."

"I don't think so. Seriously, what the hell is with you people?"

Sarah Ann fidgeted, looking around Tawny, over her own shoulder, everywhere but directly at her. "Well, you know how people are... they fall out of touch, sometimes things just get awkward, right?"

"What *happened* is that skanky whore friend of yours waltzed in with her hooker shoes and her tits out and tried to steal my goddamn husband fifteen feet from where I was standing!" A woman Tawny remembered from college but didn't know well stomped, literally stomped, her way up to them. "You've got some nerve showing up, the both of you. At least the other women here have husbands."

Sarah Ann sighed in exasperation. "Jesus, Jen, let me handle this. Tawny, we were never best friends back in school, but believe me when I say I'm telling you this for your own good. A single woman around married men is like a shark."

"… easily distracted by the scent of blood? Is this… a menstrual thing?" Tawny, of course, had been thinking of snakes earlier, and was anxious to begin with, so the mention of sharks threw her for a loop.

"Oh my God," Sarah Ann exclaimed, "how did you ever get through rush when you're this incredibly clueless? College is over, Tawny. The rest of life isn't a frat party. You and Beth need to grow the fuck up. Other people's husbands are off limits. Considering your reputations, you should both just steer clear."

At that point Kim and Jessica noticed what was going on and waded into the fray to protest Beth and Tawny's expulsion, defending Beth in particular. Tawny stood there silently, trying to piece everything together. Something had happened between Beth and Jen's husband Brendan. He said Beth started it, Beth said he was lying. Most of the women seemed to be on Jen's side.

As the other sisters argued, Tawny slipped away, trying not to let anyone see her cry. Fleeing in shame was terrible, but in her experience nothing was worse than sticking around at a party where you had been outright told you weren't wanted. She walked for a while, not paying attention to where she was going, and trying desperately not to think about how she'd failed at being human yet again. Psi Phi Epsilon had been the one place she'd ever felt like she could be herself, all of herself, not just the brainy parts, or the social misfit parts, or the gleefully oversexed parts. And now all of that was gone. Maybe it had never been real in the first place.

When she finally slowed down and looked around, Tawny was almost at the far end of campus, and she could hear Friday night parties in the distance, the muffled sound carrying through the warm night air all the way from the off-campus apartments. She stood there, taking in the view and thinking over the events of the evening, then realized she knew where she needed to go. Beth's car had still been in the parking lot, which meant she'd left on foot. Considering Jen's description of her "hooker shoes," she couldn't have gone that far in the time between her leaving and Tawny's arrival. And if there was one place Beth would go on campus...

Springer Hall loomed, huge and Romanesque, before her. Tawny started up the walk.

THEIR SOPHOMORE YEAR, SHE AND BETH WERE IN THE SAME SECTION OF an elective anthropology class, and the building in which the campus anthropology museum was housed became a favorite study-haunt of theirs. The class didn't require that much studying, but something about the museum appealed to them, and the school stored even more cool old stuff down in the basement. After weeks of being interrupted every time one of them wanted to look at the archives, an annoyed grad assistant finally gave them a key to the basement, threatening them with certain death, dismemberment, expulsion, et cetera, should they abuse the privilege.

She had always liked Springer for its odd looks and general ambiance. Plus, in one room, there were lots of neat dead things preserved in jars of formaldehyde. It was the oldest academic structure on campus, and the front-facing apex of the roof was topped with a large owl carved from red sandstone. A spotlight on the lawn lit up its solemn features, as well as the inscription that graced the front entrance: WHOSO FINDETH WISDOM FINDETH LIFE.

Owls were in fact very stupid creatures, as the space where a brain should go was mostly taken up by the enormous eyes which made them *look* intelligent by human standards. Tawny much preferred parrots. However, after watching a riveting documentary about birds of prey, she had to acknowledge that owls didn't need to be smart—they were spectacular killing machines and they didn't need calculus or quantum electrodynamics to murder thousands of rodents. The wisdom of owls was just knowing how to be an owl and doing owl things. And if weird bipedal primates think you're smart, let 'em, she figured.

"Fake it till you make it, right, buddy?" Tawny waved at the owl as she walked to the doors. She half expected them to be locked tight and the building closed up for the night.

But they weren't. Someone must be here, somewhere in the building. It could be a grad student working late, but maybe not. Maybe Beth had indeed felt the inexorable pull of nostalgia.

The interior had been extensively remodeled since she was last inside, sometime her junior year. The museum was gone as well, replaced with a large, modern-looking meeting hall.

Tawny made a beeline for the basement stairs at the rear of the building, wondering if there was even a chance that it might be unlocked. Their secret key was long gone, and if the school had stored the remainder of the museum's collection in the basement, it was no doubt kept secure most of the time.

She couldn't believe her luck. The basement door now had an automatic lock, but someone had left it propped open with a block of wood. She pulled it all the way open, groping for the light switch inside, only to find that the lights were already on.

So either Beth was indeed here, or some enterprising student had turned the place into his secret murderin' shack. She hoped it was the former.

The stone staircase was just as she remembered it, descending into the chill of a hundred years ago, when the building served as the campus library. Shelves that once formed library stacks were still lined up in neat rows, now storing an assortment of boxes, crates, and plastic tubs—probably the museum's collection. Halfway through their semester together, she and Beth had stumbled onto a long-forgotten compartment concealed in the thick stone wall behind one of the iron shelves that housed the anthropology archives.

The ancient, unrenovated basement made for a pleasant contrast with the modern main floor. She meandered through the shelves, hugging her arms against the cool air and wondering what sort of interesting relics had been relegated to this secret dungeon.

Tawny turned the corner around a shelf of boxes that a student had labeled in crayon: "HUMAN REMAINS SKULLS ONLY," and there she was. Beth was standing by the open secret compartment, holding what looked like their old notebook, affectionately referred to as "The Score." She hadn't noticed Tawny yet.

Beth looked great. Tawny knew she had a kid, but she appeared pretty much unchanged from ten years ago. She always managed to look both unaffectedly cute and sexy at the same time, a trait dudes had found irresistible. Though, her dress had the sheen of cheap polyester, and her shoes were suspiciously Target-like. Not that Target was bad or anything, but all the other sorority sisters, herself included, had worn way fancier duds to the party.

Okay, she told herself. *One, two, three, go... is what you'll do in just a minute. Make sure to go on go, not on three, or you'll throw off your rhythm. Jeez, just* go *already*! Tawny took a couple of exaggerated steps forward, making sure to walk noisily so that Beth wouldn't realize she'd been standing there gawking at her. "So… are those bitches just the worst, or what?"

Beth jumped violently and turned. "Oh! God. Tawny. You about gave me a heart attack." She stood, setting the notebook on a nearby shelf and brushing the dust from her hands onto her dress.

"I heard what happened to you at the party," Tawny said. "I was pissed. Sarah Ann kicked me out, but Kim and Jess are totally on your side, for what it's worth. When I left they were threatening to boycott future reunions if Sarah Ann didn't set the record straight."

Beth opened her mouth as if to reply, then burst into tears.

Tawny reached into her bag and withdrew a tissue, silently handing it over. Beth clutched it and sank into a crouch by the compartment, weeping. Tawny hovered nearby, not wanting to crowd her, but feeling utterly useless in the face of her storm of human emotion. Poor Beth. Tawny wanted to help her up from the floor and hug her, but she wasn't sure whether their current relationship status permitted that. They had barely seen each other since graduation.

After a while, Beth's tears lost steam and she rose to her feet.

"Sorry," she croaked, then cleared her throat. "Sorry about that. I think it's just been this super weird roller coaster for me tonight. First I was excited to be back after so long, and then I was feeling shaken after that horrible creep Brendan tried to get me to fuck him, and then I felt totally humiliated when Jen came in the bathroom where I was hiding and she started talking about what a husband-stealing whore I was, and then I saw her and realized I was just pissed. I basically told her he's a lying piece of shit. And then I came here and found our old notebook, but it's all ruined, just like my fucking life." She blew her nose.

"Sorry, that was ridiculously melodramatic. My life's fine. I just feel like absolute crap right now."

"I guess it wouldn't be Psi Phi Ep without a bunch of stupid drama," Tawny offered. "I think I had this inaccurate picture in my head of what it was like, living in a sorority. Maybe I over-estimated just how sisterly we all were. Because some of those bitches are cray."

Beth laughed, and Tawny blushed. "Did I use that word wrong?" she asked. "I heard it on TV. I thought that was how you use it."

"Oh, Tawny," Beth said, wiping her eyes with the back of her hand, "I don't think I realized for all these years how much I truly, truly missed wonderful you." She hugged Tawny awkwardly around the middle, and after a moment Tawny returned the embrace, giving her a little pat on the shoulder, her heart thudding. *Oh, please, don't fuck this up,* she begged herself.

They separated and Tawny handed her another tissue. Beth blew her nose again. "Sorry I got your dress all cobwebby. But I'm glad you came to find me. I was afraid I wouldn't get to see you at all."

Tawny shrugged off the apology with an it-doesn't-matter wave of her hand. "Is that the book?" she asked, nodding at the decaying mass on the shelf.

"Yeah. I—it's dumb, but I didn't expect it to be in such bad shape. The plastic didn't keep out all the moisture like we thought. I guess we picked a crappy hiding place." Beth laughed again, snorting a little. "Remember how we thought it would be this amazing time capsule of research for future generations when somebody found it one day after we were long dead?"

Tawny picked up the book, handling it gingerly. Damp had seeped in, despite their precautions, and she saw a thin film of condensation lining the interior of the plastic. The whole thing smelt of moldering paper and rot.

She opened it to the first page. "It's not completely ruined," she observed. "You can still read the field protocols." She carefully turned a page, and then another. "The book itself is in horrible shape, but most of the writing is still legible. Oh, geez, here's the hypothesis: 'That the presence of factors which might traditionally appeal to potential mates, such as wealth or favorable appearance, is a disincentive to the development of sexual skill, suggesting an inverse correlation between wealth or physical attractiveness and the ability to sexually gratify a partner.' That's rich."

Beth leaned to look, crowding her a little to see the page she was on.

"You know," Tawny mused, "based on the party, I guess some people think this research made us sluts."

"Ugh."

"I didn't say *I* thought it made us sluts. I think it makes us— well, basically—men."

"Good point. Nobody said anything about *his* past tonight, but I bet you Brendan slept around as much as we did in college—in four years I think he was with almost the entire Gamma Beta Pi house—on a rolling basis."

"Five years," Tawny said. "Brendan was a super senior."

Beth smiled. "Anyway, despite the rumors about the book, we never actually admitted it was a research project. Not that it lets anybody off the hook for slut-shaming us, but I guess I get why some people assumed we just liked to fuck."

"We did," Tawny objected. "Like to fuck, I mean."

"Well, sure. But they didn't know we were doing it because we'd created a scientific slam book for sex."

Tawny blinked, smiling shyly at Beth, before turning to the middle of the notebook. "Oh, man, remember him?" She pointed at the page. "Number one-zero-zero-six-one."

"I forgot how our subject numbering system worked."

"Oh," Tawny said, pleased with herself. "It's simple. All the assigned numbers were five digits. Numbers starting with one were male, numbers starting with two were female, and we used the number three for non-gender-binary people. Remember? Then they were just assigned in order of encounter after that."

"So, one-zero-zero-six-one was a man. And the zero-zero-six-one means he was, between the two of us, our sixty-first encounter?"

"Yup." Tawny nodded.

"Um, then what the hell is with those two zeros in front of it?" Beth asked, laughing. "We thought we were going to rack up fuck numbers in the four digits? In our three remaining years of college? What was *wrong* with us? That's idiotic."

Tawny grinned. "We were just planning ahead, like any prudent researchers would. Anyway, we'd have needed those extra digits if we ever expanded the project to include other associates."

"How far did we get? I'm pretty sure I remember all of mine, but how many between us both?"

Tawny turned a few more pages. "We only got to eighty-nine. The rest of the book is just empty."

"So about forty-five each. I mean, that's kind of a lot for a three-year period, but I don't get why we're apparently renowned by the entire Greek community for being huge sluts."

"You know," Tawny said, "I bet we weren't one bit sluttier than the other chicks on Greek Row, but people just remember us because we never went out by ourselves. Field protocol one was the buddy system, and we followed it religiously, so they noticed us more."

"Even with FP One," Beth commented, "looking back on it, I'm kind of amazed by some of the stuff we did. If my daughter were considering any of that shit, I'd get her in a chastity belt and under lock and key in about two seconds. Invincibility of youth, I guess. We were lucky."

"Not really," Tawny said. "We were safe because we followed the protocols. We were never assaulted, and we never even had a close call. Neither of us ever got pregnant. The system worked as designed."

"Remember how you called those brothels in Nevada to ask them about their procedures for keeping their prostitutes safe and healthy? That was a stroke of genius."

"Thanks. Although, man, it was hard to convince them at first that I wasn't prank-calling them." There was a pause as they both looked at the book. "Uh, do you want to, like, get out of this dungeon? And maybe do something gross like share an entire cherry pie at Perkins?"

Beth assumed perfect posture. "Madam," she answered, "I would be honored to commence such a disgusting exercise with you."

Tawny smiled what she hoped was a friendly, welcoming smile. This was even better than she'd hoped. "I—cool. Great."

"Oh," Beth remembered. "I forgot to ask, who was one-zero-zero, whatever?"

"I'm sure you remember—we both… researched… him. He's a state senator now." At Beth's blank stare, Tawny went on. "Kinda ugly, and he had that weird little crooked dick. He was already losing his hair junior year, poor guy."

Beth peered at the page. "Oh! It says right there in my writing, 'subject produced climactic response that threatened subsequent day's academic performance.' I remember now, he was incredible. He made me come so hard I was still shaking the next morning. I got a B on an essay test because my hand was so weak from gripping the sheets that I could hardly write."

"I'm kind of wet just thinking about that guy," Tawny said, taking out her phone and tapping on the screen.

"Just kind of?" Beth joked.

"Aw, shit," Tawny said, flashing the phone at her. "Google says he's married. He has two kids."

"Let me see." Beth leaned over to have a look at the picture on the screen. "Too bad for us. And wow, he looks better than he did then. Kind of distinguished, with his hair trimmed that way. I wonder if that lady next to him knows how lucky she is."

"I hope so. That dude is a national treasure."

"It's only fitting that he went into public service," Beth agreed.

"How the hell do these guys only have two kids?" Tawny asked.

They were both laughing. Tawny realized that for the first time in a long time, she felt really, really good.

FOUR

IN WHICH TAWNY IS REMINDED THAT TEAMWORK MAKES THE DREAM WORK

Tawny slid into the booth across from Beth, her bare legs squeaking on the vinyl seat where her dress ended. Beth did the same, unwrapping the silverware on the table and using the paper napkin to brush some of the cobwebs from her clothes.

Tawny watched in silence, trying not to show how eager she was to hang out with somebody who acted like they liked her.

A young waitress approached, but Beth stopped her before she could slap the laminated menus down on the table. "Actually, could you just bring us a pie and two forks? We want cherry. And coffee. Decaf for me."

"Regular for me," Tawny requested. The waitress left. "Remember all the times we hung out here eating dessert for dinner and mozzarella sticks of dubious origin?"

"Oh my God, I think I downed enough of those things to kill a horse."

"If we were our nineteen-year-old selves, we'd follow up our midnight feast with a frat party, and then do it again Saturday night. I never thought I would say this, but man, I hate young people. They make me feel like a vampire."

Beth looked off into the distance. "As nice as it is outside, I bet there are house parties on every corner in the student ghetto tonight. Ten years ago, you could just wander around town and find an open door and it was like, bam, instant good times. Everything was so easy back then."

Tawny had an idea. "Let's do it. Let's just go drive around until we find one."

"You want to crash a frat party? I mean, I think both of us have held up pretty well, but there's no way these kids won't know we're old people."

"Who cares? We're here, aren't we? Plus, it's late enough that everyone on fraternity row should be too drunk to recognize how decrepit and crypt-keeper-like we are."

Beth's expression teetered for a second and then Tawny saw the decision take form on her face as she slapped her hand down on the table. "You know what, you're right. I paid for a babysitter for an entire weekend, and I want to have some goddamn fun, no matter how shitty it started."

The waitress arrived then, with a pie still in its tin, two dessert plates, and a pie server.

"Please don't hate us, but can we get this to go instead?"

"Uh," the waitress faltered. "Okay... do you want that check split?"

"No," Tawny blurted out. "I'll get it."

The waitress nodded and left.

"You don't have to do that," Beth said.

Except she kind of did. Thanks to many hours of Google stalking and illegally accessing various government databases, Tawny knew that Beth's financial situation was not good. Beth was recently divorced, working some kind of clerical job unrelated to her degree, which didn't pay very well. Plus, she had a kid, and Tawny had heard that the upkeep on those things could get pretty expensive, even with two functioning parents.

"It's not a big deal," she said. "I'm… doing okay in that area. And it's the least I can do after being a bad friend and not getting back in touch for almost ten years."

Oops. Tawny hadn't meant to mention that. At least, not until further along in the evening when they were more comfortable with each other.

Beth didn't seem bothered by it. "Hey, it takes two to tango. Right before I ran into Brendan I was telling Kim and Jess that I should have held up my end. I mean, you were in England for what, five years? I could have called or e-mailed you. So for what it's worth, I was just as much to blame. I mean, if blame has to be assigned at all."

Tawny was on the verge of initiating a hug, when the waitress suddenly returned from out of nowhere with their boxed up pie and two Styrofoam cups. Beth looked doubtful about not paying her share of the check, but didn't protest.

"So…" Tawny began uncertainly, once they were in the car. "What have you been doing since I last saw you?"

Beth took a deep breath and Tawny realized she'd made a mistake. "You don't have to tell me," she said. "I just realized you probably had people asking you that the whole time at the party. I'm sure you don't feel like talking about it. And that's totally cool."

"It's okay," Beth said. "I'm tired of sharing my apparent failures"—she grinned a little here, so Tawny was pretty sure she was just joking about that—"with casual acquaintances. But you're not a casual acquaintance."

Well, that was promising. At least Beth didn't consider their friendship a total bust. They sat for a moment in silence, sipping their coffee as Tawny wound unhurriedly around the roads leading to frat row. She didn't know what to say in response to Beth's comment about failures—was it even kosher to ask someone

"Hey, how exactly did *you* fuck up at life?" She was just about to change the subject when Beth spoke up again.

"I didn't finish my doctorate. I told everybody at the reunion that I was just taking a break from school because of my daughter, but the truth is I'm not sure if it'll work out that way."

"What… happened with your husband?" Tawny asked. "I wasn't around during the, uh, courtship."

"Oh. Well, after my master's degree, with you gone, I wasn't doing… research anymore, of course, and after years of having a buddy, I didn't like going out by myself. I was three years into my program, so I didn't have time for stuff like that, anyway. I met Dan in the library one day and we started talking and then went out for a bite a few times over the next couple of weeks. I liked him. He was funny, and cute. And decent in bed. We'd been going out something like eight months and then I fucked up. I got an ear infection and the antibiotics messed up my birth control. I got pregnant."

"So he asked you to marry him?"

"Yeah. I was… kind of terrified of having a baby, and you already know marriage and kids had never been my plan, but Dan talked me into it. He was almost done with law school, and he'd already finished his MBA, so we could afford for me to take a break from my program and stay at home with our baby for a few years. He made it sound so good and safe that I said yes. We got married and then we had Jules."

"Do you like her?" Tawny asked without thinking, then winced at the tactlessness of the question. She was curious, though, because she'd never been able to imagine herself as a mother. Human gestation always seemed to her like more of a parasite-host arrangement than the tender experience most women made it out to be, but it was probably just another one of those things she didn't get.

"Yeah, I do," Beth said. "I was afraid I wouldn't. I always thought that stuff people say about how 'you'll never understand until you're a mother yourself' was bullshit. But there's something to it, much as it sort of gags me to admit that. I think it has to do with how pregnancy hormones change brain chemistry. They always say men don't feel like the baby is real until it's born and they can see and touch their child. But I was like that, too. I was a huge cow and I knew she was there—but it all seemed so abstract. I was scared that meant I didn't have any mothering instinct. So I was relieved when she was born and somebody handed her to me and I realized, thank Christ, I do like my baby."

"Wow," Tawny said, thinking it over.

"I mean, not that she isn't kind of an asshole sometimes," Beth remarked, "but I do love her."

Tawny snorted coffee out of her nose as she choked with laughter. "Are you sure it's not against some mom law to call a little girl an asshole?" she asked when she stopped coughing.

Beth shrugged. "She's not *usually* an asshole. Anyway, I think parents who think their kids never act like assholes are fooling themselves." She grinned.

"So what happened with you and Dan?"

There was a short pause before Beth answered. "Long story short, he went through a major depressive episode a couple of years ago—turns out depression runs in his family, which is one of the things you don't learn about somebody when you get married after only knowing them ten months—and then he had a sort of mental break at work, so I got a job to let him stay home and get better. We put Jules in daycare. And… about a year ago he left us and ran away with our neighbor. I don't even know where he is now. I'm sure I could find out if I wanted to, but I'm not sure there's any point. Jules doesn't even ask about him anymore."

Tawny tried to picture herself deciding to forgive someone who had betrayed her as thoroughly as it sounded like Beth's husband had done. She couldn't. She also couldn't imagine somebody deciding to leave after getting lucky enough to marry a person like Beth.

Beth studied Tawny. "So, tell me how you've been—amazing, I hope."

Tawny thought about it, trying to decide how much to say. "I guess that depends on how you define amazing. I used to think I was doing great, what with going for my Ph.D. at Oxford. I had two first-author publications there. Then I got a research job with Raytheon after school. I've invented a couple of things. I guess you could say I've been successful."

More than successful.

She was rich beyond belief, and credentialed out the ass.

She was also so lonely that she sometimes went to the grocery store and bought things she didn't need just for the friendly smile and sixty seconds of interaction she would get at the register.

"I—"

Beth leaned toward her, listening intently. Like she cared. Like it mattered to her.

Suddenly Tawny wanted to tell Beth every single thing that had happened after they'd parted ways—how she had the Ph.D. and heaps of money that had come fast and easy after she'd sold a couple of patents to DARPA, a huge house—well, two houses now—full of all the rich-people stuff that proved she should be a happy, functional adult. How every measure of her success aligned perfectly with the metrics by which people graded their lives.

How when she was supposed to be coming into her own, finding happiness and maturity, that was when life had really started to suck, because everyone she met seemed to be full up on friends already.

How she'd turned thirty a few years ago and had yet to discover anything on the other side beyond the fear that her best times were behind her.

Except she couldn't tell Beth these things. She would look like a neurotic idiot. If there was anything Tawny had learned to count on over the years, it was that she couldn't trust her social impulses. They were often wrong, even when they felt perfect.

But, she thought, looking at the expression of interest and faint concern that Beth wore, maybe she could try to rekindle something here. If she didn't scare her off by trying to be best-best-best-ever friends again too soon, if she didn't let Beth know that science was the only thing she had going on with her life—maybe she could get back a little of what she'd lost.

"You okay?" Beth asked, her eyes fixed on Tawny's. "You don't have to talk about anything you don't want to. But… you can tell me anything. We were best friends."

Were. Not *are.*

"Yeah, no, I'm okay. I think the stupid thing with the party was just bothering me."

"Oh, yeah. So what happened?"

For a second, Tawny was drowning again in the sick, buzzing sensation of rejection, hearing Sarah Ann's words—"steer clear"—over and over again in her head.

"Tawny?" Beth asked. "You kind of zoned again there."

"Oh. Yeah." She snapped back to herself. "Well, it was kind of awful. Sarah Ann told me I should leave. She made it sound like I was never supposed to come back to another event."

"That's shitty. It had nothing to do with you."

Tawny shrugged uncomfortably. "I guess I just don't get it. I mean, just because we liked sex in college, we're out to steal husbands? What actually happened with Brendan, by the way?"

"He offered me a job."

"Like, a *job* job? Working for a company?"

"Yeah. My job… kind of sucks. And he came up and said he heard from Sarah Ann I was looking. He just offered it to me. I was so excited. Then he leaned in and said he couldn't wait to fuck me." She shuddered. "The worst part was, I realized later that it kind of turned me on. Like, what's *wrong* with me?"

"Well, that I know for sure. Nothing's wrong with you," Tawny said. "Trust me, I've studied this plenty. Sometimes our bodies just respond to the prospect of sexual contact, whether it's welcome or not. Plus, stress and adrenaline and the relative novelty of the partner play into it as well." If there was anything Tawny understood, it was the excitement of a first encounter. She thrilled to first kisses, the touch of a stranger, the conquest of the unknown. It got boring after that.

"Oh." Beth pondered for a moment. "Maybe I don't feel so bad about it, then. So what about your love life? Or sex life, or both. I know we made that vow in undergrad, but I fell off the wagon for sure."

"Eh, I guess I never caught the monogamy bug. I've been pretty much waiting my entire life for something to click with that 'special someone,' but it hasn't happened yet. I'm okay with that. I've been doing a lot of internet research and in addition to being an omnisexual, I'm think I'm aromantic."

Beth looked confused. "You're a romantic? As in, you enjoy romance?"

"No, not a rrrrrromantic," Tawny took her hands from the wheel momentarily to snap her fingers like castanets. "'A' as in 'without.' *Not* interested in romance. At least, not by most people's standards."

"Okay. That makes a lot more sense."

"I mean, I have no problem being sexually attracted to people. Maybe even aliens or robots, if I got the chance. I do feel platonic love for my friends, just not the together-forever-let's-get-married kind of love." Tawny hoped her voice didn't crack as she said this. "I've had crushes on plenty of guys and girls and intersex persons, but it always evaporates after we sleep together, or by the second time, max. I might remember them fondly, but it's not the same as what people describe as romantic love."

Beth nodded solemnly. "You could make some serious money if aliens and robots ever came into the picture."

They spent the rest of the drive simulating the soundtrack to Tawny's alien-robot pornographic debut.

TAWNY PARKED HER CAR IN THE FIRST EMPTY SPOT SHE FOUND ON GREEK Row. Young men and women were milling about everywhere in the soft spring night, weaving in and out of huge old houses with every window lit up.

"What do you think? How about that one?"

"No, that one." Beth pointed to a house with the letters Zeta Chi Upsilon emblazoned on it, where a young man stood in front of the door holding a red Solo cup in one hand and a drooping rubber spear in the other. The outside of the house was decorated with what appeared to be large, fluffy clouds with golden beams of light emanating from them.

"What the hell do you think is going on there?"

"I don't know, but I'm totally down to find out."

"Don't forget the coffee." Tawny grabbed their to-go cups and Beth carried the pie as they got out of the car and walked to the ZXY house. Hopefully they wouldn't be outed as the desperately uncool ancient relics they were.

Up close, the frat sentinel was wearing a Wagnerian horned helmet and a rhinestone-bedecked plastic breastplate that had apparently been salvaged from a child's costume, as it was many sizes too small for him. The sounds of a full-on rager echoed from inside the house.

"Greetings, fair nymphs, and-or goddesses!"

"Hi!" They both smiled brightly at him, but Tawny let Beth lead the way. "We're from Psi Phi Ep, and we're uh, here for"— Beth looked up at the hand-lettered sign taped to the wall—"the 'Come as your favorite mythological figure and end of finals' party."

"Wait, before I can let you in, you have to prove your divine credentials. For in addition to being Caleb, junior in Sports Economics, I am also Heimdall, guardian of the entrance to Asgard." He stifled a belch.

Beth thought for a moment. "Okay, I'm… the Morrigan, Celtic goddess of death. You can tell because I have some leftover shrouds on me." She pointed out the cobwebs still clinging to her black dress.

"Right on. What about you?" He brandished his spear at Tawny.

Tawny faltered. She wasn't exactly up on world mythology, but Beth stepped in to save her.

"This is Sekhmet, the Egyptian lion goddess known as the Red Lady—"

"She ain't no lady!" A young woman in a crop top and jean shorts gave Tawny a friendly smack on the ass as she wobbled past them out the door and was noisily sick on some nearby shrubbery.

"Jesus, Emily," Heimdall said, turning in her direction. "Are you okay?"

"Not Jesus! I can't turn water into wine, just wine into puke," Emily said, between heaves.

Heimdall yelled over his shoulder at a group of girls in the house. "Sophie! I mean, Xochiquetzal! Your friend is drunk as fuck and she needs water and someone to take care of her!" He turned back to Beth and Tawny. "Anyway, welcome to Olympus, queens of heaven! Partake of our ambrosia!" He flourished dramatically toward a large plastic garbage bin full of radioactive-looking red liquid.

"Ambrosia, huh? What's really in it?"

"The nectar of the gods?"

"Dude. Come on."

He sighed. "Okay, it's jungle juice."

Tawny shot a glance at Beth, full of the psychic imprint of jungle juice–induced horrors. No wonder Emily was ralphing in the bushes. "No, thanks," Beth said. "We brought our own drinks. Strong stuff, too."

"French roast in the hooooooouuuuuuse!" Tawny held aloft the to-go cups in a "raise the roof" gesture.

Beth followed suit. "And we brought pie!"

"Whoo!" A group of students cheered from behind Heimdall at the mention of pie. A young woman wearing a gold lamé toga and a plastic toilet seat on her head—she wore a nametag that read "Cloacina, Goddess of Sewers"—raised her cup. "As the great Saint Augustine of Hippo once said: 'Oh Lord, make me chaste… but not yet!'" She chugged her jungle juice and her fellow revelers did the same.

Beth smiled and shrugged. "*Plus ça change, plus c'est la même chose.*"

As they stepped past Heimdall, another guy gestured toward a room where hip-hop was blaring. "You girls want to dance with some swole dudes?"

"Swole? Oh, I don't know about that—" Beth started to say, but then Tawny grabbed her hand and pulled her forward.

"Yes, we absolutely do."

FOR THE NEXT TWO HOURS, THEY FREAK-DANCED, WATCHED A FEW KEG stands, and brought many a boy to the yard with their milkshakes. Eventually, Tawny headed to the kitchen in search of water, and after a short while, Beth wandered in after her, fanning herself.

"There you are. Hey, I don't mean to be a wet blanket, but are you ready to head out soon? While it's very flattering to be grinded on by heavily-muscled dudes a decade younger than me, I think I grew out of this for a reason."

"Sure, and anyway, I'm kind of hungry and our pie was devoured by hungry bros." Tawny pointed at the tin, which now lay dented on the counter. It was empty, save for a few crumbs and red smears of cherry filling.

"Good point. We should call it a night."

Tawny couldn't bear for their evening of fun to be over. "We don't have to. I'm at the hotel up the hill, and we could order all the pie we want through room service. Honestly, I'd love to just hang out and shoot the shit with you. It's been so long."

Beth smiled. "I was kind of hoping you'd say that. Let's leave the kids to their fun and go do grown-up things like eating room service ice cream and giving each other manicures."

"Farewell, swole bros!" Tawny called, leading the way back to the front door.

They waved goodbye to another chorus of friendly whooping, and from somewhere nearby, the voice of Xochiquetzal said, "It's your turn to hold *my* hair."

FIVE

IN WHICH DANGER IS FORECAST
AND FORTUNES SEALED

"HOLY SHIT." BETH STARED AROUND THE HOTEL ROOM—REALLY, A SUITE of rooms. "This place is huge and swanky."

Tawny clicked on the TV for background noise and a potential distraction from any awkward situations that might arise. She desperately wanted this to go well.

"Make yourself at home. By which I mean you have full permission to flop on either of the beds—I'm totes gonna." She kicked off her high-heeled sandals and launched herself onto the heap of clean sheets and neatly arranged ornamental pillows.

"Do you have company?"

"No, I always get two beds. That way I can keep my stuff on one and sleep in the other."

"That, quite frankly, is brilliant." Beth hopped onto the second bed. They both stretched out and rubbed their feet.

"Can I see the book?" Beth asked after a moment.

Tawny grabbed it from the nightstand and passed it over to her, reminiscing as she watched Beth turn through the pages.

One Saturday night, near the beginning of their sophomore year, they'd started out with a case of beer and a discussion about the Zeta Chi Upsilon brother Tawny was seeing. She was annoyed because, while a girl could hardly ask for a sexier guy, he was surprisingly lackluster in the sack. Both times she'd slept with him, he seemed confused that being dazzlingly good looking wasn't enough to bring her to ecstatic climax. Sadly, he was a bit lazy when it came down to it. It seemed like such a waste.

The talk had morphed into one of those marathon, life-defining conversations that people seem to have in abundance during college. Comparing notes about sexual experiences, the two of them developed their central hypothesis. By the time the early morning sun crept in through the windows, they were almost sober and lay sprawled on the floor with a huge five-subject grid notebook that would ultimately become known as "The Score." In it, they recorded their few college conquests to date, with brief descriptions of each encounter. Each one was ranked by their sexual competence, as objectively as possible, on a simple scale of one to five points.

Beth had explained some of the historical and anthropological context. "Basically, every society is obsessed with controlling women's sexuality! The same behavior that has been acceptable for men for millennia is considered horrifying and wrong if a woman does it. The Romans actually thought cunnilingus was dirtier than anal sex."

"God, our culture is so screwed up," Tawny said.

"We should turn this thing into a slam book for fucking," Beth said.

"Yes!" Tawny said happily, clapping her hands together. "And, you know, this could be kind of valuable information, from a research perspective. Really, we'd be doing humanity a huge favor."

The result of this conversation was a thrillingly exciting adventure, in which they each bedded a good number of men (and women—even at that point Tawny knew she was an omnisexual) and recorded their findings. At some point rumors got out about the project and they had to resort to keeping the book hidden at all times. It became—perhaps unsurprisingly—a semi-mythical hot-ticket item that a lot of the men and women on campus would have gone to great lengths to acquire. Near the end they were frequently approached by people who wanted to pay them, either for the fabled book itself or for information contained within it—for all kinds of reasons.

Some were men who suspected they hadn't fared well and wanted to get rid of the evidence that proved it. *What evidence?*

Some were men who thought they'd done all right and who were hopeful that the girls might be willing to leak their performance around campus. *Sorry, no can do. It might make it look like the guys we don't talk about weren't good, and nobody needs all of campus thinking he's a crummy lay… even if he was.*

Some were men wanting to know how they'd done and interested in any constructive criticism that might improve their game. Usually Beth and Tawny accommodated these requests willingly, since they viewed themselves as having a humanitarian obligation to help anyone interested in such self-improvement.

And some were women trying to conduct what amounted to background checks on new boyfriends. *Sorry. We'll let you know if he's a mean drunk, but you have to learn about his dick yourself.*

Despite the confluence of inquiries, they both kept to their general policy of denial that any such book existed. They also strictly maintained the personal privacy of their subjects. It seemed somehow unethical otherwise. The exception to this rule, of course, was when a man had done something during an encounter that made them think he represented a physical threat to women in general. In these cases they spread the word as diplomatically as possible to the women on campus that they should watch themselves with those certain guys who had shown a proclivity for getting too aggressive or otherwise dangerous when they had a girl alone.

By the end of senior year, they'd gradually abandoned the project. It was a combination of factors—senior theses and graduation were time-consuming if you cared about your education at all, which they both did—and they had become a bit too famous on campus. People were all too aware now of the girls who kept score—and not all of them wanted to put themselves under the microscope. Even if said girls did have an impeccable reputation for keeping the specifics of their encounters in confidence.

And here they were, ten years later. Now what? How could they reconcile their reunion with the demands of life that would reassert themselves as soon as this magical weekend was over?

Tawny knew other people would find it silly, but sometimes when she was puzzling over a social conundrum it helped her to picture a command line interface inside her head. She'd feed it the problem and the parameters of the situation and let logic tell her what should happen next.

The facts were these:

Beth had money trouble, and a job she disliked, she didn't have a boyfriend or probably even any good sex toys, and Tawny suspected she spent most of her time being worried about things.

Tawny was a literal billionaire, she had a job she loved that she could do from home, she didn't want a significant other, if she wanted them she could afford a whole roomful of dildos, and she didn't worry about much, except whether she would ever, ever have meaningful companionship again.

Which gave her this:

```
> BETH -$ -PARTNER -DILDO +STRESS
> TAWNY +$ +JOB -PARTNER +LONELY
>>> HOUSEMATES <<<
```

Two single women in their thirties, and one of them with a kid? Well, that was wrong—she was solving important life problems, not pitching a three-camera sitcom. Try something else.

```
> TAWNY -BETH +20YRS
>>> CAT LADY <<<

> RECALC -CATS
>>> HOWARD HUGHES <<<

> RECALC -CATS -URINEBOTTLES
>>> PRINCE -MUSIC <<<
```

Ugh. Well, try another.

```
> BETH -$ +20YRS
>>> TRAILER PARK FEMME FATALE <<<
```

Fuck. Well—

"What're you thinking?" Beth looked up from the book.

"Oh. Well, just that…" Tawny felt suddenly shy. "I'm glad we're here. I mean, I'm sorry the reunion turned out to suck. But I don't feel as bad about it now." She glanced at Beth. "Do you want to do something tomorrow? I get it if you had other plans or if tonight sucked too much and you just want to go home."

"Actually, I was just trying to decide whether to ask you the same thing," Beth said. "I don't even care what we do. We can hang out here talking and eating all weekend for all I care. I don't think I realized how much I'd missed doing stuff like that."

"This might be a weird thing to suggest," Tawny began, gesturing at the book, "but that thing is in bad shape and—"

"Are you thinking what I'm thinking?" Beth asked. "Make a new copy? Preserve it?" She looked eager at the prospect.

"Yes!" Tawny said with excitement. "I mean, if nothing else, for sentimental reasons."

"I'm in," Beth declared. "The copy place is just up the street. Or we can buy a notebook and transcribe it by hand."

"Sure, whichever, we'll figure it out."

Maybe the computer in her head was on to something after all.

"Let's raid the mini bar!" Tawny bounced up from the bed and opened the little refrigerator, surveying the selection of small bottles.

"Wait, aren't these things, like, super expensive?"

Tawny knew that sometimes people got weird about the generosity of others, but she couldn't think of a way to casually mention how she'd become a billionaire without bringing up stuff that would raise far too many questions.

"Sure, it normally would be expensive, except I'm in one of those loyalty rewards programs and I blew a bunch of my points this weekend. Everything is comped."

"Seriously? *Everything?*"

"Yeah, if we wanted to we could spend all night drinking Cristal and calling psychic hotlines for free."

"I always wanted to do that."

"Call a psychic hotline? Do those even exist anymore?" Tawny grabbed the landline phone and dialed a number. "Guess there's one way to find out."

"What are you doing?"

"Testing something."

The sound of elevator music floated out of the phone receiver, followed by an automated message. "You have reached Miss Clea's hotline. Please enter your credit card information to be connected with one of our psychics. $4.99 for the first five minutes, plus $3.99 for each additional minute."

"It works! The future is ours!" Tawny entered her credit card number, giggling.

"What, you just knew that phone number off the top of your head?"

"Sort of. When I was a teenager I'd sit around dialing random 1-800 numbers with random sex words, and one time I hit on 1-800-NUT-SACK. As it turns out, that number belongs to a psychic hotline."

"Did you get your fortune told?"

"No, at the time psychics were way less interesting to me than nutsacks, so I hung up."

"Hey, it's ringing again!"

This time, a woman answered. "Welcome to Miss Clea's House of Aquarius. Part the veil of time and learn what the universe has in store for you," she intoned in a terrible fake Jamaican accent that sounded like a mangled Irish lilt.

"Hi, Miss Clea. My name's Tawny and I'm here with my friend Beth. We'll put you on speakerphone so you can talk to us both."

"Hello, ladies. I'm sensing… is one of you a Libra?"

Beth stifled a laugh. "No, but we definitely have some questions about our destiny."

"Let me call the spirits and all of the past, present, and future will be revealed!" A maraca sounded in the background. "Okay, the spirits have come. What do you wish to know?"

"Uh…" Tawny hesitated. It occurred to her that the question she most wanted to ask was not something she wanted Beth to overhear.

"We can always begin with matters of love," Miss Clea suggested. "Everyone wants to hear about love."

"Gross, no." Beth stuck her tongue out.

"Wait, what's this?" Miss Clea said in a not-very-convincing surprised tone.

"I don't know, what?"

"Ahem. Danger, I see, in your futures!"

"What kind of danger?"

"Let me consult the cards."

"I thought you were consulting the spirits," Beth protested.

"The spirits speak… through the cards," Miss Clea replied peevishly. "Do you want to hear this or not?"

"Sorry, we'll be good."

"All right, then. I'm having a vision of a blue car—"

"Holy shit, *my* car is blue!" Tawny burst out.

"It is?" Beth asked.

"Well, more like a blue-gray. Or gray with a bluish sheen. I guess you could call it slate. Or gunmetal? Anyway, Miss Clea, are we going to meet our demise in a gruesome accident?"

"Uh, no… more like mild-to-moderate danger. Ah, yes, it becomes clear now—you should get that alternator belt looked at. The spirits… cards… portend a most bumpy ride and a big bill at the mechanic that could easily be prevented with a regular maintenance schedule."

"I'll get right on that."

"Oh my God, Tawny." Beth had been watching the TV guide scroll across the screen, when she sat straight up and grabbed the remote. "The Super Mario Brothers movie is on. Remember that?"

"Yeah, we watched this with Jess and Kim and Xiaowen on Terrible Movie Night. It was the best-worst thing ever. The… burst thing ever."

"Our duty as good humans demands we watch it now."

"Hey, Miss Clea, you down for catching a movie with us?"

"It's your $3.99 a minute, honey."

"Great! Pull up the streaming site and you can watch along. And, I mean, the spirits can chime in too if they have any input."

"Sounds delightful."

"I know, right? You're gonna love this."

"Bob Hoskins is a national treasure," Beth yelled at the phone.

Midway through the classic Goomba dancing scene, Beth got up to go to the bathroom. As soon as she was out of sight, Tawny grabbed the phone and switched off the speaker.

"Hey, Miss Clea?" she whispered.

"Yeah?"

"I genuinely need your help on something. I just reconnected with someone I've been close to in the past, but we haven't seen each other in years. I'm afraid that after this weekend, they'll disappear again."

"And you want to take things to the next level?"

"That's one way of putting it. But what if I scare them off by coming on too strong?"

"Then they weren't truly the one for you anyway. You should let them know how much they matter before it's too late. At least, that's what the spirits are telling me."

Tawny would have asked her for some specifics about taking that leap of faith, but Beth came back from the bathroom at that exact moment and Tawny put down the receiver and switched Miss Clea back to speakerphone.

Beth waved her back to the TV. "Oh, I love this part."

Tawny set the phone on its side. Onscreen, John Leguizamo's Luigi confessed his star-crossed love to the Princess.

"But Daisy... I wanna be with you." He pronounced it "witchoo."

They both giggled hysterically. Tawny seized the moment.

"You know, this reminds me of something."

"What's that?"

"Well, much like Dennis Hopper in his iconic role as King Koopa, I'm super busy all the time." Worst. Segue. Ever. *Dumbass*, she berated herself. "You know, with my experiments and all."

"You're devolving people into dinosaurs and fungi?"

"Only on weekends. Most of the time it's just a lot of math. And lasers."

Considering that her super-secret project did in fact involve things moving backward through time, Tawny was tempted to tell her everything right then and there, but she restrained herself—if she went too far, she might scare Beth away and ruin everything. But Beth looked curious. Maybe this would work out.

"Anyway, I've been working on an important freelance project, and it's eating up all my time, and well, my house and all my affairs in general have just sort of collapsed. Not structurally, of course. Before I bought the house I checked all the foundations myself."

"I think I get what you mean." Tawny realized that Beth was being very patient with her. *Get to the point!* she told herself.

"So I was thinking... I could use a personal assistant. Someone to manage all my stuff while I'm sciencing. And you mentioned that you hate your job and I know you're super smart and competent and good at this sort of thing"—she knew she was babbling, but if she didn't get it out now, she'd lose her nerve—"and my house is more than big enough to accommodate not only a live-in assistant, but also any children they might have—did I mention it's in a great school district? Suffice it to say, maybe it's the sleep deprivation talking, but I hereby offer you the job of personal assistant." She looked at Beth. "To me," she added.

There was a long pause, broken only by the sound of Miss Clea, softly singing along with "Walk the Dinosaur" as the end credits rolled.

Beth dissolved into giggles again. "Yeah, I wish... well, at least I know I'm not the only one who's had too much from the mini bar!" she teased.

Tawny looked at the floor.

Beth abruptly stopped laughing. "Wait—are you *serious?*" she asked, blinking in surprise. "You would really do that?"

Tawny shrugged.

"But this is the first you've seen me in years! What if I've turned into a nut and you ask me to do this and then you get stuck with a crazy person for an assistant!"

"I was just messing around. Anyway, you don't seem like a crazy person."

"I might be," Beth said. "Because I kinda want to say yes."

"Just forget it," Tawny said. "We're drunk."

Beth groped for the phone handset on the carpet between them. "Miss Clea?" she asked. "Are you getting this?"

"Yep," said a bored voice on the other end of the line. Whoever she was, their phone psychic had given up the fake Jamaican accent somewhere around the beginning of hour three.

"Well, should I do it? Should I move in with my former college roommate and best friend whom I haven't seen in something like seven years?"

"Probably?" Tawny could almost hear the woman shrug with indifference.

"Let's do it," Beth told her. "I haven't felt like this in years. It's been ages since I did anything more impulsive than try a new ice cream flavor."

"That's for a good reason. We shouldn't decide something like this when we're sloshed," Tawny said. "I don't know what I was thinking suggesting it."

"You're not sloshed," Beth argued. "You always had a hollow leg for booze. You knew what you were saying, and I think it's a good idea."

"We can talk about it in the morning," Tawny said. "I'm sorry I said anything. You already got one ridiculous job offer tonight. You didn't deserve another."

Beth stared at her, taking her measure, before pulling her phone out of her pocket.

"What are you doing?" Tawny asked anxiously. "Put that away."

"You always underestimate yourself socially," Beth said. "You get hopeful with somebody, and then you get scared that you overreached and you withdraw."

"Maybe," Tawny said. "But we can talk about it later. We have all day tomorrow and Sunday to figure it out."

"I know all your tricks," Beth said, tapping at her phone's screen and holding Tawny at bay with her other arm as she tried to reach for the phone. She held it to her ear, leaning as far from Tawny as she could get. "Besides, we'll need tomorrow and Sunday to get all my shit packed up."

"Hi Ted," she said into the phone. "It's Beth Bird. I'm sorry for the abrupt notice, but I have to tell you that I've received a very lucrative offer and won't be returning to work again." Tawny stopped trying to get the phone away from her and slouched against the bed with a little sound of dismay. "I'm afraid you'll have to punch fuck PaperPride yourself this time," Beth continued. "Thanks for understanding!"

"God, I can't believe you did that," Tawny groaned. "When you sober up you're never going to forgive me for letting you quit your job."

"When I sober up?" Beth asked innocently. "I'm not drunk."

Tawny raised her eyes to meet Beth's, an excited, scared thrill of disbelief fluttering through her. "You mean you actually want to do this?"

"Shit yeah, I want to do this. You're the best friend I ever had and you just handed me a golden ticket. Let's get some sleep, and then you can help me decide what to say to the hag who runs my kid's daycare."

Tawny laughed. "I'm sure we can figure something out."

"I'm gonna be honest," Beth said. "My main goal is to use the words 'culture of violence' in an unironic context."

SIX

IN WHICH BETH BECOMES THE
PROUD PARENT OF A WIZARD

BETH PULLED HER CAR UP BEHIND THE MOVING VAN, LOOKING AT TAWNY'S neighborhood and trying to decide whether it was what she'd imagined when she'd accepted the job offer a week ago. This place was so… ordinary. Upscale, but more suburban than she'd pictured for someone like Tawny. The subdivision was new, almost shadeless, with trees still dwarfed by the houses. Beth had done some advance research about the neighborhood that week during a break from packing, trying to decide what options she would have when Jules was ready for school in the fall. It was one of those intentionally planned communities, with retail and schools in walking distance, and houses big as McMansions, except that none of them looked the same. The surprisingly stately homes occupied huge lots, spaced well apart from each other, but arranged so that Tawny's street looked more cozy than the size of the houses should have allowed.

This house, simply put, was incredible. Built in the Mediterranean style and landscaped in a way that made her think more of Florida than the Midwest, Tawny's home was nestled at the end of a long drive. Beth wasn't sure how a house with three balconies facing the front could nestle, but it managed.

"Wow," Jules said from the back. "This is our new house?"

Beth broke out of her reverie and undid her seat belt. "Yep. Wow is right. I guess we should go inside and see Tawny and have a look around, huh?"

The front door was propped open for the movers, who had arrived before them and were busy at work moving Beth's small household into Tawny's great room. "This place is big," was all Jules said as they moved aside for a man carrying stacked boxes.

"Beth? Are you guys here?" Tawny called as she came into view. "Hi!" she said, giving Jules a little wave. "These guys are almost done moving your stuff, I think. I thought we could look around a little and then have lunch. After we eat I can show you the neighborhood."

"This place is big," Jules said again.

"I guess it is," Tawny agreed. "Want to see your room?"

Jules looked around, frowning slightly. Beth wondered what she was thinking. "All right," she agreed, extending her hand to Tawny, who hesitated for a moment before taking it.

"I'm going to duck into the bathroom first," Beth said. "Find you in a minute?"

"Sure," Tawny said, pointing with her free hand. "Just off the kitchen, through there. We'll be upstairs."

"Where are your kids?" she heard Jules asking Tawny as they walked away through the house.

The kitchen was the nicest one she had ever seen in someone's house, with swaths of pink marble covering every surface, an island and serving bar about a mile long, and a display of expensive cooking implements that had clearly never been used. It looked like someone had asked a handful of people what the "best" things were to put in one's house, and after hearing their recommendations had gone to the Le Creuset and Williams-Sonoma websites and ordered one of everything.

Forgetting the bathroom in her curiosity, she pulled on the handle to a tall cabinet and stepped back in surprise at the rush of cold air that engulfed her. It was a walk-in refrigerator. Beth leaned inside to look, fascinated. She'd never heard of a person having a walk-in fridge in their home. Tawny's, which was probably big enough to support the operations of a small restaurant, contained three things—a quart-sized carton of whole milk that bulged alarmingly at the sides, a bottle of not-from-concentrate orange juice, and some leftover Asian takeout of indiscernible age.

She closed the fridge door, feeling dazed at the thought that, starting now, she'd be doing all her cooking in this kitchen that was bigger than her old bedroom. The washroom Tawny had pointed out was just off the kitchen and she used it hastily, eager to see the rest of the house and settle in.

"Jules?" she called as she climbed the staircase at the center of the house. "Tawny?" She heard the pounding of feet as Jules ran down the hallway.

"Mom! Come see my castle!"

"You have a castle? You mean, like a dollhouse?" Beth questioned, looking at the huge chandelier hanging over the staircase. Whoever had done Tawny's decorating, they were good.

"Come *see* it!" Beth let Jules pull her by one hand up the stairs to the second level. She wanted to slow down and look at her surroundings—was that an *elevator?*— but Jules kept impatiently tugging her along.

Tawny stepped out onto the landing as they approached, looking nervous. "I hope this is okay. I mean, they say you shouldn't spoil kids, but I just thought, this is a big change, maybe Jules would like something nice, and, I mean, we don't have to keep this, although now that I mention that, I shouldn't have shown her already, I guess…" She seemed to realize that she was meandering, and trailed off.

"I'm sure it's not that big a deal—oh." Beth gawked at Jules's new room. Like everything else she'd seen in the house so far, it was a prime example of a room being its own platonic ideal. There had never existed a more perfect representation of a little girl's room.

The walls were a gentle blush color. The furniture and trim were white. Everything else was the garish princess-pink that Jules loved most—the comforters on the brand-new, gleaming white bunk bed that sat against one wall, the curtains, the wall art, the cushion on the stool that accompanied the child-sized vanity positioned next to the bed, and the painted seats and top of the also child-sized table and chairs on the other side of the bed. Tawny had rounded out all of this with a built-in bookshelf that ran the length of the room opposite the bed, which was pre-populated with books, puzzles, and games.

But the *pièce de résistance* was the castle, complete with tiny keep and turrets, which filled the entire far wall of the room and was built right against the balcony that faced the front of the house. She crossed to look at it more closely. "Jesus, is this— Tawny, is this built into the wall? This is incredible." The castle was taller than her, with a real wooden door on the lower level, and a top platform with a sturdy-looking rail. It even had a slide that allowed quick access from the top back to the floor.

"Don't worry," Tawny said as Beth ran her hands along the textured faux-stone plastic exterior of the toy castle. "It's very safe. The door can't be barred from the inside, so you can't be locked out. And… I made sure they built the ceiling inside high enough for us to fit inside, if we sit. Plus, the slide swings out of the way to make it easier for us big people to get to the balcony. So…"

Jules ran up to Tawny and hugged her around the middle. "I *love* my castle," she exclaimed before breaking away and throwing open the door to the keep. Beth heard a clambering sound and then Jules peered down at her from atop the castle. "I cast a spell," she announced.

"What kind of spell?" Tawny asked. "Are you a witch?"

Jules considered the question. "No," she decided. "A wizard. Are there princess wizards?"

"Sure," Tawny told her. "I don't see why not."

"You didn't have to do all this," Beth said. "I was... going to get her some new stuff myself after we got moved in," she finished lamely. She'd planned to take Jules to Target and pick out a bed and decorations as soon as she got her first paycheck.

"Are princess wizards better than regular wizards?" Jules asked.

"Probably," Beth said.

"I know I didn't," Tawny hedged. "But... I just wanted today to be special. I can afford it. And... I wanted her to like me."

"Well, she definitely likes you. I'm guessing she likes you more than me right now." Beth watched Jules wave at them from the castle, trying to decide how she felt about Tawny spending so much money on her and whether it was wrong to be okay with it.

Tawny much be a *lot* richer than Beth had originally thought. "Doing okay," was how she had put it the previous weekend. What did that mean, exactly, if she could afford to casually deck out a little kid's room like this in a week's time? If she lived in a brand-new three story house outfitted like this?

"I'm sorry," Tawny said, staring at the floor. "I didn't mean to mess this up. I always do this. I can—"

"Tawny." Beth stopped her. "It's okay. It really is. This surprised me, but you didn't do anything wrong. And Jules obviously loves it. I think... I think I'm just worried about not wanting to be a mooch or take advantage of you."

"Oh, no, I would never think that about you—" Tawny said, but cut herself off when Jules stuck her head out one of the windows on the floor level of the castle.

"Tawny? Can we get curtains for my castle?"

"Honey, don't—" Beth began.

"Yeah, sure—" Tawny started at the same time.

They looked at each other. Tawny gave Beth a tiny shrug. "It's just curtains."

"All right," Beth said. "But just so you know, Jules—this is a special occasion. You won't be getting presents like this all the time just because we're living in a nicer place."

"Presents," Jules said disdainfully. "I have a castle."

"Can we come in?" Tawny asked. "Princess-Wizard?"

"Yeah. If you show me how to make potions."

"Sure," Tawny said. "After lunch."

They ducked their heads and went inside the castle. Tawny was right—Beth could stand almost all the way up. Tawny took a seat at a table so small that it made her look comically over-sized, and reached over to flip a switch that lit a number of small plastic torches installed on the walls. The torches bathed the space in a pleasant, comforting light.

"I mean, wouldn't you have just died to have something like this when you were a kid?" Tawny asked as Beth joined her in one of the small chairs. "I'm not sure if I built it more for her or for me."

"It is really cool," Beth agreed, looking with mild awe at a faux-stone lion figure that crouched in one corner of the keep. "I'm torn—on the one hand, I don't want her to develop an entitlement complex. And I know you said it was okay, but I don't want us to take advantage of you. On the other hand... this is so amazingly, stupidly awesome."

"I promise I won't spoil her. Well, not *too* much, anyway. I read some books about children this week so I would know how to be a good role model."

Beth laughed despite herself. "I don't know if you can learn that from a book or not. But you'll figure it out."

"I just wanted to say—" Tawny began hesitantly. "I just wanted to say, I'm glad you're both here. I almost backed out of it last week and I'm glad you stopped me. I'm… excited to have people around. And I hope I didn't screw it up by getting things off on the wrong foot."

"You didn't. And… me too," Beth said, surprised by the rush of emotion that accompanied her words. "I've been looking forward to today all week," she continued after clearing her throat heavily. "And I'm looking forward to starting over. I missed having a friend like you."

"Yeah."

Beth heard a whooshing sound. Realizing that Jules had come down the slide, she and Tawny turned just as she appeared at the door to the keep. "This slide is a security risk," Jules informed them.

Beth burst out laughing and stood to leave the castle. "How so?" she asked, stifling her laughter when she saw Jules's serious expression.

"Anybody could climb up there. Even without magic."

"We could make a spell to keep them out of the top," Tawny suggested as she ducked her head to follow Beth.

"I don't know," Jules said, looking dubious as she twisted a lock of her thick brown hair around one finger. "It would have to be a big spell."

"You're in luck, then. I'm a big wizard." Beth watched as Tawny stood up to her full height. "See? Get me a wand." She pointed at a toy box across the room.

Jules ran and rummaged through the chest.

"So," Tawny remarked, "I guess we have a spellcraft lesson, and then… lunch? I ordered a delivery from the grocery store earlier so we wouldn't have to leave until we felt like it."

"OH, SHIT, YOU DIDN'T TELL ME YOU HAD A POOL!" BETH SAID AS THEY carried their food out onto the patio. The rear of the house looked out over a large patio and a spacious, immaculately groomed backyard which terminated in front of another structure that was of modern construction, but had been built in the style of an old-fashioned carriage house. "And a hot tub? Wow. That'll be great after I finish unpacking."

"I got us some Gewürztraminer for just that purpose. And I'll help you unpack." Tawny opened a container of chicken salad and spooned a little onto a plate. "Hey Jules," she called. "Come try this."

"I guarantee you she won't eat that. It has celery, and mayonnaise... and chicken."

"She doesn't eat chicken?"

"She barely eats anything. There are like four remotely healthy things she'll eat and about a thousand horrible things she's fine with. The pediatrician says it's a phase."

"Wow. That sounds like a nightmare."

"Yeah. It's kind of crazy-making. Sometimes she changes the rules on the four things she'll eat and doesn't tell me."

Jules came over to the table, squinting doubtfully. "What's that?" she inquired, pointing at the plate.

"Nothing," Tawny said. "I changed my mind about giving you any."

"Why?"

"Your mom says you wouldn't like it."

"Why?"

"I don't know. Because you're picky."

"Hmm. True," Jules conceded. "But, what is it?"

"Don't worry about it," Tawny said, reaching for the plate. "Your mom brought you out some cheese and crackers."

"But what *is* that?"

"Bird poop."

"What?" Jules screwed up her face.

"That's her 'are you lying?' face," Beth put in, straining against the urge to laugh.

"*Are* you lying?" Jules demanded.

"Seriously, you're asking me that?" Tawny asked. "Bird poop is nature's best kept secret. Anyway, it's cool that it's not your thing. I'd kind of rather have it for myself. It's expensive anyway."

Jules eyed the plate again. "I want to try it," she told Tawny.

Beth stared at them, afraid to interrupt whatever miracle was taking place in front of her.

"Nah." Tawny picked up a cracker and scooped up some chicken salad, then popped it in her mouth.

"Tawny. Please?"

Tawny chewed slowly, pretending to think about it.

"Do you want me to get *depressed*?"

"Depressed? That bad, huh?" Tawny slid a fork across the table.

Jules took a tentative bite, wearing a face that said she was ready to spit it back out immediately if it displeased her. "Is this *really* bird poop?" she asked, rolling it around in her mouth.

"Yep. Can I have it back now? I mean, you don't like it, do you?"

"Maybe," Jules said, taking another forkful while Beth looked on in awe. "What kind of bird pooped this? It's kind of... good."

"Different birds," Tawny said, picking up the container. "This one says—oh, albatross, that's a rare one—okay, so this one is albatross, duck and red-tailed hawk. And owl. That must be what the chunks are."

"What's an albatross?"

"It's a very large bird," Beth explained. "Usually it lives by the ocean."

"Why?"

"They eat fish."

"Why?"

"Because they live by the ocean."

"What's a red-tailed hawk?" Jules had almost finished the glob of chicken salad.

"It's a bird that makes a sound like this." Tawny made a surprisingly realistic imitation of a hawk's cry.

"Do that again!"

She did.

"Why is it crunchy?" Jules wanted to know.

"Probably mouse bones?" Tawny guessed. "From the owl."

"Really?" Jules crunched the celery bits gleefully between her teeth. "Poor mice."

"Want a cracker?" Tawny held one out.

Jules took it and scooped up the last of the chicken salad. "Can I go play? Tawny has a turtle sandbox," she told Beth, chewing loudly. "With shovels."

"Sure. Remember to put the lid back when you're done, so cats won't poop in it."

"Gross." Jules wrinkled her nose. "I wouldn't eat *that*." She flounced away.

"What are you, a kid whisperer?" Beth asked. "You got her to eat something with more than one ingredient. And nobody cried."

"I don't know. Maybe kids just like gross stuff?" Tawny speculated.

"I'm vaguely disgusted with her, but still dizzy with the possibilities. What else can we get her to eat under the guise of it being bird shit?"

"Ham salad. Tuna salad."

"Risotto?"

"Oh, yeah, I bet I could talk her into that. I love risotto. Do you think she'd go for Chicken a la King?"

"Maybe."

"What about fettuccine alfredo?"

"Oh, great idea. I make good alfredo sauce, too."

"That sounds awesome. I don't always take the time out to sit down for proper meals."

"Let's do that from now on," Beth suggested. "You wouldn't know it to look at what I've been up to the last few years, but I love cooking. And it'll be good for all of us."

"Well, it'll be good as long as we can invent enough new kinds of animal poop to feed her," Tawny said, laughing.

Beth grinned. Taking this job was the best decision she'd made in a long time.

SEVEN

IN WHICH TAWNY MAKES
AN UNLIKELY ALLY
AMONGST THE PARROTS

TAWNY HAD ALWAYS BEEN UNEASY AROUND LITTLE KIDS—SHE WAS SO tall and ungainly, and they were so… small. It didn't help that her own time as one of them hadn't exactly been a basket of kittens and rainbows. And she'd never had much going on in the way of maternal instincts. On the odd occasion one of her fellow scientists spawned, Tawny had always fled the scene before they could make her hold the baby. What if something happened to it on her watch?

So her happiness about Beth's decision to accept her offer was abruptly tempered by the realization that she would have to live with a child. A child she'd never met, to whom she wasn't even related. She wasn't a cool auntie or a long-time friend of the family that Beth's little girl would recognize or trust. Tawny had no idea what to do with a five-year-old. Jules was too young to be governed by snake law—that shit was only for high school and above. Kids wouldn't come when you called them—they had to be coaxed, she heard. If you spooked them, they'd try to hide, generally under the stove or in a box, though they could be lured out with food. Or was that cats? Tawny didn't have one of those, either.

In an effort not to ruin everything at the last minute, she had prepared several possible opening lines for their first meeting:

"Hi there, little girl. You like farts, right? Farts are funny. Let's talk about farts."

Or:

"You may have noticed that unlike your mom I don't communicate well with other humans, but that doesn't mean I'm a robot. Even if I was a robot, I would never shoot you with my laser eyes. I'm totally not a robot, though."

Or maybe even:

"Don't go under the stove, there are spiders. Here, I got you this can of tuna."

The worry set in for real on their trip back to Beth's apartment in the city to begin the moving process. What if Jules hated her? No matter how awesome their newly revived friendship might be, Tawny couldn't imagine Beth utterly forsaking her child's feelings regarding their living situation. And Tawny wouldn't want her to do that. Maybe she could bribe Jules. But with what?

"Hey Beth, I was thinking, about meeting Jules for the first time—I know kids can be leery of unfamiliar things, but is there anything she likes? Do kids like specific things at her age? I assume she has object permanence now."

"Yes, she does."

"Well, there's that at least." Tawny decided not to mention the can of tuna in her jacket pocket.

"Tawny, I know you don't have much experience with kids, but you'll be fine. Jules likes all the same stuff we did at that age. Princesses and ponies and neon pink but also astronauts and

King Arthur. Though I don't want to think about her acting out weird, vaguely BDSM-spectrum games with her Barbies the way I did when I was five."

"Oh man, I remember that conversation, back in undergrad. I think that was when I knew we would be best friends—when we each confessed all of the crazy sex things we did to our toys when we were kids. It wasn't just us, I remember other chicks admitting it too."

Beth smiled. "It's an important moment in any young woman's life… the day she realizes there are other girls out there who are total weirdos just like her."

The rest of the drive had just been them joking and reminiscing, but then, all too soon, they arrived at Beth's apartment complex, a collection of squat brick buildings with either concrete "yards" or flimsy-looking outdoor balconies. Tawny waited with trepidation, hovering a few steps behind as Beth led the way into her apartment and had a short conversation with the babysitter, who looked surprised to hear that Beth was moving.

Beth was so natural with people. Tawny watched from the side as she explained everything, touching the girl on the elbow and talking about how much she had helped them and how much Beth appreciated her. At the end, Beth handed her an envelope and they hugged.

"I'm going to go wake up Jules from her nap so she can say bye to Chris," Beth told them before disappearing down the short apartment hallway.

The babysitter made a couple of awkward attempts at small talk, but Tawny was too nervous to muster the energy required for a conversation with a complete stranger. She answered in monosyllables until the girl gave up and pretended to look at her cell phone. Finally, Beth emerged, holding hands with a sleepy-looking little girl.

The babysitter knelt and gave her a hug. "I'll see you Tuesday, Ju-Ju-Be," she said in a friendly voice. "After that I won't see you for a while, but we'll have an amazing time this week. And we'll make some cookies that *don't* turn out gross."

Jules nodded. It looked like she was still half-asleep.

While Beth showed the babysitter to the door, Tawny studied Jules, who definitely took after her mother. She had the same dark, glossy hair and big brown eyes, with which she scanned Tawny warily.

They watched each other while Tawny desperately tried to think of something to say to her, until Beth closed the door and turned back to them. "Jules," she said, "this is my friend Tawny. She's a scientist."

"Hi." Tawny's heart was pounding. She hoped her discomfort wasn't noticeable to Beth and Jules. "I'm your mom's friend." *She already said that, idiot!* Tawny silently yelled at herself. "I am indeed a scientist." *She said that, too!*

Thankfully, Jules picked up the thread of conversation. "Scientists know a lot of stuff, right?"

"Usually in a highly specialized way, but yes."

"Yeah, well… I read *The Hobbit* in only three days."

"That's very impressive," Tawny said. "You must be about as smart as this parrot I used to know."

Jules gave her a suspicious look. "What kind of parrot?"

"He was a kakapo named Bingham from New Zealand. They're flightless, nocturnal, ground-dwelling Strigopoideans that evolved to fill the ecological niches normally occupied by mammals. A biologist friend of mine worked with kakapos and she said that Bingham was as smart as a six-year-old."

"A six-year-old! Mommy, did you hear that?"

One thing Tawny did remember about her childhood was that at Jules's age, every year was a big deal. "Yeah, people used to think they were dim-witted little creatures, but it turns out, they're just kind of shy about their intellectual abilities."

"Just like me. Mrs. Hyde thinks I'm a dim-witted creature, too." Behind Jules, Beth winced visibly. She had told Tawny all about the evil hag who ran the daycare with an iron fist. "What do kakapos look like?"

Tawny relaxed slightly. "Have you seen budgies before?"

Jules nodded.

"They look kind of like that, only much bigger and fatter. They have to be very fat to be considered good looking to other kakapos." On impulse, she grabbed a pillow from the couch and shoved it under her shirt. "They run like this," Tawny squatted down, folded her arms up by her sides and launched into a lumbering jog-waddle. Jules shrieked with delight and imitated her. They raced up and down through the living room like bottom-heavy velociraptors as Beth watched with an expression on her face that was somewhere between laughter and jaw-dropping astonishment.

"High… uh… wing?" Tawny suggested, pointing an elbow at Jules.

"Fat parrots!" Jules yelled, bumping Tawny's outstretched arm with her own.

AFTER THAT, THINGS HADN'T BEEN SO DIFFICULT. TAWNY AND BETH HAD started the packing process, arranged for movers, and everything was finished within the week. Only a few days after moving in, Jules was already trotting around the house like she owned the place, flapping her arms and making twittering noises. She even watched David Attenborough documentaries on the BBC with Tawny on Wednesday nights. Had Tawny known that kids could be this into parrots, she would never have been so terrified of them.

Of course, she'd gotten spectacularly lucky with Jules. There were probably plenty of stupid kids out there who didn't like nature films or anything else Tawny found fun. Jules was almost as good a companion as her mother, who was already the best thing that ever happened to Tawny. It was amazing, the difference friendly companionship could make in a person's life. Tawny felt herself becoming less like Prince-minus-music as soon as they unloaded the last of their stuff. Every day she was a little more grateful to her past self for having the courage to make the job offer.

Things were looking up—not only had she discovered a heretofore unknown talent with children, she'd figured out a solution to her own "Great Matter," as she'd been thematically thinking of it. The whole thing had been Beth's idea, not that Beth knew this.

Tawny was relaxing one afternoon in the breakfast nook with a preparatory stein of mead—she still didn't like it very much, but she knew old-timey people drank mead, so she was practicing not being grossed out by it. It had been a long day in the lab and she was watching the latest episode of one of her favorite premium cable historical boob dramas, *Henry's Women*—strictly for research purposes!—when Beth walked by and did a double take.

"Is this that show about Henry Eight?"

"Henry Eight? You mean Henry the Eighth?"

"Yeah, sorry, it's historian shorthand."

She stood there, watching the screen for a few minutes after Tawny nodded her understanding. "Wow. This shit is terrible," she said after a while. "It's *all* kinds of wrong."

"Really? How?" It occurred to Tawny then that involving Beth in her preparations in some way might be a wise move. She had been a history Ph.D. candidate at one time, and she was smart. Maybe Tawny could pick her brain for useful tidbits.

"Okay, where to even *start*…"

"I know what you're thinking,"—Tawny defended herself—"this is absolute crap. But after sciencing all day, I need a palate cleanser for my brain. Something as stupid as possible. And all my reality shows are on break right now."

"Hey, no judgment here," Beth said. "Well, okay, I'm judging the creators of this show," she amended. "But no judgment on you, I mean. I get the needing-mindless-TV thing. *I* spent the morning with Jules, you might recall, who is developing alarmingly fascist attitudes toward her toys—er, never mind…" She trailed off.

"You were saying?" Tawny prompted. "About the show?"

"So, that woman." Beth pointed to a blonde actress dressed in a powder-blue gown. "She's supposed to be Jane Seymour, right?"

Tawny nodded. "Uh-huh." Beth was awesome at this.

"So, what's she doing?"

"She appears to be fellating the King while he fingers her."

"No, I mean plot-wise."

"Oh. They're about to get married, but first she wants him to have his current wife, Anne Boleyn, killed off."

"Strike one! It's true Henry was already courting Jane Seymour while his marriage to Anne was in its death throes, but Jane refused to let him put it in her until he put a ring on it. Also, she had a reputation for being a pretty decent person. Whether that's the case or not, she likely wasn't publicly rooting for the Queen's death."

"Wow. I had no idea." Inspiration hit Tawny in a sudden flash. She looked at Beth, trying to decide how she could pump her for information without tipping her off that something was up. "When exactly did all that happen?" she asked, trying to sound casual. "I mean, for Anne Boleyn's execution and all that."

"Anne was beheaded at the Tower of London on May 19th, in the year of our Lord fifteen-hundred-and-thirty-six." Beth adopted a foofy English accent and flipped one hand around over her eye like a monocle.

"Damn, you're good. But I'll see your imaginary monocle and raise you an imaginary fancy moustache." Tawny raised her hands to her mouth, pinkies extended. She couldn't help being impressed at how anybody could know all this stuff just off the top of her head. It wasn't like Beth had been studying for this.

"But," Beth continued, "she was arrested right at the beginning of May. So there's strike two for *Henry's Women*, it's Christmas on the set."

"Maybe they had to film it in the winter because they spent all their budget on His Majesty's computer-generated dong?" Tawny suggested.

"Good point, there's no way that thing is natural." Beth began to sing, wearing an exaggeratedly solemn expression. "Deck the balls with veins a-plenty, fa-la-la-la-la-la-la-la-late." Both of them busted up laughing.

"Mommy, why are you singing Christmas songs? Is Christmas soon?" Jules emerged then from her post-lunch nap, and Beth had flushed bright red and changed the subject to something more child appropriate.

So that had been the end of that.

But the exchange made her realize there might be some gaps in her research. Beth's seemingly endless stores of historical knowledge would be just the ticket to close those gaps. Strangely, she'd hadn't even considered Beth's degree when she made her the job offer. At the time of the reunion, she'd barely begun the live organism stage of testing—so she hadn't been looking for a partner in the venture. It was hard to say then whether her invention would ever be more than just a hopeful theory.

But now, thanks to her skill with virtual photons, it was a (theoretically) viable model. She just had to take the machine for a trial run, and provided that went all right, she could tweak things to perfection and then figure out how to talk Beth into trying it with her. It was time to reap the benefit of her years of hard work with a much-deserved vacation. All the hard stuff was behind her.

EIGHT

IN WHICH BETH TAKES DELIVERY
OF A MYSTERIOUS PACKAGE

"Breakfast!" Beth yelled, switching off the burner under the scrambled eggs and transferring the heavy enameled pan to a trivet on the counter. "Jules!" The little girl looked up, impatient at the interruption. "Time for breakfast. Go find Tawny and tell her, okay?" Grumbling, Jules slipped down from her chair and left the room.

It would be a few minutes before they ate. Beth laid slices of cheese over the eggs and clapped a lid over the pan, slipping the food into the oven to keep warm before starting to butter the small stack of raisin toast she'd prepared.

The last few weeks had been good ones. She enjoyed being useful again, and running a household with plenty of resources to do it on was fun. It was hard to guess how rich Tawny might actually be, but her wealth seemed almost bottomless. On their second day there, she'd been handed a credit card with her name on it, so she could take care of household expenses and incidentals with complete autonomy. "My accountant made me put a monthly limit on it," Tawny confessed apologetically. "I picked ten thousand, but you can let me know if that's not enough and I'll get it changed." Beth had assured her she'd probably be able to manage running the house on a mere ten thousand dollars a month.

She heard Jules skipping into the room ahead of Tawny as she finished buttering the last of the toast and moved everything to the table. "Beetle toast!" Jules exclaimed. "Yes. I will eat it."

Tawny caught Beth's eye and they both smiled. Raisins and eggs were among the foods Jules never would have touched in their former life, but Tawny had convinced her that raisins were the chewy sundried remains of dead beetles and that eggs enhanced her "biochemical signature," increasing the odds she would one day develop superpowers.

"Nice horses," Tawny said to Jules, sliding her chair in and reaching for the pan of eggs.

"They're slaves," the little girl replied nonchalantly.

"Well, that sucks," Tawny replied. "I'm totally judging you for that."

"Honey," Beth interrupted, "We talked about this. Remember? Pretending things is okay, but having slaves is a very bad thing. Nobody wants to be a slave."

"They don't mind, they're getting paid," Jules said.

"Then they're not really slaves," Tawny pointed out.

"No," Jules agreed. "They just call themselves that because they love working for me so much."

Tawny shrugged agreeably. "Whatever, weirdo."

Jules cackled happily. Beth reached over and stopped her before she could "feed" cheesy eggs to one of the ponies.

"The ponies can stay on the counter while we finish eating."

"The slaves, you mean," Jules said as her mother removed the toy horses.

"No," Beth said in a firm tone. "I meant ponies." She turned back to her seat, tripped, and barely caught herself from falling face-first into the table. Tawny half rose to come help her, but Beth waved her off.

"What the hell, Jules?" she demanded, looking down at the equine chain gang tethered to her chair leg with copious amounts of string. "How many of these damn ponies do you have, anyway? They're all over the house!" Beth stooped and lifted up the chair, yanking the string up and taking the ponies with it.

Jules and Tawny shared an inscrutable glance and turned back to Beth with uniformly innocent expressions. "Just… *some…* ponies…" Jules offered.

"Well… why were they tied to my chair?" She set the pony chain on the counter.

"I didn't want the prisoners to escape."

Beth gave her daughter a long look as she returned to her seat and picked up a piece of toast. "I hope this isn't some strange harbinger of your future as an exploiter of social injustice."

"I think it's more like she's learning to tie knots at school," Tawny suggested.

"I hope that's all it is." Beth laughed despite herself. "No more ponies tied up on the floor, okay? It's hazardous."

Jules watched them, her soft brown eyes studying them both intently. "I wouldn't need all these toy ponies if I had a *real* one."

"Yeah, no. That's not happening," Beth said. "Like, one-hundred-percent not happening. Don't even let yourself pretend there's a world where your mommy is open to taking on the responsibility of a horse."

"Why?"

"We could always—" Tawny began.

"No."

"All I'm saying is, there's a stable not so far from here that boards horses. We wouldn't have to take care of any actual animals ourselves. If she was interested in that when she got older, I mean."

"Yeah, Mommy, I—" Jules started.

"Fine, I agree to a *future* conversation about something horse related. I agree to *nothing* horse related right now, except that if you ever want to see a horse in real life you have to stop leaving toy ponies all over the place."

There was a long pause. "Yeah. That seems fair," Tawny said.

Jules nodded sagely. "Okay. We're getting a pony *later*. Deal."

"No, there's no deal—"

"Mommy. It's okay. Agree to disagree."

"Did you teach her that phrase?" Beth inquired. "It seems like I've been hearing it a lot lately."

Tawny made an exaggerated expression of ignorance. "She could have learned that anywhere."

"Well, it's pretty much the worst idiom of all time."

"Agree to disagree," Tawny said, barely containing her laughter.

"Great joke, Tawny," Jules congratulated her. "You do great jokes."

"Ugh," Beth said, laughing. "You guys are the worst."

Jules took a bite of raisin toast and chewed it thoughtfully. "We could get a dog, though," she suggested. "Or a giraffe. I could feed it from my window."

Beth groaned. "Finish eating. We have to get ready for school."

"Hey—do you mind if I tag along?" Tawny asked. "I'm waiting on some calculations to process, so I can't get much done in the lab this morning anyhow. I wanted to pick your brain about some stuff, if you don't mind. Maybe we could grab a cup of coffee."

"Sure," Beth agreed, curious what she wanted to know.

"So, what was it you wanted to ask me about?" Beth asked Tawny. "Chai tea latte, please," she told the young woman behind the counter.

"Oh, uh, well, it wasn't anything major," Tawny said, opening her purse and staring into it. "You remember how I was watching that show last week, *Henry's Women*? I just wanted to know more about that time period. It seems interesting, is all." She glanced up at Beth, flushed slightly, and rummaged in her bag.

Beth picked up her drink, wondering what had brought on this sudden bout of awkwardness. It hadn't taken long for her and Tawny to fall back into the easy companionability they'd enjoyed in college, but every once in a while Tawny still got a bit funny about something. "Okay," she said. "First of all, be aware that *Henry's Women* is more or less just cable television soft core porn. From a historical perspective, it might as well be *Throne Wars*. In terms of veracity it has very little going for it. It uses historical figures and their names, but it's only loosely based on actual fact. Although, the costumes aren't bad."

Tawny collected her coffee from the barista. "So… the Tudors weren't really having that much sex?" She seemed disappointed.

"Well," Beth said, taking a seat at a small table, "It's not that. It's just that for TV they change a lot of facts and events for purposes of dramatization—oh, shit, I think I know that guy." She jerked her head toward the door. "No, don't look. Act normal. He's the dad of one of Jules's classmates."

Along with the many mothers who dropped their children off at Rising Stars School, the private preschool and elementary which Tawny had insisted on paying for Jules to attend, there were a handful of men who did the same. The handsome red-haired man who had just walked in the door was one of them.

Beth took a sip of her coffee and looked hard at Tawny, hoping she'd recognize that they should stop staring at him.

"Look at those cheekbones," Tawny said appraisingly. "He's really good looking. But good looking like somebody who wasn't always. Like he grew into it from a gawky teenager. The hot guys who didn't grow up hot are always the best. And you always had a thing for guys with red hair."

"I think his name is Lance," Beth whispered, not looking in his direction. "I've said hi to him a couple times. Always generic conversations, though. His son is that little boy Jules was talking to when we dropped her off."

"You like him, don't you," Tawny said. It wasn't a question.

"No. Well, maybe a little," Beth said, half under her breath. "But not really. I think I'm just sort of boy crazy right now," she said. "I… haven't had sex since way before the divorce. But I seriously need to not sleep with other parents at my kid's school. I have no business even thinking about getting involved with somebody, anyway. Remind me I'm crazy."

"You're not crazy," Tawny said. "He's cute."

Beth didn't realize how blatantly they were staring at him until he spotted them, smiled in recognition, and made his way over.

"I know you," he said. "Beth, isn't it? Jules's mom?"

"Yes," she replied. She felt her cheeks flush as she realized she'd addressed his crotch, and stood to greet him. "Beth Bird. And… this is Tawny. Tawny, this is… Lance, right?"

"That's right," he said. "Oh, don't get up on my account," he protested as Tawny also rose to shake his hand. "I was going to sit down with a crossword for a few minutes, but I wouldn't mind some company instead." He looked at Beth as he said this.

"Uh—sure," Beth said, sinking back into her chair. "That'd be nice," she added.

"Great." He beamed at her before turning to walk up to the counter.

Tawny watched him go. "He totally likes you."

Beth studied him doubtfully from behind. "You think so?" He was wearing khaki shorts. They made his ass look nice. Everything about him was so trim.

"I *know* so. Did you see that smile? He's into you. I'm sure he's been lusting after you since you first met him. He drops his kid off and every time he sees your tits under your top he can't wait to run back home and take care of business." Tawny was giggling by now.

"Shut up," Beth said. "Besides, he's probably married. No way I'm opening up a can of worms like that."

"I bet he's not married. I bet he's a single dad."

Lance collected the coffee and returned to the table, taking a seat across from them.

"Is your kid that cute little red-haired boy with the overbite and the turtle backpack?"

"*Tawny*," Beth hissed.

"What?"

Lance just laughed. "Yep, that's my Tim. No hiding it, he's going to need braces. Poor kid—they make you wait until they're older."

"That makes sense," Tawny said, nodding. "Children's skeletons keep growing for a long time, so it'd be a lot of wasted pain if you did it too early. Plus, baby teeth."

"Yeah, that kid's going to have some rough school pictures for a few years." Lance took a long sip of his coffee, glancing at them both in turn.

Tawny stood up abruptly. "Where are you going?" Beth asked. "We just got here. And didn't you want to talk?"

"Oh... I have something I have to take care of in the lab. But you should stay and chat." Tawny turned to Lance. "You should come over and join us for dinner this weekend. I bet the kids would enjoy playing. We can use the outdoor kitchen and still keep an eye on them in the pool."

Beth narrowed her eyes at Tawny. Inviting people over didn't seem like her style. She was trying to fix Beth up with this guy. It was sweet, but not what she was looking for at present. "You don't have to do that," she said, shooting Tawny a warning look. "I'm sure you're busy."

"Actually, that'd be great," Lance said.

Tawny gave Beth a look that said, *see, here's where he'd mention his wife if he had one!*

"We don't get out to see other people as much as we should. So I'd love to. And I bet you're right—I've seen Tim with Jules. They'd be friends if they didn't have to pretend so hard to the rest of the class that the other one is icky."

"How does Tim feel about chicken?" Tawny asked. "It's the only protein we can reliably get Jules to eat."

"We love chicken," Lance said.

"Great. Because Beth has gotten very, very good at making chicken."

He laughed. "I bet."

Tawny grinned. "Let's do Tandoori style since we're cooking outside anyway. And, well, great meeting you, but I gotta head back to the house. But… we'll see you next Saturday? Say… four o'clock?"

"Sounds good!"

"Beth—don't forget to trade numbers with Lance. I would, of course, but I have to dash. Nice meeting you," and Tawny was gone in a hurry.

Beth watched her go, trying to decide if she was annoyed, terrified, or relieved to have been left alone with him. He was wearing a light cologne and the sweet, manly scent of it had been making her nipples stand up for the last five minutes.

"How'd you meet?" Lance asked, drumming his fingers absently on the table. His hands were big, and strong looking. He wasn't wearing a ring. Not that that meant anything. Beth forced herself to raise her eyes to meet his. She *really* didn't need to be thinking about what those hands would feel like on her skin.

"Oh, it was ages ago," she said. "We met in college, of course."

"Of course," he agreed. "Are you new to the area?"

"Yeah, just moved here last month. What about you?"

"About a year ago. I did well with some business ventures a few years back, and I've been lucky enough that now I can spend a lot of time with my son. I had one of those dads who was never around. I didn't want to be that kind of father." He swirled the coffee in his cup. "So, Tawny works in a lab? Sounds interesting."

His lips looked soft. She wondered if Lance liked to bite. "Uh… yeah. She's kind of the ultimate breadwinner, I guess. She does contract research. I don't understand most of her work, to be honest. I studied history."

Why, *why* hadn't she worn something a little nicer than jean shorts and the T-shirt she'd received as a gift for having donated to their local library?

"You sound like a good team. Complementary skills and all that," he commented.

"Yeah, I guess we are," Beth said. "You should see her and Jules when they gang up on me, though. It's unreal how good they are at it. We had the most idiotic conversation this morning about ponies and whether we would ever get one. Tawny said maybe someday. I said hell no."

"Oh, God, the pony conversation is the worst," he agreed.

"What, do little boys have a thing about ponies too?"

"Not exactly. Specifically, Tim requested a 'war horse' for his birthday. Suffice to say, he did not receive a war horse."

Beth laughed. "Kids are such crazy weirdos. So what other stuff will Tim eat? I want to make sure we're prepared on Saturday." Maybe Tawny had been right to invite him over. It wouldn't be so bad for the two of them to have a friend in the neighborhood, she decided, especially one with a kid Jules's age. She couldn't sleep with him, since there'd be no escaping him if things got awkward, but there was nothing stopping them from being friends.

"Tim's not too picky—he'll eat Tandoori chicken, for sure. Loves potatoes and rice. And corn. And ice cream. He's not too bad about trying new things."

"I'm jealous," Beth said. "Tawny's the only one who can get Jules to try new foods. She's the only person who can convince her to eat anything remotely nutritious. Somehow she does it so Jules thinks it was her idea."

"That's the way to do it. Kid ideas are great, you realize. Adult ideas suck."

Beth smiled and reached for her bag before standing up. "I should get going. I have a bunch of stuff I need to get done today."

"I hear you there," he said, standing up himself and extending one hand. "Should I bring wine on Saturday?"

"That'd be great." She gave him a friendly shake. He was taller than she'd realized at first. And he had such a nice, strong grip.

Beth met his eyes, trying to decide how willing she was to risk making a terrible mistake and embarrassing herself just for the sake of a little fun.

Beth leaned impulsively toward Lance. "I know we just met, but... do you want to do something crazy?"

His breath hitched a little. He was only inches away, and she could smell the pleasant, combined aroma of coffee and his cologne. She could hardly believe she was about to do this. He was practically a stranger.

She deliberately dragged her gaze down his body, lingering on his best features, making sure he could see her doing it.

He swallowed heavily. "What did you have in mind?"

There was something in his voice that suddenly set her aflame. Setting her hand on his knee, she slid it slowly up his thigh. She held his gaze for a long moment, savoring the need between her legs, enjoying his expression of frank interest mixed with slight disbelief.

"Wait a minute or two for appearances," she said, "then meet me in the bathroom. It'll be unlocked." She stood, swinging her purse up over her shoulder, and forced herself to walk away without looking back.

While she waited, Beth could hardly resist the temptation to get started without him. She hadn't done anything like this since long before meeting Dan, and she was incredibly turned on. She looked at herself in the mirror and ran her hands lightly over her nipples, which were hard and standing at attention, telegraphing her desire through her bra and the thin T-shirt. She hesitated, wondering if he would show up, hoping someone else didn't open the door instead.

Then she heard a soft knock on the door and he opened it, slipping quickly inside. "I've never done anything like this before," he said, locking the door behind him.

Beth sucked in her breath at his obvious arousal. He was big, that much she could tell, and hard as a rock. She shrugged her shirt off over her head, and his gaze immediately dropped to her breasts. Thankfully, she'd worn a half-decent bra that day. It might even match her underwear.

Lance slowly dragged his eyes up to meet hers, as if asking for permission to approach her. Beth held his gaze, slowly licking her lower lip, challenging him to do something about it.

"You are so goddamn hot," he said, pressing her against the wall for a savage kiss that she returned with equal fervor.

"Then you'd better fuck me," she ordered him as soon as they came up for air.

He tore roughly at her shorts, fumbling with the fly as he continued to kiss her. He was rough, and he used his teeth a little too much. She fucking loved it.

Lance finally relieved her of the jean shorts, then yanked her panties down, but before he could reach for his own pants, she put her hand on his arm and stopped him. "First you watch," she said at his look of confused disappointment. "Do you like what you see?" she asked as she unhooked her bra and let it fall to the floor.

His hands immediately moved to her breasts, squeezing them and stroking her nipples with an expert touch. "Very much." His voice was husky, convincing her he felt the same eagerness she did.

His touch was setting her on fire, but Beth backed away and leaned against the wall, slowly moving her hand between her legs. She watched his eyes, locked on her as she began to stroke herself in a gentle rhythm. Watching his reaction, she slid a finger inside, then two. She was so aroused that it ached, but she forced herself to go slowly. She smoothed her fingers over her clit, spreading herself to give him a better view.

He liked to watch, all right. Looking at his face, she wasn't sure how much longer he'd last like this. She might not even have to touch him.

She slid her fingers back inside, then out again, loving the effect it had on him.

"Lance." Beth looked straight into his eyes. "Are you ready to fuck me?"

He couldn't unzip his pants fast enough.

She needed this so badly.

They were too desperate for any more kissing, or fondling, or any other sexual niceties. This was raw.

Lance pushed her roughly against the wall again and Beth whimpered as she felt the tip of his cock touch her outer lips.

"Jesus," he said, "you are so fucking wet." He reached down and guided himself inside her, sheathing his full length in a single motion.

"Oh, God," Beth gasped, clawing at him as he lifted her up to get a better angle. She needed both hands to hold herself up against him, but he obviously knew what he was doing. His hand dropped to where their bodies joined, his thumb kneading her clit in rhythm with his thrusts, applying just the amount of pressure she needed.

It occurred to her for a brief moment to wonder whether anybody could hear him slamming her against the wall, and then the thought was gone, lost in the wave of sensation. His hips slapped against hers, and she thought he might be close. She couldn't wait to feel him convulse inside of her, couldn't wait to hear what he sounded like when he came. Beth tensed herself, concentrating on the feeling of his incredible cock. God, she was so close, just another moment and—

The doorbell chimed loudly.

Goddamnit.

Beth froze and craned her neck to listen, hoping whoever it was would go away.

She was responsible for receiving and unpacking all of Tawny's deliveries, which were generally for lab supplies and other equipment, but often she didn't even make it to the door by the time the driver deposited the package on the porch and left. It wasn't a hot day. Most of the stuff Tawny had shipped to the house wouldn't suffer from being left outside a little while.

No such luck.

After the third chime, she splashed out of the tub, thoroughly pissed off, and threw on the filmy nightgown she'd worn into the bathroom. She yanked her robe off its hook and jammed her feet into slippers before running down the stairs and across the house to the front door. "Just a minute," she shouted, hoping her voice would carry.

Outside, a young man with some of the worst acne scars she'd ever seen was just beginning to fill out one of the yellow sorry-not-sorry-we-missed-you forms as she opened the door. She looked at him with immense irritation. Why would he ring the doorbell so many times if he was just going to leave it anyway?

The kid was at least ten years younger than her, and not attractive, but despite her irritation, Beth couldn't help being extremely aware of his pleasant… maleness as she signed for the package. Under the robe, she was still keenly aware of how wet she remained from her disappointingly interrupted solo session. "Uh—" she said, then cut herself off as she realized she'd almost spoken her thoughts aloud. *I'm sexually frustrated. You look like you might be sexually frustrated too. Any interest? All I need is five minutes of your time and a total commitment to never seeing each other again!*

She scribbled her name and fairly slammed the door in his startled face. The last thing she needed to be doing was inviting nineteen-year-old delivery drivers into the foyer for casual sex. Ridiculous. She was somebody's *mother*, for God's sake. Which was the reason she was back here at the house fantasizing about fucking a near-stranger in public, rather than actually doing it.

On the upside, she was pretty sure Lance had no clue she'd wanted to throw him down on the floor of the coffee shop and ride him rough.

Beth glanced at the mantle clock as she passed through the living room carrying the package. Almost ten—later than she'd thought. That meant the grocery delivery would be here soon, and then she'd need to prep lunch, pick up Jules, serve lunch, put chicken in the fridge to marinate for dinner—in other words, not much time left for getting back to her bath. She sighed, shrugging to herself.

"Win some, lose some," she said aloud. Anyway, perhaps she'd been spending *too* much fun time in the bath recently—her hand was kind of sore. She flexed it, making a mental note to take something for the ache.

She dropped the package on the kitchen counter and fished a box cutter out of a drawer. Tawny received enough packages—several a day at minimum—that by the end of her first week Beth had become an expert unpacker. She made a neat slit through the packing tape and opened the box flaps. "What the fuck?" she muttered.

The box contained a plastic wrapped costume with a cardboard insert labeled SEXY CAVEWOMAN COSTUME, featuring a photo of a smiling woman wearing a skimpy animal-print dress. In the corner of the insert, in tiny letters, was printed: KEEP AWAY FROM OPEN FLAME. Not surprising, considering the costume appeared to be made of the cheapest synthetic material the world had ever seen.

Well, that was a bit weird. It was even stranger in light of the delivery she'd accepted yesterday of a MEDIEVAL PRINCESS costume, complete with a pink cone-shaped hat with a long, filmy streamer flowing from the tip. When she'd joked to Tawny about it being a bit early for Halloween costumes, her friend had stammered some awkward reply and made a clumsy attempt to change the subject.

Beth had dropped it and pretended that the exchange wasn't weird. It was one of those moments that made her uncomfortably aware that in addition to being her friend, Tawny was technically also her employer. Thankfully, the moment had passed, although the next time Beth went out to the lab, she noted that unlike most of the deliveries she brought in each day, the princess costume had been put away somewhere out of sight.

Her phone buzzed on the counter, and she picked it up, wondering if Tawny wanted something from the house. It was a text from Lance: *Hey! It was great meeting you and Tawny today. I didn't mention my partner because he was originally supposed to be out of town this weekend, but that changed. Mind if I bring him along?*

Beth blinked at her phone, nonplussed, then replied: *Sure! Sounds great!*

So. Lance was gay. Good to know.

Beth was suddenly immensely grateful that she hadn't been brave—stupid?—enough to ask him to fuck her in a public restroom. She shook her head, relieved. She could live with the permanent friend zone. At least she hadn't humiliated herself.

And did he think she and Tawny were a couple? Beth thought over their conversation at the coffee shop. Shit. It definitely could have sounded like she and Tawny were Jules's two mommies.

She'd get this package out to the lab, and then she'd figure out the least awkward way to clarify to Lance that she and Tawny were gay-friendly, but not gay themselves. If Tawny was busy enough with whatever she'd rushed back to do, Beth could quietly leave it for her without comment or acknowledgment. Whatever she was buying these costumes for, it must be something that embarrassed her, and with the "SEXY CAVEWOMAN" label on this package, she had a few ideas what it might be.

It didn't seem like Tawny to be shy about sex, but then again, she'd only lived here a month after years of separation. Regardless, Beth intended to respect her privacy. She didn't want Tawny to change her mind about the value of their arrangement.

THE LAB WAS HOUSED IN THE CARRIAGE HOUSE AT THE BACK OF TAWNY'S property, but was just a short walk across the back patio from the kitchen. Beth quietly eased the door open and slipped inside. There was a table just inside the main lab area where she often left new supplies. She would leave the package there, ideally without drawing any attention to her presence, and then would go about her day, doing her best not to wonder what odd costuming might arrive tomorrow.

Her slippers were quiet on the concrete floor, underscoring what seemed like an unusual silence. She hadn't spent much time in the lab, but Tawny liked to keep a small radio playing, and the sounds of her working with various electronic components or other materials were often audible to anyone dropping in. She could hear water running somewhere, but not much else. Suddenly the hair on the back of her neck pricked up with fear. She'd seen a headline last week—a man working in his garage had accidentally electrocuted himself and died instantly.

Don't be silly, she told herself. *Tawny knows what she's doing.* But she found herself walking toward the main lab all the same. "Tawny?" she called shakily.

No one answered.

Maybe she'd stepped back into the house for a moment. Although, Beth would have passed her on the little stone walkway that led to the house, if that were the case.

The running water sound was coming from the back of the building. Beth knew there was a small living area at the back of the carriage house, behind the lab. She'd never had cause to go in there herself, but sometimes Tawny slept out here when her work kept her up late. She took a breath and walked toward the sound, cursing herself for being so irrationally worried. She was going to look like an idiot. Tawny was just in the bathroom or something, and she'd come out and find Beth here and wonder why she had gotten so scared over *absolutely nothing at all.*

But there was no one in the bathroom. The sound of water was from a shower that had been left running. Steam billowed from the shower, but there was no sign of Tawny. Perhaps she'd stepped into the other room. "Tawny?" she called again, more loudly this time.

All that excess moisture wasn't good for the ceiling and walls. Beth looked around again, unsure if there could be some important scientific reason that her friend might leave a hot shower running with no one around to use it. After a moment, she decided she should turn it off. Then she'd find Tawny. They'd all have a good laugh at dinner over the fact that Beth had gotten frightened over something so silly.

She hoped.

The shower handle was on the far wall. Shitty design, she thought. It would be impossible to shut it off without getting wet. Tawny must have turned on the water and left, but the bath mat just outside the shower was dry. Had the water been left running so long that the bath mat had already dried? Or did Tawny have a remote control that allowed her to start the shower from the outside? Beth looked around but didn't see any switches, buttons, or handles.

No helping it, then. She stepped into the shower, flinching from the scalding water. Steam blinded her as she reached for the handle and gave it a hard pull.

PARTE THE SECONDE

PROLOGUE

IN WHICH... ???

Tawny SLIPPED THROUGH THE DOOR AND EASED IT SHUT, TRYING TO MAKE as little noise as possible. Of course, that was a moot point considering all the Darth Vader sounds she was making with the gas mask on, but whatever.

Her rapid breathing was misting up the inside of the face piece. She reached up under her chin and touched a button. The miniature windshield wipers she'd installed in the mask cleared the fog to reveal Beth, sprawled out in her bed, fast asleep.

She moved to the edge of the bed, then switched on her headlamp. Beth didn't move. Good. At least with the sleeping gas filling the house there was no risk that anyone would wake up and disrupt her plans.

She couldn't fuck this up. Beth had to be unconscious for this part, or everything would come undone. Lives hung in the balance.

Tawny raised her scalpel.

NINE

IN WHICH TAWNY LEARNS THAT
THE PAST IS A FOREIGN COUNTRY
WHEREIN THEY DO THINGS DIFFERENTLY

Tawny had chosen this exact moment in history for well-thought-out reasons, which boiled down to: Anne Boleyn would be out of favor and therefore out of the way, but Henry wasn't yet married to Jane Seymour—who had by all accounts refused to give him any sexy times until he'd disposed of his second wife. Result being: the King would be horny as a goat, with no acceptable sexual outlets available to him.

Tawny took a deep breath and looked around at the stone walls, the tapestries, the arched passage leading out to the courtyard where she could hear all the nobles talking.

She was here, and her nerves could go fuck themselves. Well, not literally, since with any luck she'd need them for fucking other people.

Everything would be fine, she decided. Hers was not the first maiden voyage in history to be very slightly under-prepared, and look how many of those had succeeded in spite of it, *lots,* she reminded herself.

She wasn't nobody.

She'd invented *time travel*, for God's sake. She was about to utterly blow some sixteenth-century minds.

The machine worked—that was really all that mattered.

And when she went home she'd figure out a way to tell Beth and get her on board.

Everything would be fine.

After all, she'd done almost enough research to meet the Malcolm Gladwell standards for expertise on the subject of Greenwich palace, Henry's preferred royal residence. Tawny was pretty sure most people didn't know the palace was called *Placentia*, a fact she found equally gross and reassuring. She knew obscure shit like that. She was fucking *prepared*.

Then what about those weird accents, genius? her nasty little inside voice snickered.

Maybe the acoustics were off in here because of some weirdness with the architecture. Maybe it had something to do with sixteenth-century building materials. Maybe her ears had gotten plugged during the time travel process—just like flying. Maybe—well, it didn't matter. She was going to do this. They were just snakes, and she was braver than that. It didn't hurt that, thanks to living with two other humans for a month, her social skills had improved, almost to the level she'd been at in her sorority days.

Good.

Right.

Tawny squared her shoulders, lifted her forehead from the tapestry she'd been leaning against, and took a deep breath.

"Who're you, then?" She swallowed a startled yelp as a pair of strong hands gripped her by the shoulders and spun her around.

Her captor was a man, about her height, with a Tudor rose on his black and red tunic, and a sword hanging at his belt. A palace guard, she guessed.

Tawny suppressed the scream that was her first impulse, knowing better than to draw still more attention to herself. At least this guy was alone. He gave her a little shake about the shoulders. "Come on, who are you? I've not seen you at court before, and by your looks, you're about mischief or worse."

"I'm a"—*time traveling seductress*, her brain interjected—"visiting noblewoman from far away. I'm very wealthy and powerful."

This guard was her first sixteenth-century person, and she was oddly surprised to find how… human he was. She realized now that she'd been envisioning the past like a Disney ride staffed by animatronic simulacra of people. But this guy was real. She could see the stubble on his jaw, smell the heady combination of male musk and some kind of herbal scent he wore. His nose had been broken at least once, and now it sat crookedly on his face in a charming sort of way.

"Creeping around like a common thief? I think not. I know who's being hosted at the palace, and you're not in the rolls, whoever you are." He shook her again. "I'll have your name and then we'll see what the Chief Warder wants to do with you." His voice was deep and rolling, and just as not-British-sounding as the court people she'd been eavesdropping on. She hadn't planned for this.

"I—ah—I—"

Tawny couldn't think of anything else to do, so she grabbed his hands and shoved them up against her breasts, which were already squished practically up to her chin in her attempt to give herself some hint of cleavage.

He blinked rapidly. "What're you—"

"Shh… you don't want anyone to hear us, do you?" she whispered, guiding his fingers to the metallic ribbon lacings of her bodice. The sudden reversal of circumstances seemed to work— he looked confused, but that didn't stop him from unlacing her and slipping his rough, calloused hands inside her chemise to stroke her small, pert breasts.

Tawny was a little surprised to realize that the combination of danger and stress—not to mention the guard's rugged good looks—made her quite excited. She wanted him. Badly. Her nipples hardened under his fingers, and she felt the familiar aching heat uncoil in her core. Taking advantage of his momentary stupefaction, she shoved him against the wall and down onto a nearby bench, hiking up her skirts and petticoats to straddle him. It should have felt awkward and ungainly, but sex always afforded her an unexpected grace and fluidity, like a mermaid diving back into the sea after trying to walk on land.

"This is… a… dream?" he asked, his hands moving over her breasts and body as if they had a will of their own. When she didn't answer, he pushed her conical hat back and ran his fingers through her hair with surprising gentleness. He took one pink nipple in his mouth, sucking and then biting, then licked a tight circle around it.

Tawny moaned quietly as she ran her hands over his pants—*breeches? tights?* she wondered, *well, doesn't matter anyway*—and found his erection where it strained against his clothes. It was her turn to unlace him. She couldn't see his cock around the fullness of her skirts, but it sprang free into her hand and it felt good and hard and ready. Thank goodness she'd had the sense to wear crotchless panties under all the other foofaraw.

She stroked him and he closed his eyes with pleasure, fingers still working through her hair. Tawny impaled herself on his cock, guiding him inside her with one smooth motion as she slammed him hard against the wall. She was so hot and wet as he slid into her cunt that she spread her legs as wide as she could to take him in even deeper. In response, he grunted and wrapped his arms around her, crushing her to him as they started to move together in a delicious pounding rhythm.

He was uncircumcised, to her surprise, and between that and the situation and the angle of their bodies, he somehow brought her close to climax with remarkable speed as he pumped beneath her. Tawny felt her pleasure building as she ground her hips against him—and when she crested over the wave she curled herself around him and bit his neck to keep from crying out.

She felt the sudden tightening of his muscles then, the urgent thrusts that meant he was about to come. An unwelcome thought intruded on her post-orgasmic haze—she couldn't afford to get her princess outfit stained right before meeting the King!

"Ah, fuck. Sorry, wait a second." Tawny pushed herself off of him, trying not to giggle at his look of shocked dismay, then dropped to her knees, grabbed his cock and took him in her mouth. She relished every inch, running her tongue up and down the sides, and met his eyes with hers.

"Oh, Christ!" he moaned. "Are you—are you some kind of she-demon, come to steal my soul?"

"Mmm-hmm, sure," she murmured, licking in faster and faster circles around the swollen head of his prick while she gripped the shaft and ran one hand up and down its length.

It didn't take long after that. He bucked his hips, gasping, and then she was swallowing his heat as it flooded her mouth. From the corner of her eye she saw him press his fist against his mouth to stifle his groans of pleasure, then lie back, panting.

Tawny gave him a fond final lick before rising to her feet. He looked up at her for a moment in a daze that seemed comprised of equal parts wonder and fear, then stood, wobbling a little. It made her smile to see him unsteady on his feet—satisfaction at a job well done. She was grateful to this nice man; she felt considerably more confident after this encounter than she had a few minutes ago. What had she been so worried about, anyway?

"Run along, now, dear. I've got… important noblewoman things to do." She reached around and gave him a friendly pat on his firm, well-rounded ass. It seemed to startle him back into action. They stared at each other for a long moment while he was plainly struggling to work out what he should say. Finally, he backed away from her, stuffing himself back into his tights—yes, definitely tights—then turned and ran.

Tawny re-laced her bodice, wiped her lips on a table runner under a nearby marble vase, and adjusted the streamer on her hat. She strode into Henry's court with a smile on her face and a song in her heart.

ONCE IN THE COURTYARD, SHE REALIZED SHE'D BEEN WORKING HERSELF into a neurotic fear-fest for nothing. This shit was even better than she imagined—a sea of people, as brightly colored as the birds in the documentaries she and Jules watched every week. She saw less in the way of cleavage than she'd been expecting from TV, but gems and pearls and gold chains and brocade and velvet rustled and shone everywhere she looked. It was impressive. Nobody had a hat quite as awesome as hers, though.

They—Tawny and about thirty of the well-dressed noble types, plus a roving swarm of people who were apparently their servants—stood in a long gallery, with two arched exits leading out into a courtyard. She caught a glimpse of well-manicured greenery. The walls were decorated with elaborate murals, carved paneling, and richly embroidered hangings.

She scanned the area for her target. The blonde woman with the full cheeks and Cupid's bow lips must be Jane Seymour. Tawny recognized her right away. *Good portraiting, ye olde artists!*

Of course the Queen wouldn't be around, as she was confined to chambers, but where was the King?

Tawny had hoped there would be a herald to announce her presence (and all the titles she'd made up to seem legit), but as no one in the crowd had volunteered, well, she'd just have to dive in. *Snakes*, she reminded herself.

"Good gentles," she began, wincing inwardly as she stumbled over the second word and made it sound more like 'genitals.'

"I prithee seeketh thy king." She'd practiced this speech a few times. The old-timey lingo didn't quite roll off the tongue, but it wasn't as tough as she'd feared, either.

"Well? Whence be… eth the noble ruler of Ye Olde Enga-land?"

Thunderous silence.

They must, she realized, be stunned by her futuristic beauty—all the courtiers and even their servants simply stared at her. One boy, dressed in royal livery, had frozen, open-mouthed, in the act of pouring wine into a goblet that changed positions when its owner whirled around to face Tawny. The steady trickling of the wine hitting the floor was the only sound.

Well, she hadn't planned on what she'd do if the denizens of the past were too dazzled to speak to her.

"What is this? Don't just stand about, make way! Let me see!" A bold bellow echoed from behind the mass of nobles, who murmured apologies and moved to either side of the courtyard in a susurrus of silk and velvet.

A thrill coursed through her. Directly in front of her, a man sat in a magnificent gilded chair, propped up by cushions. Henry! One leg was stretched out in front of him, resting on an ottoman.

Tawny knew he'd still be busted up from the jousting accident (the cliff-hanger third season finale on *Henry's Women*), but even the later paintings of him portrayed a tall, barrel-chested man, red-bearded, with piercing blue eyes and tights stuffed with a package that put Jareth the Goblin King to shame.

The guy in front of her was a hot portly mess.

If her undergraduate research had taught her anything, though, it was that looks and sexual prowess did not always correlate.

Tawny marched toward him in her best approximation of stately dignity, ignoring the tingle in her limbs and the flutter in her stomach that always preceded a new conquest.

"Bring her." The King straightened in his throne and snapped his fingers. Two of the noblemen and three guards strode toward her.

She held up a hand. "Nay, ye merry gentlemen! Though I be but of the fair sex, I canst indeed walk with mine own two feet."

"The lady can speak with her own two feet as well, it would seem," said one of the nobles, a tall, handsome young man with red hair.

"Y-eek!" They hoisted her up, and half dragged, half shoved her over to the King, pushing her toward his feet. She stumbled forward and would have fallen if the huge plastic hoops and stiff boning of her multitude of petticoats hadn't hit the ground first and bounced her back up to a standing position.

"Uh, okay then." *Whatever you do, don't say 'okay,'* she privately corrected herself. "I mean, shit. I mean—" Then she got her first good look at the King.

Henry was even more disappointing up close. Heavy bags under his eyes, blotchy skin, and a Taftian paunch the likes of which she'd seldom seen. The thought of letting him touch her, of getting his sweat on her, turned Tawny's stomach. But it wasn't his weight that disgusted her. No, it was the look on his face she found revolting—a prideful sneer born of the self-assurance that comes with holding absolute power of life and death over millions of people.

Well, that and the oozing sores, if she was being honest with herself. The fabric of his tights was stretched like sausage casings over his legs, and blood was seeping through the fabric onto a gilded cushion.

"Noooooooope," Tawny said, and hiked up her skirts to flee the scene. The court gasped as one. Crap. That had been a mistake. Now that she'd shown her ankles, Henry would be inflamed with lust. She dropped her skirts, only to find that her path out was blocked by several guards whose stance indicated she wasn't going anywhere.

"Who *is* this woman?" the King demanded.

The courtiers demurred, a gentle buzz of speculation running through the crowd, but no one answered at first.

"Whoever she may be, the poor creature may have taken a hit to the head, Your Majesty," someone said finally. The speaker was the same tall, good-looking young man who had joked about her feet. He looked quite a bit like the King. "Or perhaps," he continued, drawing out the moment, "Lord Chancellor Cromwell has brought a new fool into your employ." Everyone laughed.

A sudden hum, almost inaudible, swelled up behind her, something no one in this place but Tawny would have recognized—the sound of electricity. Then she heard a familiar voice from behind the archway.

"What the shit is this shit? Oh my God."

And Beth, sopping wet, dressed in only a bathrobe, staggered into view. She must have found her way into the shower somehow. Tawny all but wept with gratitude.

"Beth," she mouthed in silent desperation. "Help."

She watched, pleading inside her own head, as Beth gaped at her for a long moment in stunned confusion, then seemed to recover and orient to her situation with incredible speed. "I fear our messengers were waylaid, elsewise Your Majesty would have known of our coming," she said. "The rigors of travel have taxed Lady Tawny. I am afraid she is not quite herself at present."

That was putting it mildly.

Tawny watched the crowd of nobles, trying to decide whether they were falling for the stuff Beth had said. They ought to be, she'd said words like 'elsewise' to them. It sounded really legit.

The King was talking to one of the men next to him. Tawny ran to Beth. Beth was more than a head shorter than her, but she instantly felt safer at her side. Staring at the King and wondering what on earth would happen, it took her a moment to realize Beth was saying something to her.

"What is this, a roleplaying thing? The graphics are incredible. Not a generic sprite in the bunch."

Tawny stared at her. Roleplaying? Sprites? What was she talking about?

Graphics—Christ! Beth thought this was a video game!

She didn't understand that everything here was real, with real consequences. She might do anything.

Oh. Fuck.

"Beth," she hissed as one of the guys next to the King began a long sentence, addressed to them, with a lot of words that sounded ridiculous in his weird not-English accent. She suspected the gist of it was that they had a lot of 'splainin' to do.

Beth was looking at the guy, not at Tawny. Not good.

"Beth!" she whispered.

Beth looked up at her with an impatient expression. "Not a game," Tawny whispered again. "Time travel!"

Beth continued to stare up at Tawny for a long moment, a strange expression occupying her features as the words sank in.

"Ah," she faltered briefly, obviously trying to recover her composure. Then, Tawny watched, awestruck, as she turned to address the King and his court. "I am Elizabeth, daughter of the Duke of… Saterland. I'm afraid I must apologize most strenuously for this strange display of hysterics. Please—prithee forgive us, Your Majesty. We were set upon by ruffians after landing in England, and the men of our traveling party dispatched." Beth adopted an exaggeratedly tragic expression. "We ladies escaped, but were forced to complete our journey alone, with only the most inadequate of supplies." Beth made a vague gesture indicating Tawny's and her odd state of dress.

Before she could go on, the asshole ginger kid cut in. "Your Majesty,"—everyone in the court turned to face him. Fuck, he was probably important—"I think it plain to all here that these two baggages are spies—extraordinarily unapt spies, mayhap, but spies all the same—and they should be taken into custody at the Tower until they surrender their... secrets." His blue eyes roamed over Beth as he spoke.

"Spies?" Beth drew herself up to her full height—and while she was petite by modern standards, she was taller than many of the women in the room. "Our raiment and demeanor may seem strange in the way that those of any traveler from distant lands might, but I assure you, sir, that if you are ignorant of Frisian customs, it is through no fault of ours." She sniffed theatrically. Tawny recognized that sniff from Beth's dramatic rendition of the evil Mrs. Hyde. "Spies we are not!" Beth concluded.

"Ah, yes! Frisians! I thought as much!" The King stood momentarily in his excitement, then plopped back into his chair. "I was, of course, waiting to see if any of my court would puzzle it out."

What a smug dickbag. No way was she having sex with him, now or ever.

Plus, the King was just *way* too excited to have a couple of Frisians at court, whatever Frisians were. Tawny wondered if it was a kind of old-timey job that women used to have, like librarians or teachers. She hoped it didn't have anything to do with prostitution.

"If it please Your Majesty," Beth said, "the Lady Tawny and I have traveled far and suffered much. Would that we were not so fatigued by our journey. Else we fain should share our sad tale. With your leave, Majesty, we would retire to private chambers for a time to rest and regain our senses."

"Of course," the King said, moving one arm in what was obviously meant to be a magnanimous gesture. "Let it never be said that the Crown knows not how to indulge the sensibilities of a lady."

Beth favored him with a brilliant, grateful smile of obeisance, and curtsied again. Tawny copied the movement, a bit awkwardly, but the effort seemed good enough for Henry.

"Steward!" he called. "Fetch two maids to convey to guest apartments these two good ladies of our humble ally Frisia. Swiftly, anon." He settled back into his chair, looking pleased with himself.

Beth had done it.

Single-handedly, with zero notice or preparation, she'd not only convinced the King of England that they were no threat to the Crown by conjuring up a story covering who they were, where they were from, how they'd ended up in such a dire state, and why they were now here—she'd also gotten them assigned a suite of rooms instead of clapped in chains in a dungeon somewhere. And that was about five seconds after learning that time travel was real and that she was 500 years from her own era. She even knew how to talk like them. What would she be able to do when she was actually prepared?

She should have told Beth about all this before she'd gone. There was *so* much to explain, and now she was probably pissed off at having met the King for the first time in her bathrobe. A lump rose in Tawny's throat just thinking about it. Why hadn't she told her?

"There is to be a feast most grand this even, and you must come and regale us with tales of your land! And tomorrow, you must come a-Maying with us!" someone was saying to her.

Tawny snapped back to the present. Past. Whatever. "Uh… great?" she managed.

She noted a look of mild dismay on Jane Seymour's face at the King's obvious interest in these two mysterious strangers and wished she could tell the poor woman not to worry. There was no way Tawny was getting anywhere near Henry's royal scepter after having seen the wound suppurating beneath the hosiery stretched tight as a drum over his leg. She wished she could tell *herself* not to worry while she was at it.

In a moment two maids arrived to escort them to their guest chambers. Beth took her by the hand. "Come along, dear, it's time to make ready for the festivities." She was probably only being nice because everybody was still there watching them. The sooner Tawny could get her alone to explain the whole mess, the better.

They made their way through the staring crowd.

"Yes, get out of those wet clothes," the ginger kid called out as they left the courtyard. "I'm sure your fellow *Frisians* would be aghast should you catch a chill and die!" He didn't look pleased at having been outmaneuvered.

Beth shot him a glare. Well, hopefully he wouldn't be their problem for much longer.

"What the fuck is a Frisian?" Tawny whispered to her as they followed their maids down the corridor.

"We are," Beth said. "For now."

TEN

IN WHICH BETH EXPLAINS THE
RETROSPECTIVELY OBVIOUS HAZARD OF
SUBSTITUTING TV DRAMAS FOR RESEARCH

BETH WAS DIMLY AWARE THAT THEIR JOURNEY THROUGH THE PALACE TO their assigned quarters ought to have been an assault on her senses—except she couldn't seem to tear her eyes from Tawny's atrocious princess costume. The dress bore an uncanny resemblance to one from Jules's dress-up trunk—it was of equally period-inaccurate construction, and made in the same obnoxious hot pink color. She also wore a matching cone-shaped streamer hat. It looked worse in person than it had in the picture on the package.

It was hard to imagine how someone who had seen every episode of *Henry's Women* could have settled on this get-up for meeting the real Henry. The dress wasn't period appropriate for the sixteenth century. It wasn't period appropriate for *any* century.

Next to her, Tawny stared resolutely at the backs of their maids, avoiding Beth's gaze. She drew a shaky little breath, which Beth recognized as one of her friend's anxious tics. And no wonder she was anxious. Beth hoped she understood how irresponsible she'd been to come here all by herself, woefully unprepared, and dressed in clothes that would have made her stand out as a freak no matter what time she visited. Had she done any research at all about the Tudors before she came to visit them in person?

The inside of this massive pile of stone—she thought it might be Greenwich, which was situated on the Thames in London and had been one of the King's favorite haunts—was brighter than she expected in an era without electric lighting. Natural light streamed through the huge floor-to-ceiling windows facing the river, and although it was midday, sconced torches lit the corridors as well. The place looked every inch a palace, with heavy tapestries lining the stone walls to ward off the damp, and paintings of various Tudor nobles hung at intervals.

They passed a man, high in station, judging by his clothes, and Beth wondered as he strode by whether he was anybody she'd ever read about. As he passed she felt a gentle draft on her skin and the heavy floral bouquet of rose oil wafted toward her, with a hint of spice that made her think of her latte from that morning.

Smelling—she was physically smelling the sixteenth century. She couldn't decide whether the thought made her giddy or whether it terrified her beyond measure. Maybe it was a little of both.

Beth was bursting with questions for Tawny, but she couldn't begin that conversation in front of their maids, who in addition to being denizens of the wrong century, had most likely been ordered by at least one person to watch them and get the goods on whatever it was that Frisians did when they were alone. Judging by the level of fascination apparent in the court, these women had little better understanding of Frisians than Tawny.

The maids turned, taking them down a short hallway and opening a seemingly random door, through which Beth could see a suite of comfortably appointed guest quarters of the type commonly assigned to visiting nobility.

"I'm Kate. Mary here will see to your bath, m'lady," one of them said to Tawny. She spoke slowly and carefully, presumably because she'd realized Tawny was having difficulty understanding everyone. "I'll help you ready your lady's toilet," she said to Beth.

Great. They thought Beth was Tawny's maid. It wasn't surprising, considering Beth was dripping wet and dressed in a sopping bathrobe.

Tawny piped up. "Oh, but we'll both need baths—so maybe we should just get that out of the way now?"

Mary raised an eyebrow. "A bath... for your servant?"

"I'm not in sooth Lady Tawny's servant," Beth explained, nudging Tawny. "I'm her kinswoman."

"Oh, yeah, um—" Tawny gave her head a little shake. "Now that I've recovered from mine... swoon... I totally remember that the Lady Elizabeth is... mine... relative, and should be treated accordingly. She just had to take charge for a minute while I was out of it. I get why you'd think that, with her clothes and all, but she's not my servant. She outranks me, actually."

The two maids exchanged a long look.

"Yes, m'lady and... m'lady," one of them said. "We'll be back in a twinkling." They curtsied and left.

Tawny stood there as the maids withdrew, staring at the floor, her lips moving slightly. Beth thought she might be counting. "First things first," she said. "You are one-hundred-percent telling me this isn't a Holodeck? Because a Holodeck I can kind of start to understand."

Tawny raised her eyebrows at the question. "Uh... no. It's not a Holodeck."

"So I heard you right, in the courtyard. This is... time travel."

"Er... yes."

"So, help me out here. I take a package to the lab, and then I realize somebody left a shower running. I turn it off. Now I'm in the actual court of King Henry. Correct?"

Tawny nodded.

"Then spill."

"Are you sure you want to actually hear this? Do you need some time to freak out a little bit first? I mean, you just learned time travel is real, and that you got blasted five hundred years back in time to a place with no electricity. By accident. Maybe you need some time to get used to the idea. I could just explain it later, after we've gone home."

Beth shook her head. She had the feeling Tawny was afraid to tell her the whole story. "No. I'm here now. And it's obviously real. I don't see what good freaking out is going to do now." That might change if she stopped long enough to think very hard about their situation, but it didn't seem helpful to bring that up. "So I'd rather hear it now."

"Uh." Tawny raised her eyes briefly to Beth's, then seemed to decide something. "Well... this might sound stupid with all the shit I've done that seems great, and with my house and all the money and everything," she said, then stopped. "But my life has basically been on the skids since I graduated."

Beth frowned. "How so? You're incredibly successful. And you're celebrated in your field."

"Yeah, except I'm kind of... not. I mean, I'm accomplished, but... nobody likes me. At least in college I had some friends. Or, I thought I did. But after that, nobody wanted to put up with me. Things were okay when we had the project and then they just... weren't anymore. All the men my age were either hunting down marriage partners or playing the field with twenty-year-olds. Or, it was okay to have sex with me, be 'fuck buddies' or whatever, but there was... always this weird veneer of disdain, like doesn't this idiot know she's too old for this? Like grown-ups can't just bang whoever they want whenever they want?

"And, not all of them were rampaging choad-warriors, but the decent guys just wanted to keep their heads down and get through their post-docs, and the hyper-competitive assholes wanted to humiliate me at lab meetings. I mean, there are women scientists, but not that many in my field, and it's so hard to get credibility that it's not like they want to go out and pick up men in the name of science.

"Anyway," Tawny continued, "before the reunion I realized just how alone I was. I was living like a recluse. I'm not like other people and they all find me weird and unlikeable. But... not you. So I thought, if I could find you again... and then I did and you weren't a snake and I realized things could be okay again."

Beth listened in silence, her mind whirling.

There was a small vanity nearby holding an array of ladies' toilet items. Tawny picked up a boar-bristle brush lying on it and studied the handle, avoiding Beth's gaze. "And I realized something else," she said. "The only time I was ever truly happy was when we worked on the project together. And then I had this breakthrough on something I was researching, and I realized time travel might be possible. And one thing just sort of led to another after that."

Beth stared at her. "Are you saying—" She took a steadying breath. "Are you saying you invented time travel so you could go into the past and fuck famous people?"

"Well... they don't *have* to be famous," Tawny said.

"Okay. Tawny." Beth took another deep breath and turned away from her friend, toward a window that looked out upon a small enclosed garden area outside. "You have given me an amazing opportunity by hiring me, and you've turned my entire life around, so don't think I'm not grateful for that—but I can't believe you would do something this fucking stupid."

She heard Tawny move closer, could practically sense the waves of anxiety rippling off her. "I—"

"You broke the rules." Beth cut her off in a low voice, a little surprised to realize just how angry she was. "Field protocol one is the buddy system! Number *one*! And I'd wager just being here in the first place is breaking *some* kind of universal law and now we'll all get sucked into a black hole and die and never see our own time again! We don't even *have* a protocol to deal with this shit! The King could have ordered you *killed*, did you even think of that?"

There was a long silence behind her. Beth turned and felt immediately horrible. Tawny looked stricken, her eyes brimming. "I—" she began again. A tear broke free and trailed down her cheek.

"Oh, honey," Beth said, softening. "Come here." She pushed Tawny into a nearby plush chair and perched next to her on its arm, smoothing her rumpled hair comfortingly. "I didn't mean all of that. I'm sure we won't really die in a black hole. We won't—right?"

Tawny sniffed loudly. "No, we won't." She leaned her head on Beth's leg, a look of abject misery on her face. "I didn't build it on wormhole theory."

Beth opened her mouth to ask what that meant, then thought better of it. "It's just—how could you do something like this alone? What if something terrible had happened? Jules would be devastated if we lost you. *I* would be devastated."

"I… made a will before I went," Tawny mumbled. "And I guess I'm still not used to thinking that way. Before you, there was nobody to miss me. If I choked on my lunch and died, they wouldn't have discovered my desiccated corpse for weeks. Months, maybe. I don't even have a pet to eat me after I die."

Beth stroked her hair and let her talk.

"Nobody likes me except you. And Jules… that's why I didn't tell you. You wouldn't have let me do it alone. And I couldn't take you with me the first time. I'd never tested it on humans. I could barely bring myself to send the first guinea pig through. If I took you with me and something went wrong…"

Beth stopped cold and clapped her hands to her mouth in horror. "Oh, God. Jules. I can't believe I forgot her. Tawny, we have to get home right now! She'll be out of school in like an hour, and if I'm not there to pick her up—" She sprang to her feet, looking around the room. How the hell were they going to get back? How come *that* hadn't been her first question? Her throat choked up with tears of panic.

"Hey—hey—hey, calm down, it's okay!" Tawny rose and clasped one of Beth's fluttering hands in her own, looking straight into her eyes. "We can go back whenever we want, and it doesn't matter. It'll only be five minutes after we left. Jules will still be at school. She'll never even know we were gone."

"What?" Beth caught her breath. "So we can choose what time to go back to?"

"Well, not quite—it's always five minutes, but yeah, time won't pass at home like it does here. We could stay a week and it wouldn't matter, apart from the fact that we'd be a week older when we went back home."

"Why five minutes?"

"It's a quirk of the time travel model I used. I'm not sure why, but with the guinea pigs they always came back in five minutes. Well, four minutes and forty-nine-odd seconds. At first I thought you could only stay in the past five minutes, but then I sent back some test droids and their on-board instruments showed they'd been gone for hours, even though it was still just the five minutes in our time."

"So that's what you've been doing this whole time we've lived with you?" Beth asked. "Sending robots into the past to determine its potential for sex tourism?"

Tawny frowned. "Well… that's not *exactly* how'd I'd put it. Anyway, we can go home any time we want." She held up her thumb and forefinger. "I implanted a set of controls for the machine under my skin here. It can't be lost, and all I have to do to fire it up is to click them together three times fast. When I go, I'll hold on to you."

Beth relaxed a little. "Okay," she said uncertainly. "And that will work? To take me with you?"

"Sure, I think anything I'm touching will transport with me."

"You think? Or you *know*?"

"I know," Tawny said. "I mean, I didn't arrive here naked."

"Girl," Beth said, "it might have been better if you did. That dress!"

"It's not *that* different from the ones on *Henry's Women*," Tawny defended herself. "Which I now understand is a festering sack of lies, anyway."

"Speaking of which, why did you pick, out of everyone in the history of ever, the most obvious possible choice? I've never known you to be that basic about your sexual partners."

Tawny looked down. "I figured it was the obvious choice for a reason. Everybody knows Henry got down with a lot of women and it didn't seem likely he'd reject me. I didn't… I didn't want to come all this way for nothing."

Beth paused before answering, choosing her words carefully. "That's something you're worried about? Rejection?"

"Well… it's been a while. My self-confidence isn't what it was," Tawny said to the floor.

"I get it."

"I couldn't ask you for help, and then all my other preparations took up my time, and then I just had to try the machine or lose my nerve completely. Henry wasn't the very first person who came to mind, but I thought he'd be the easiest one to start with."

Beth laughed.

"What?"

"It's just… what could be difficult after you solved time travel?"

Tawny gave her a small, hopeful smile. "Believe it or not, getting something to move backward through time was the easy part."

"What's the tough part? Do I even want to know?"

"Oh, you know, getting to the right place without ending up trapped in the earth's core or scattered into a trillion pieces. Here, for example. I had to take the best-preserved plans from Christopher Wren's archives—which weren't even for the *original* palace, by the way—and then compare them to a drawing of the palace kept in the Bodleian library at Oxford, so that I could work backward from there to here, figuring out which of the palace's structures were added after Henry's time." Tawny stopped for breath.

"Are we at Greenwich Palace?" Beth interrupted.

"Yeah. Did you know he called this place *Placentia*? Ew."

"It's Latin. It means something like 'pleasant place to live.'"

"Well, it sounds gross," Tawny said. "Anyway, I had to do all that before I could even build an accurate computer model of this structure so I wouldn't risk beaming myself into a wall. And when I say accurate, I mean with an error margin of no more than plus or minus five centimeters, and taking into account the exact positioning of the earth, this palace, everything, that existed on this day, in this year." She paused, apparently thinking of what else to add.

It must have been difficult, Beth reflected, to be working on something like this and not be able to talk to anybody about it.

"Oh," Tawny went on. "And on top of that, Henry and Anne had been renovating the palace. So I had that to worry about as well."

"Jesus," Beth said. "I guess I'm starting to understand why you didn't have time for adequate preparation on the cultural-slash-linguistics front."

"Oh, so about that—here's a history question for you. Why the hell does everybody sound so weird and not... British at all?"

"This was just before the Great Vowel Shift," Beth posited. "English pronunciation was a lot different before that. And in addition to the vowels, they also pronounce more of their consonants than we do. So that's a big part of why it doesn't sound like our English. What they speak is called Early Modern English in our time."

"Yeah, well... when I first heard it I got so freaked out I thought I'd have a Great Bowel Shift," Tawny replied, and Beth sputtered with laughter.

"I'm still having a hard time believing this is real," she said when she recovered. "That was the real Henry I saw. And the real Jane Seymour."

"Yeah," Tawny agreed. "It's weird. They're famous but they don't know how famous they *really* are. That people are still talking about them hundreds of years in the future. That people in the twenty-first century think they're super fuckable."

"Did you see Cromwell?" Beth asked. "I don't think I saw him in there. But I could have missed him. Or maybe he doesn't look like his portraits."

"Which one is he?" Tawny asked, furrowing her brow. "Didn't he kill a king?"

"No, that's the Puritan one. He won't be born for another seventy years. This one, Thomas Cromwell, is one of the King's most important ministers. I'm sure you remember him from *Henry's Women*—he always has on that little black hat. We're lucky he wasn't there, in fact. He'd probably see right through my impromptu story about being Frisian."

"What is a Frisian, anyway?" Tawny asked.

"Frisia is… kind of like Holland before it was Holland. It's part of an area of Europe called the Low Countries."

"And he would know we weren't from there?"

"Cromwell's a very educated man and he's likely been to that part of Europe. And it's his job to know everything that's going on. You've seen *Throne Wars*, right?"

"Sure."

"Cromwell is kind of like the Hand of the King and the Master of Coin rolled into one."

"Ah." Tawny nodded in understanding.

Beth picked up the hairbrush Tawny had looked at earlier and examined the handle, trying to decide if it was mother-of-pearl, and mentally cataloguing the other faces she'd seen in the courtyard.

She set the brush down and picked up a small stoppered bottle, raising it to her nose. More rose perfume. She handed the bottle to Tawny. "Check this out. Most people who could afford it liked spicy scents like nutmeg. But everybody here's all decked out in roses because they think it'll impress the King."

Tawny took a cautious sniff. "Why roses?"

"It's the heraldic bloom of the Tudor family. Personally I think it's a little cloying, but I mean, what are you going to do, tell a king that Bath and Body Perks did it better?"

"Wow. I can't believe you," Tawny said. "You already figured out where we are—can you guess *when* we are?"

Beth did some quick mental math. "Let me see," she thought aloud. "The King's leg is wounded, and he's gained weight. He had a jousting accident in January 1536, so it has to be after that. Jane Seymour was with him, but she's not Queen yet. So Queen

Anne is still alive, and probably hasn't yet been arrested. It must be—the end of April, 1536."

"Wow. Yeah. It's April thirtieth. How the hell do you know all this?"

Beth shrugged, secretly pleased at the expression of open awe on Tawny's face. "I *was* a doctoral candidate. And I've always had a photographic memory for this type of stuff. Don't ask me to do any math, though. I'm expecting *you* to limp Jules through algebra and geometry when the time comes."

"What about that smartass ginger kid? Is he anybody?"

"The one who couldn't stop zinging me? I think that was Henry FitzRoy," Beth speculated. "I thought he'd look kind of wimpy, from the portrait of him that survived, but he's tall and handsome instead. Maybe the portrait was done when he was younger. He definitely looks like his father."

"Who's his father?"

"Oh—the King. He's Henry's son."

"Whoa—whoa—whoa." Tawny looked at her, brow furrowed in confusion. "If he has a son, why all the wives and brouhaha about getting a male heir? That guy looks plenty old enough to be a king if his dad croaks. Which means he had to be born way before Henry ditched Catherine of Aragon… right?"

"He's a bastard," Beth explained.

"Well, sure he is, but—oh. You mean an actual bastard."

"Right. He's not a legitimately born heir. That doesn't mean he could never be legitimated, but it complicates things. Anyway, Henry adores him. He gave him a double dukedom when he was just a little kid, so FitzRoy outranks practically everybody in England. Even his name is special—FitzRoy means 'son of the King.' Anyway, it's a moot point. He dies in summer 1536 so none of this matters. Sad, really."

Tawny frowned. "That is sad. And weird. I know that people not constantly dying young is a relatively modern convention, but he looks fine to me."

"Yeah. Nobody knows, but supposedly it was a respiratory illness. Plague, maybe. It could be anything. And who knows, people with royal blood died from all kinds of weird genetic problems that weren't understood at the time. Kind of an odd story, actually—he didn't have the fancy state funeral you'd expect for somebody with a title like his. They kept it quiet and buried him fast and discreetly. Some people think that means he was poisoned, but I never bought that. More likely, it was plague or sweating sickness, and they buried him right away to avoid starting a panic. Sorry… this is probably boring for you to listen to."

"Not at all," Tawny said. "You should write books about this stuff. You make them sound like real people, not like boring facts from a history class."

"They are real people."

They stood there for another minute in silence before Tawny spoke again. "By ye olde God's teeth, I wonder where the hell is our bath?"

Beth shuddered. "Tawny, I love you, but you have to drop the 'ye olde' stuff. That was never a thing. *Ever.*"

"You're shitting me. Aren't you? 'Ye olde' is totally a thing. It's everywhere!"

"Nope. It has to do with this extra letter their alphabet had, called *thorn*, and—never mind, it's not important. I'll explain it later, if you even care."

"What about 'God's wounds,' can I say that? I heard somebody say that in the courtyard."

"God's wounds is fine. Just don't overdo it. And don't say *totally* to them. It sounds absurd."

"Man. I wish I'd asked you about all this before coming here. I'm—I'm sorry you ended up here by mistake. I swear I didn't think anything like that would happen. Please don't be too mad at me."

"It's okay. Really. I forgive you for breaking the rules—this time."

"Uh. There's more."

Beth raised an eyebrow. "Go on."

"Well, while I was trying to figure out how best to approach the courtyard, I happened to bump into a guard, and he was pretty cute and I needed to relieve some tension, and I also had to make sure he didn't throw me in a dungeon—so I shoved him against a wall and rode him like a pony. I think he thinks I'm a succubus or something. He mentioned she-demons."

They high-fived.

"You didn't tell him you were from the future, did you?" Beth asked suddenly.

"No, *obviously*," Tawny said, looking offended. "I mean, how on earth would I explain that? These people don't even have air conditioning."

"Fair enough," Beth agreed, grinning. "And—you didn't make any 'predictions' about the near-future to impress any-body? No Connecticut Yankee stuff or anything?"

"Well, aside from the Game Boy I brought to give the King—no, no, *kidding*!" She waved her hands placatingly at Beth's sudden grimace. "It was a Game Boy Advance. I mean, he's a *King*, for God's sake!"

Beth didn't laugh. "They don't fuck around with witchcraft here. Seriously. Don't do anything strange."

"I guess that isn't too different from avoiding the NSA at home. And it means *Henry's Women* did get something right."

"Wait, what? The NSA?" This was the first Beth was hearing of this.

"It's nothing, really. I just, you know, have to make sure not to do anything time travel-related in public. We have an arrangement." Tawny waved her hand dismissively.

"Oh. Well… there's definitely going to be a conversation about that later. But they talked about witches on that show?"

"Yeah, they had Anne Boleyn running around in Stevie Nicks-ish black dresses using charms on everybody to make them love her… and based on your expression, I'm guessing that isn't an accurate portrayal."

"I can't even." Beth shook her head. "So how was he?"

"The guard? Not bad for a quickie."

"I suppose you didn't have time for 'Protection and Inspection,' then?"

"No, but that's one thing I'm not worried about. I'm on the shot and some prophylactic antivirals, and anything like the syph' would have no defense against modern antibiotics, so I planned on dosing up with some penicillin once we get home. Though, on reflection, we should both check ourselves for lice later."

"I guess you were more prepared than I thought."

"For old-fashioned germs it's like shooting fish in a barrel, except with a machine gun and simple-minded, slow-moving fish. At least, until antibiotic resistant chlamydia and AIDS hit the scene. We'll be safe from pretty much any communicable disease up through the 1940s, venereal or otherwise."

Beth's heart fluttered with surprise. "We?"

Tawny gave her a look like she'd been punched in the gut. "You… aren't going to do this with me?" she asked. "But I thought… Field Protocol One."

"I… didn't realize you thought I was in," Beth said. "I mean, seven years ago, yeah. But I have Jules now. I can't just run off and… time… bang every person I find fascinating. We should probably go home soon."

For a second, Beth thought Tawny might cry, but she stood up straight instead. "You're *really* going to skip out on the chance to attend a feast at the court of Henry the Eighth? You, the *historian*? Don't you want to see all… this?" She gestured at the room and Beth looked at their surroundings and understood what Tawny was actually saying—she'd be giving up something no other modern eyes had ever seen.

"I mean—you're already here," Tawny argued. "You'll be back at almost the exact same time, it'll be like you were never gone. We can stay for the feast, we can go home right after dinner! We'll come back here and I'll fire up the machine! Nobody will ever even know!"

Beth's resolve was wavering. "Well… but what about *your* plans?" she countered.

"I already got what I showed up for. And I don't want Henry anymore. I'm content."

Beth bit her lip and thought about it for a long moment. It was a dangerous place, at a dangerous time, but they weren't likely to get caught up in any palace intrigues in the course of a three hour feast. And… she would be the only twenty-first-century historian to have been a guest at the table of a sixteenth-century monarch.

"You know what?" she said, feeling an excited smile take form on her face. "Let's do it. For old times' sake, if nothing else."

"Really?" Tawny looked thrilled beyond belief.

"Really. But I hope you like whole animals stuffed with other whole animals."

"Will there be giant turkey legs and shit like a Renaissance Festival? They eat that all the time on *Henry's Women*."

"Doubtful. Turkeys aren't indigenous to Europe."

"Aw, man," Tawny grumbled. "Is *everything* on TV a lie?"

Beth snorted. "Before I forget—why is your time machine a shower?"

"Oh, you'll like this, there's a funny thing about water and the human body—"

"My ladies! Your bath." The maids appeared, with reinforcements, carrying an enormous copper tub between the two of them. The five sturdy young men following them lugged several kettles of steaming hot water.

A third maid arrived straight on their heels, with gowns for each of them. She held one out for Beth's inspection. "As you lost your accoutrements, the King thought it best if you had raiment fitting your station." After a significant pause, she added, "M'lady," clearly unsure of what to do with her distinguished, but odd, guests, who were also possibly spies.

Beth smoothed her hands over the dress—a sparkling garment of dark blue and gold velvet brocade, embroidered in an elaborate floral pattern shot with silver thread. It was the most beautiful gown she had ever seen. It was hard to believe she'd get to wear this lovely thing.

The maid held the second dress up, evaluating Tawny with a doubtful eye. The garment might have reached her mid-calves, if that.

"Ah," Tawny stammered, "I'd rather just keep... the garb of mine own country. Frisia." The maid stared at her. "Verily," Tawny added, looking hopeful that this might conclude the exchange.

"Prithee excuse my cousin," Beth interrupted. "She has little experience with the English tongue."

The third maid nodded curtly and withdrew to the hallway outside, obviously relieved to be done with them both.

Beth turned and winked at Tawny. "Yea, verily. This night our milkshake shall bring all the lads to the sward."

ELEVEN

IN WHICH TAWNY
ENJOYS JUGGALO ANTICS

TAWNY'S COMPANION AT DINNER, LADY CATHERINE WILLOUGHBY, MADE for rather animated conversation, as she seemed to smile and clap her hands excitedly with almost every other sentence. "Just wait until the morrow, there'll be swans!"

Tawny hated swans because of an unpleasant childhood encounter that had left her with a broken arm and her grandfather expelled from his nursing home. She couldn't decide if the prospect of swans on the morrow appalled or intrigued her. "Why?"

"Because it's May Day! Swan is eaten only for especial occasions. Holidays, you know. Or perhaps you don't. Do Frisians not celebrate the first of May? It's delightful here. We'll all go out riding in the wood, and His Majesty and the men will hunt while we ladies gather flowers. We'll be just as wood nymphs in the train of Diana! Oh! And tennis in the afternoon."

"That sounds, uh, really great. Will the King be able to play?"

Lady Catherine paused, giving her a look tinged with suspicion. "Word of His Majesty's mishap traveled as far as your country?"

"Oh, probably not, but the Lady Elizabeth and I were traveling through France when all the town criers went ape with the news." Tawny smiled brightly. Thanks to Beth's excellent cover for them, she didn't have to pretend to have their bizarro-English down pat, and she was much more at ease.

Tawny and Beth were seated close together at one of the middle tables, near where Henry and Bastard-Henry-Junior were toasting and chortling up a storm. According to Beth, being placed so close to the King was quite a compliment. Henry's courtiers were indeed snake-like, wary of her, but no one besides FitzRoy was in a striking mood. Also, she giggled to herself, all the snakes around here wore turtlenecks.

On the right, she was separated from Beth by the loquacious Lady Catherine, a jolly, red-cheeked young woman with her hair hidden under a hefty gable hood. On her left was a stolid, black-bearded fellow with a sexy eye patch. He smelled faintly of onions and had barely spoken since they were seated. Catherine, on the other hand, was ablaze with chatter and excitement for each dish as it came to the table.

"Here comes the next service. Saints be praised, we no longer have to eat frumenty with porpoise anymore! Methinks those great awful fish monsters were not what the Church Patriarchs had in yore conceived for Lent."

"I know, right? Who doesn't hate fish monsters... that are totally not mammals?"

Lady Catherine gave her a bit of a funny look, and Tawny realized belatedly that Beth had specifically told her not to say "totally" to these people. Or maybe Lady Catherine just didn't know what mammals were and was covering up her embarrassment.

Tawny gave her another brilliant smile, and the conversation moved on, to her relief. She had faked her way through a solid hour of the feast, using the same techniques that had served her in other unfamiliar situations—smile, nod, and make positive-sounding noises every so often to evince the approval and positive regard she was supposed to be feeling as part of the interaction.

Even with her previous plans for a steamy encounter with the disappointingly gout-ridden King now firmly dashed, there was still plenty to enjoy. The people-watching alone would have made the whole trip worthwhile. There were strolling minstrels, assorted pomp and pageantry, and elaborate candle fixtures—Tawny had to hand it to the sixteenth-century crowd for their ingenuity in dealing with the sad lack of electricity.

And, of course, there was the food.

Lady Catherine was obliging in identifying each dish for her, and even Sexy Eye Patch (she hadn't caught his name and was afraid it would be rude to ask) explained a couple of things. There was a seemingly endless parade of spiced meats—roast beef, hen boiled with leeks, leg of mutton with a "galladine sauce" that tasted kind of gingery, rabbit, partridge, pheasant, and venison. Servants brought out trays brimming with pies stuffed full of larks' tongues and quince, eels and lampreys galore, fruit tarts, cheeses, salads made of last year's dried marigolds, and floundery sea creatures called turbots. Everybody oohed and ahhed at the appearance of "manchet," which made her laugh when it turned out to be just plain white bread. Still more impressive were the marzipan figures of the Seven Wonders of the Ancient World and a host of fragrant confections made from more types of cream than Tawny had ever heard of.

Apparently the Tudors didn't do courses; all kinds of dishes, salty and sweet, were brought out in groups, though they did get more elaborate as the feast went on, with the jellies of peacock—seriously, what?—giving way to whole pheasants with their feet and heads covered in gold leaf, which she half-expected would soon be surpassed in turn by a bedazzled ostrich.

Tawny, whose love of novelty extended to food, tasted everything she could get her hands on. The custom here was for servants to bring each dish—on gold and silver platters, of course—to the royal table first, then promenade it around to the other diners, who could choose various morsels as they liked.

At the start of the feast she had already loaded up a plate before she noticed there were no forks. Her fellow feasters were using little daggers to cut up their food, and then they speared and ate it from the tip, like that wasn't dangerous or anything. No wonder these people got mouth abscesses, like, constantly.

She panicked—not only did she not have one of those little knives, she did *not* want to eat that way—when she realized that most of the food was already in hand-edible form. There were linen napkins aplenty, and young men patrolling the tables with bowls of hot water decorated with flowers for a quick wash-off in between dishes. Tawny grabbed a piece of pheasant and dug in.

Some time later, she had started on yet another delicious pie when she heard Beth mutter, "Are you fucking kidding me?"

Tawny turned to witness a scene straight out of a Renaissance Festival: King Henry the Eighth beaming as two serving men presented a giant silver platter with an honest-to-God turkey on it, steaming and golden-skinned. He insisted on carving off one of the pterodactyl-sized legs, holding it aloft like a sword in one hand as he raised a glass to the bounty of the New World with the other.

Tawny couldn't keep the ecstatic grin from her face.

Beth face-palmed. "Turkey. It's a damned turkey," she said, mumbling into her hand.

"Oh, that." Lady Catherine motioned dismissively. "We've had turkey at court since I was a girl, nigh on ten years. Not any great wonder, in my esteem. Even His Majesty is losing his affection for the bird. Well, he was, until the cooks discovered turkey, stuffed with goose, stuffed with chicken, stuffed with partridge, stuffed with pigeon. As regards the spoils of the New World, I'm far more curious about the 'Spanish Secret,' aren't you?"

she said with a wink. Tawny was just about to ask what kind of delightfully naughty thing that might be, when the King's voice boomed out over the chatter in the room.

"Lady Willoughby! Your sylphine tones are required! Since so many of our court poets are indisposed,"—the room hushed at this comment about court poets, Tawny noticed curiously—"only you can do justice to my art. Well, you, Sir Thomas, and Sir Francis Bryan. And, of course, my lad Henry here." He clapped his son on the back.

"Oh, huzzah indeed," Catherine muttered under her breath. Then she jumped to her feet and curtsied, followed by Sexy Eye Patch, who made a deep, courteous bow toward the royal table. "Excellent, Your Majesty!" declared Lady Catherine. She, Sexy Eye Patch, the other man, and the King's douchebag bastard son all assembled to one side of the royal table.

"We await your pleasure, Your Majesty."

"Of course you do," the King said, beaming. "The song shall be a court favorite, 'Pastime with Good Company.'" Everyone cheered, but Tawny thought more than a little of the applause was made with less than sincere gusto. The quartet the King had selected launched into a four-part harmony—Lady Catherine did in fact have a lovely soprano voice—accompanied by some of the minstrels strumming and tootling on various old-timey instruments, including a miniature trombone of some kind.

Beth took advantage of the sudden vacancy and slid into Lady Catherine's empty seat next to Tawny, crystal goblet in hand.

"What's the 'Spanish Secret?'" Tawny whispered. "Not syphilis, I hope?"

Beth shook her head. "Chocolate."

"Oh, man," Tawny said, "these people are gonna be so unprepared for that shit, not that their cuisine isn't amazing and all, but marzipan, comparatively, is no great shakes."

"Speaking of marzipan, according to my new friends Lady Salisbury and Sir Richard over there, Henry is showing off at this feast to impress Jane Seymour, since he's about to get rid of Anne. Hence all the ridiculous food and it isn't even May Day."

"We've only been here a few hours and you're already networking. How do you do it?" Tawny realized that she was speaking through a mouthful of lamprey and hurried to finish chewing.

"You're doing pretty well yourself. And I've been talking up everyone near me to keep Henry's punk son at bay. He's been slinging barbed comments and the occasional backhanded compliment my way all night. If there were an opening, no doubt he'd have come and perched at my elbow to deliver still greater vitriol."

"What a little shit."

Despite being a little shit, Henry FitzRoy had a fine tenor voice. As he sang, he kept sneaking looks at them. Not that she blamed him—Beth was radiant after her bath and grooming. She fit in seamlessly, unlike Tawny, who in addition to knowing next to nothing about the culture was taller than every woman in the room, and at least half the men.

Beth fidgeted with her goblet for a moment, staring into it. "I just wanted to say... I'm having a great time. I know things got off to an awkward start, and I know I was mad at first, but now that we're here, I haven't felt this awesome in months. Make that years. I mean, working for you turned things around for me and Jules, but this—this is one of the most amazing things I've ever experienced. I'm so happy you wanted to share it with me."

Tawny's heart leapt. "Seriously?"

"Seriously." They smiled at each other and shared a moment of companionable silence.

"Hey, have you tried this stuff?" Beth asked, breaking the lull. "It's called hypocras. I've read about it before, but it's so much better than the descriptions make it sound."

Tawny took a sip. "Whoo, that is sweet! Here, if you like that you should try some of these awesome gilt sugarplums." She took one from her plate and held it out to Beth, who tasted it.

"Oh, that is good. Here, you have to try one of these stuffed fruitcakes," Beth said. "There's something in here called 'force-meat,' and it tastes way too good for its name."

After a while the song ended and everyone applauded. The members of the quartet bowed and curtsied to Henry, then started back to their seats, only to be held in place by a crook of his royal finger.

"Not yet, friends. The Crown yet requires your services. The next song will be my latest composition, given me in a dream by the loveliest of the Muses: 'My Love, With Angel Wings.'" At the royal table, Jane Seymour beamed. "And then bring in the jugglers!"

"Did he say Juggalos?" Tawny asked.

At that precise moment, mimes in black-and-white face paint appeared in the hall, and Tawny, laughing, could tell that things would be better than okay.

"GOOD KING WENCESLAS LOOKED OUT—ON SOME SCHMUCK NAMED STEphen—"

"I don't think that's how it goes," Beth interrupted her.

"No, no—I got this. Something-something, twist-and-shout—oh-I-cannot-eeee-ven! Hey, it rhymes!" Tawny burst into uncontrollable giggles as she and Beth half-danced, half-staggered, arm-in-arm down the hallway, trailed by their aggrieved maidservants. They'd been attempting to sing "Good King Wenceslas" ever since they left the feast—it was the most

Renaissance-spectrum piece of music Tawny knew—without successfully finishing a verse yet.

They emerged into a larger chamber and swung each other around like square dance partners, immersed in the golden glow of moderately drunken *bonhomie*. Tawny knew she was grinning like an idiot, but she couldn't help it. This was exactly what she'd envisioned—the spirit of their glory days returned at last.

"I think I should've passed on that last glass of hypocras," Beth said, wobbling a little. "Oh, and I just remembered something. What did you mean before when you said I'm not a snake?"

Tawny stopped in front of a large tapestry depicting a court scene very similar to the one she'd walked in on earlier that day, except with more cherubs and lions. Something felt strange. "Did you hear something?" she asked. "Just now?"

"No, did you?" Beth looked around, bracing herself against the wall with one hand.

"Shh." Tawny held her breath, trying to pinpoint the unnerving sound—and realized that it wasn't a sound at all, it was silence she'd noticed—the eerie stillness that surrounds the horror-movie victim when she runs into the woods.

"Hey," said Beth, "where did our maids go?"

And then the masked men surrounded them.

Half-a-dozen beefy dudes in black domino masks, dressed in what looked like all-black versions of the uniform her guard had worn earlier that day, swarmed out of the shadows. The men stood in a circle and stared at them, but said nothing. One of them cracked his knuckles in what he evidently thought was a menacing fashion, until one of his comrades smacked him in the shoulder.

"Beth, what do we do?" Tawny whispered.

"Distract them and run?"

"Distract them with what?"

"Ahem." One of the men cleared his throat.

"Uh—hi there." Tawny waved at him.

The speaker sketched a mocking bow. "Prithee, my ladies, your company is requested by a personage of great import for some postcibal entertainment. We are here to… escort you thither."

Oh, God. Henry. He must want one or both of them for sex things. She wasn't familiar with the term *postcibal*, but it sounded a little like *postcoital*. Maybe it was an ancient version of that word. Whatever they were in for, it would be totally gross.

"Have you taken leave of your senses? Are you not aware that we're important too—as in *foreign dignitaries*!" Beth was clearly feeling that hypocras. "You have no claim upon us—we answer only to our sovereign."

"And you perhaps are not aware that you have no choice in this matter. Surrender, and you'll not be harmed!"

Definitely sex things.

With a flick of his wrist, the man produced a slim blade from a scabbard at his side and brandished it at them. Well, more flourished than brandished. But the fact remained that they were surrounded by masked goons and their leader was pointing a literal sword at them. Beth and Tawny shared a long, eyebrow-raising, vague-gesturing, lip-reading moment as they tried to decide what to do.

"Take them," said the masked leader.

"Eat thee a confluence of dicks!" Beth yelled, cheeks flushed.

The men gaped at her a moment, then exchanged beleaguered glances with each other.

Tawny leapt up and dislodged a tapestry from its hangers and hurled it at the three men closest to them, who toppled over amidst a chorus of "Zounds!" and "Oddsbodikins!" She grabbed Beth by the arm and they hiked up their skirts and ran right over their fallen foes.

"That was some action hero shit, honey!" Beth exclaimed breathlessly as they ran.

The masked goons were in hot pursuit. "Quickly, men!" she heard behind them. "Remember, he wants them unhurt!"

"Tawny, quick, which way are our rooms?" Beth cried. "We have to use the clicker, but we can't let anybody see us!"

"No, no, let's get outside, that's the first place they'll look! I know the way, don't worry."

Beth nodded and Tawny took the lead. They darted down what seemed like an endless succession of hallways, never able to shed their pursuers for long enough to safely activate the device.

Their clothing didn't help—within minutes, Tawny's lungs felt like they'd been stuffed with glass and stomped on, thanks to the goddamn corset she was wearing. Soon she couldn't hear Beth over the sound of her own labored breathing.

This part of the palace was deserted and oddly dim, with only a few guttering torches in the wall sconces. It still synced up with the maps Tawny had painstakingly memorized, though, and the emergency exit she'd picked was right around the corner.

"Okay," she wheezed, "those windows shouldn't be guarded and we can—Beth?" Tawny turned around. Beth was nowhere in sight.

"There's the other one!" Two of the men in black came charging down the hall at her. Tawny about-faced and fled, chest heaving. She couldn't go much further without stripping off her ridiculous get-up.

Heavy footfalls echoed behind her—she'd have to hide and find Beth once the men were gone. Tawny turned down another passage, passing a heavy wooden door. She back-tracked, and leaned against it, listening for occupants.

"I think she went this way!" No matter if the room was occupied, now. Tawny gripped the heavy iron ring, flung the door open and darted through, pulling it closed behind her as quietly as possible and stubbing her toe in the process. She stifled a litany of terrified exclamations, all of them some variation on 'fuck-fuck-fuck', as the sounds of her pursuers reached the door—and subsided into the distance as they went right past. She slumped forward against the wall, limp with relief.

"If my lord and husband has sent a cut-throat, he might have chosen someone *slightly* less conspicuous," said a female voice behind her.

Tawny turned around, groping at the bric-a-brac on the nearby mantle for something she could use as a weapon, then stopped when she saw the speaker. The woman who emerged from the shadows was unmistakable. Short and slender, dark hair and darker eyes, even wearing the necklace she'd last been painted in.

"You must be the latest well-bred doxy come to vie for Henry's affections. Welcome to Hell," said Anne Boleyn.

TWELVE

IN WHICH BETH SEDUCES A GENTLEMAN BARELY HAVING REACHED HIS MAJORITY

BETH HAD RUN DOWN SEVERAL DARK CORRIDORS, THE SOUNDS OF HER pursuers clapping fast behind her, for several minutes before she realized she had lost Tawny. Another moment after that, she ran straight into a dead end and stood there, chest heaving, staring with woozy dismay at a large tapestry depicting a brightly plumed budgerigar perched on the edge of a dish, eating seeds from a hand extended to it from out of frame.

It was hard to decide whom she was more worried about—herself, since she was hammered on spiced wine, or Tawny, since she knew nothing of the culture and would fast get herself into trouble. Although, Tawny had the clicker that would get them home.

The thought occurred to Beth that she should be seriously concerned. No matter how modern their dinner companions fancied themselves, the truth remained that in a few short weeks this country would execute its Queen on charges of treason and witchcraft. While Beth had the distinct advantage of not having pissed off the King by failing to birth a viable male heir, she was still a stranger with a less-than-expert grasp on their language, whose cover story wouldn't stand up to much scrutiny. Tawny could duck around a corner and blink home any time, but Beth might get stuck here if she couldn't find her before that happened.

All of this flew through her mind in the few seconds before the footsteps pounded around the corner and two of the men stood there, seeming to leer at her as they approached.

"Brigands!" she screeched, backing away. "Thou pied… pied… asses! Poltroons!"

They closed in, indifferent to her shouting.

"Thou, motherfucker," she cried, clawing at the man on her right as they seized her, one at each arm, "art as a candle, the better part burnt out!"

The two men exchanged an aggrieved glance and the one she had yelled at appealed to her reason, loosening his grip a little. "Prithee, lady, come in peace."

"I shall not, thou sniveling, sanguine coward!" Beth spat, struggling violently against their grasp. "Thy antics do not amount to a man!"

The man to her left sighed. "Methinks the lady is sorely distempered," he said to his companion.

"Swine-drunk," the other agreed.

"I heard that!" Beth snapped at him, jerking her arm roughly away. "*Thou'rt* sorely distempered! Thinkest thou I be deaf?! Or what?"

"Lady," the first man said, sounding regretful, "By my troth, I would not accost a woman of gentle birth, but you leave me no choice." He took her firmly by the arm and motioned to the other man, who fished in a pouch at his waist and withdrew a scrap of cloth, to which he applied a stinking, corrosive fluid from a small vial.

They had ether in Tudor England? Beth thought crazily as she fought against the first man, who had pinned her against him, both arms uselessly trapped behind her. "Shh," he whispered to her. "You shall not be harmed. Cease this madness." Lacking arms, she commenced thrashing her legs at this. They were beyond doubt the words of some kind of Tudor sadist. What would become of her?

She heard something tear as one of her kicks connected not with the second man but instead with her unwieldy gown, and then he moved deftly to one side and raised the cloth to her face. "Raper!" Beth screamed before she began to choke on the sickly smelling rag held over her nose and mouth. Her legs failed beneath her then and she slumped helplessly into the arms of her captor. Her sight went black, and then her hearing endured a few more moments, although the words quickly lost any meaning.

"Verily," she heard one of them declare in tones of frank amazement. "The alchemist's potion hath done its promised duty."

"In sooth," the other agreed, "it be a miraculous modern age in which we live."

If Beth could have giggled, she might have.

AT FIRST SHE HAD A HAZY SENSE THAT HOURS HAD PASSED, BUT AS REALITY shaded itself back in, Beth realized foggily that someone had removed the cloth from her face. It must have been only minutes. In patches, her consciousness returned. She was in a sumptuously appointed chamber, well lit by a combination of wall sconces and a low-hanging chandelier that held a host of flickering candles.

There were too many details to take in all at once. She was tied fast to the elaborately carved cushioned chair in which she had been propped, her wrists bound to its arms. Beth coughed away some of the harsh sting from her throat, fixing her eyes uncomprehendingly on the carpet in front of her seat. It was an ornate floral pattern of the type common in the Tudor period.

Suddenly she realized that people were talking close behind her where she couldn't see them. "—shrieking like a wraith."

"And you used the sweet vitriol?" a clear young male voice asked. "It hath rendered her unanimate." Sweet vitriol, she seemed to recall, was the archaic term for ether. So she'd been right.

"We were sorely vexed to administer the potion, my lord, but she fought like a wild thing," she heard next, spoken in a tone approaching admiration. Whether it was admiration of her vivacity or of the ether's efficacy, she couldn't tell.

"Yes," the clear voice said. "I am little surprised at this. The lady imbibed overmuch at the banquet. Thank thee for conveying her safe to me. That shall be all I require from thee this evening."

"Aye, my lord," one of the men said, and she heard their soft footfalls on the rug and then the sound of a door opening and closing.

She heard someone, probably the owner of the young male voice, move somewhere behind her. The clink sounded then of glass tinking gently against glass. Someone pouring wine, perhaps.

Beth blinked hard and looked around the room for anything that might give her a clue as to the identity of her captor, or reduce her disadvantage in this situation. She saw only the average personal quarters of someone high in station—stone walls lavishly decorated with tapestries, rugs covering nearly every square foot of the no doubt cold stone floor, and the usual furnishings that might be seen in such a place. Desk, table, chairs—and an extensively ornamented four-poster canopied bed with curtains and a thick spread on which a hunting scene was embroidered in golden thread.

She was still a little drunk, but the ether had taken some of the rancor out of her, and the adrenaline rush that accompanied her capture had sharpened her senses. Beth felt very alert as she lifted her head to survey her gaoler.

"I see you have awakened," the voice said, and then he came into view.

FitzRoy.

Beth took him in—he was a tall, physically imposing man like his father must have been in youth, and handsome, with light red hair and the same sharp blue eyes. He'd changed from his banquet finery into a simple linen shirt and hose. It was a rather becoming look on him—not that she cared much for that at the moment.

"You drugged me," she accused. "How dare you? I am your royal father's guest!"

"I did," he admitted, "but t'would not have been needed had you come peacefully."

"With no explanation and at the point of a marauder's sword? I think you might expect most ladies to refuse such an invitation," Beth answered haughtily.

This short speech failed to have the desired impact. "What is a marauder?" he asked curiously.

"It is a Frisian word. It means... a bad man who attacks people," she said, wondering whether the word had perhaps not been in common usage at the time. Hopefully she could pass off any more of her unwitting anachronisms as Frisian idiosyncrasies.

"Oh," FitzRoy said. "Well, would you have some wine? Or, mayhap you have taken enough spirits this eve. Some watered ale, perhaps?"

Her throat was awfully parched, now that she thought of it. She nodded and he picked up a cup from the table nearby and brought it to her. "No biting," he warned her as he lifted it to her lips.

Beth took a generous swallow. "Do you often find yourself in peril of being bitten by women?" she asked peevishly.

He froze, holding the cup to her mouth, and surprised her by responding not with a clever retort, but by blushing deeply with evident embarrassment. His fair complexion flushed bright red, from his cheeks, all the way down his neck into his shirt.

Beth had forgotten how young he was. Despite the situation, his bashfulness struck her as rather sweet.

It occurred to her then that FitzRoy had called her *you*, rather than the *thee* reserved for speaking to someone of lower station, such as the men he had sent to take her. He still appeared to consider her a member of the aristocracy, then. Perhaps he believed some of her story after all.

She could work with this.

"Your Grace," she said bluntly, "Will you tell me why you have brought me here? I hope it is not for the purpose of committing bawdy wickedness against my person."

Her accusation had its desired effect—if anything, he reddened still further. "No," he said after a moment, withdrawing the cup and standing there stiffly before her, clutching it in his grasp.

She opened her eyes wide and blinked innocently at him. "Then I would know your reason."

"Respectfully, lady," he replied, "I do not know how much of your strange tale is a lie, but I would wager the answer is 'much of it.' I meant to bring you and your companion for some discreet questioning, but she seems to have evaded my men."

So Tawny had escaped, then. That was something. Beth wondered where she might be holed up, and whether anyone was still looking for her. Would she be able to venture out in search of Beth?

"You believe I am a spy," she said flatly.

"Yes," he said. The embarrassed flush had faded, and he appeared to be getting his bearings. "I believe you are a spy sent to undermine my father's rule of England. I would learn your secrets and cease your meddling."

"I assure you I am no spy. Allow me to tell you of my innocence, noble sir," she said, feeling more confident now.

"Prithee," he said dryly, gesturing for her to begin before pulling up a chair for himself.

Beth thought fast. What else did she know about him? He was born in summer 1519 to one of Queen Catherine's ladies in waiting. The Queen, she recalled, was pregnant, making her sexually inaccessible to the King, who had sought his pleasure elsewhere. The King had done far better than mere acknowledgment of his bastard son. Rather, he had given him a double dukedom and welcomed him to court as befitted a royal prince of unimpeachable birth.

If she remembered correctly, FitzRoy was married around age fifteen to the daughter of a duke. He was now seventeen, and one of the King's most viable potential heirs.

With a rush of comprehension, she realized that this last fact must be the reason for all his grandstanding at dinner, and for his inquiry into her potential espionage. He wanted to become King. To do that, he needed to impress his father.

"Well?" he asked impatiently.

In that moment Beth understood with utter clarity what FitzRoy needed to hear from her.

"Your Grace, may I speak frankly? I shall give you the real truth of why I am here, if you in turn will give me your oath that I will remain unharmed at your hands. You and I are not enemies at all, and in sooth should be the best of friends."

Happily enough for her, FitzRoy seemed intrigued by her assertion. "I give you my word," he said, "if I judge your story to be truth and not the vile lies of a spy."

"My lord father sent me to England with an entourage," she began. "We lost the men of our party to an attack by ruffians, which accounts for our strange appearance when we arrived at court. However, in my explanation to His Majesty I omitted certain details concerning the reason for our visit."

"Go on," he said, frowning slightly.

"My lord father learned in recent months that after the King's accident, the Queen Anne had fallen into disfavor owing to… recent disappointments." She paused delicately for effect. "Subsequent to this, my father learned that the Seymour family was attempting to marry Sir John's daughter to His Majesty in the event that the Queen were set aside. I was sent to do anything in my power to prevent Jane Seymour from becoming the King's new wife and queen."

"Why would the Low Countries care who becomes Queen?" he asked.

"The Seymours are rivals of my family's mercantile interests. We have heard, even in our remote land, that the King was for a time terribly ill."

FitzRoy frowned at this, but nodded.

Beth continued. "Should the King produce a son with a Seymour queen, that child would become his heir in the stead of Princess Elizabeth… or another." She nodded at him to indicate that she well knew whom that other heir might be.

His expression clouded. "True," he acknowledged. "Yet I must again ask, why should Frisians concern themselves with English 'heritance?'"

It wouldn't do to speak too casually of the death of a reigning monarch. "If the unthinkable should ever happen," she said, choosing her words with care, "if His Majesty should be taken from England too young, before his heir were of age, it might mean a Seymour regency. And failing that event, the Seymours would still wield undue influence in English politics… and industry."

Wary interest dawned in his pale blue eyes. "And this friendship of which you spake?" he asked cautiously. "In what way do our causes converge? I can see no reason why you should prefer any particular outcome beyond preventing a Seymour from one day controlling the realm."

"True," she conceded, "at minimum my father hopes to prevent a Seymour ascension. However, he also knows that you, my lord, would prove a strong, independent ruler—one who will consider fairly the trade interests of not merely a single line, but all of England. You were raised as a royal prince all your life, and you will attain your majority soon. There is no more suitable heir in all your country." She was really laying it on, but Beth hoped her speech might convince him to untie her.

"In fact I already have," he said moodily.

"Have what?" she asked, confused.

"Attained my majority." He rose from his seat and turned away from her, staring pensively into the distance.

"But you…" she trailed off, unsure what to say next.

"My age of record is not my true age. In sooth, I am older—eighteen years, already. My father wished to conceal my date of conception when he brought me to court—I would risk his wroth were I to publicly declare myself. And yet—" He left off, fist clenched in frustration.

Beth felt a pang of sudden compassion for him. "You are a man in years," she said, "but forced to masquerade as a boy."

"You are an unkind lady," he said without much heat, "to remind me of this fact."

"I crave your pardon," Beth said, and meant it. "If it offers you any comfort, my lord, well does this explain why you appear manful beyond your years." She didn't entirely mean that—he looked plenty young—but some part of her wanted to make him feel better.

"Indeed?" he asked with interest. "Trow you that others may have made this selfsame observation?"

"It is wholly possible, my lord," she assured him. "Doubtless they share your trepidation at incurring the King's disfavor. They dare not share their suspicions."

"Good madam," FitzRoy said, "Will you take my apology at my ill conduct, sprung as it was from my overcaution?" He moved to loosen the bond securing her left wrist.

"Gladly I would," Beth said, touched despite herself by his apparent sincerity. "You acted on your loyalty to the realm."

He nodded in agreement as he finished undoing the knot at her wrist and moved to the other. He had a light, gentle touch that reminded Beth of her first college boyfriend. Up close, she could smell his clean, pleasantly musky male scent. He didn't wear the rose fragrance his father preferred, but smelled rather of something spicier, with hints of citrus and nutmeg.

FitzRoy brushed her hand as he picked apart the rope knot, and she wasn't very surprised by then to feel a stirring between her legs. He was very handsome—probably the spitting image of his father at eighteen—and something about him was strangely appealing. Perhaps it was that despite his adolescent bravado in public, in private, he had turned out to be a more earnest and thoughtful person than she'd expected. Or maybe it was just that after her long period of uninterrupted celibacy, any attractive man in close quarters was enough to set her afire. Even if he only had eighteen years to stack up against her thirty-three.

Any port in a storm, after all.

He finished untying her and let the rope fall away, his hand lingering unnecessarily by hers for a moment, leaving her to guess whether it was on purpose or not. The heat of his hand warmed her skin, even though he wasn't touching her. Slowly she raised her eyes to his, wondering what it was she saw there. He blushed and pulled his hand away, and to her surprise her own cheeks grew warm too.

FitzRoy cleared his throat, rising to his feet. "Will you—will you take more wine?" he asked. "If you prefer it less strong, I will water it."

Beth nodded her speechless agreement, rubbing her wrists and wondering what on earth had come over her. When she was home again, she decided, she would buy a decent vibrator and put an end to this idiocy once and for all. It was all very well for Tawny to have sex with whomever she pleased, but Beth wasn't a free agent like Tawny. She had Jules to think about.

But no one will ever, ever have to know, argued a tiny voice inside her.

"My lady," FitzRoy said, handing her a cup.

"Thank you," she said shyly, taking a sip. Like the hypocras she'd enjoyed at dinner, it was delicious and tasted faintly of cinnamon. Thankfully, it was considerably weaker than the hypocras.

After a moment of awkward silence, he spoke again. "I should like further discourse on your plans for the Seymours, but the hour has grown rather late. Shall I... escort you back to your chambers?"

Was she imagining it, or did he sound reluctant? Was he only offering because he knew it was what a gentleman should do?

"I must be mad," she said, sure she'd later regret the words, "as you brought me here under rude circumstance, but..." she paused, unsure of how to tell him she wasn't yet ready to leave.

"But your duty compels you to persevere despite your weariness?" he suggested promptly.

"Yes," she said with gratitude. "And—I am not so grievously weary," she offered. "I might enjoy passing some 'time in good company' this evening."

FitzRoy beamed at her reference, lighting up his whole face.

With embarrassment, Beth felt her stomach give a little flip-flop at the sight of his brilliant smile. He really was terribly good looking, with that careless mop of red curls and the good-natured expression he wore when he wasn't trying to be sharp and witty. She wondered what kind of king he might have made. A good one, perhaps—educated to be conversant in politics and royal etiquette, but with the natural humility of any bastard-born child.

"Did you know," he commented, resuming his seat, "my father wrote that song about Queen Catherine?"

"I heard that once," Beth said politely.

"Queen Catherine was never unkind to me," he mused, "tho' she had much cause to be. She was a good lady. Pity that my father forgot how dearly he once loved her. And the Queen Anne, for that matter."

"Might he be reminded?" Beth asked. "If he were to take back Anne, perhaps your status as heir would be settled once and for all. I heard the Queen has been poorly of late. Whereas Jane…" she trailed off. Jane Seymour was plainly in robust health and Beth already knew that in a little over a year she would produce Henry's only legitimate male heir to survive childhood. Not that her new friend Henry FitzRoy would be around to mourn that occasion.

"I fear not," he said. "My father—well, you would not know the strength of his will as do those of us in his court—is a man set upon his own course. Lord Chancellor Cromwell is among the few who hold any sway with him, and he has no reason to take up my cause." He hesitated, then added, "My father has… changed since his wounding."

Beth knew what he meant. The King, a formerly jocular and generous man, had experienced an abrupt personality change after his jousting accident. Historians speculated that it was due to a traumatic brain injury suffered as part of the incident.

"We might yet prevent a Seymour union," he went on, "if we had some means of discrediting Jane and making her unfit for royal marriage. Still, I regret to stoop to such villainy. She gives every appearance of a gentle, virtuous soul."

"Perchance you are right," Beth agreed. She was tired of talking about the Seymours, but wasn't sure where to turn the conversation instead. "Your Grace," she said, lifting her cup, "what sort of wine is this? It is delicious."

"It comes from Italy, I am told," he said, studying her.

"Ah," she said. "I have never been there. I hear it is very different to both our countries."

"Speaking to the customs of our countries—may I ask you something rather private?"

"Of course," she said, curious what he wanted to know, and equally curious whether she could lie sufficiently to answer it.

"Why would your father send his daughter on such a dangerous errand? You are plainly close in age to me and Lady Willoughby. You are too young a woman to bear such a burden."

In truth, Beth was well over ten years older than them both, but she'd also had the lifelong benefit afforded by a modern diet and dental care.

"An Englishman," FitzRoy continued, "would never press his daughter into such service."

No, Beth thought, an Englishman would rather whore his daughter out to a king for political favor. "My father is in poor health, and has no sons to act in our family's interest," she told him, "and in Frisia things are different than they are here." This was of course nonsense, but he didn't know that.

"It is difficult to imagine," he said. "He had no plans for you to marry? Such an unkind fate for a lady."

"He did," she said, "but I was widowed near as soon as I was wed."

"Truly?" he inquired, looking speculatively at her. "That is a sad tale. You are too young to be a widow."

Something about the sweet sincerity with which he said this made Beth want to kiss him and tuck him into her skirts to be taken home with her to keep for all time.

"You are too kind," she murmured.

FitzRoy raised his cup and took a lengthy draught of wine. He had not, Beth noticed, diluted his own wine as he had hers.

"And, er…" she began, "what of you, Your Grace? Your lord father hath made you a good match, is that not true?" It might steadfast her resolve to remind herself that not only was he too young for her, he was also already married.

He poured himself a second glass of wine and downed most of it in a single swallow. "You must call me Henry," he said. "And if I may speak openly? My marriage is one in name alone. I have not seen my wife in over a year, nor at any point been permitted to enjoy"—he gave a little cough and left off awkwardly for a moment—"her company."

Beth had read several sources speculating that FitzRoy's arranged marriage had been an unconsummated one, but she always assumed that for a handsome adolescent male coming of age in this particular court in this particular time period, he must have had more than his share of dalliances. There were plenty of comely young maids about.

"Your Grace—" she said in considerable shock.

"—Henry," he corrected her.

"Henry," she continued. "Are you in whole troth telling me you are—" She didn't want to insult his adolescent pride by calling him a virgin, but there weren't many more dignified ways of putting it. "You have not yet enjoyed the pleasures of a woman?" she finished inelegantly, feeling her cheeks grow hot.

He flushed red again, but held her gaze. "Well," he said boldly, "have you?"

"Enjoyed the pleasures of a woman?" Beth quipped, then giggled.

Henry blushed again, but joined in her laughter.

"Forgive me," Beth gasped, wiping the tears from her eyes as her mirth subsided. "I drank too much wine at the feast, and now you've given me still more wine. I am a silly thing. You must ignore my foolishness, Your Grace."

"Henry," he corrected her again, dragging his chair close enough that his knee nearly brushed hers, and draining his glass of wine. Beth's pulse quickened with anticipation.

"Perhaps I too have had overmuch wine," he said, setting his cup on the table. "I think it has given me innatural courage. I hope you will not find me ungentlemanly." He leaned in and gave her a gentle, uncertain kiss on the lips.

THIRTEEN

IN WHICH BETH LEARNS THAT
WHILE THE PAST IS A FOREIGN COUNTRY
THEY DO SOME STUFF THE SAME

It would be a terrible crime to let this sweet young man die a virgin, Beth decided abruptly. She couldn't change the course of history, but she could give him a good tumble before he went.

She leaned into him, encouraging him, enjoying the soft tentativeness of his touch on her arm. "Henry," she whispered into his mouth, playing her tongue against his, then left off as he grew bolder and deepened his kiss.

He broke their embrace and pulled away, but only after lingering another long moment. "Aye?" he asked, looking as though he expected to be scolded for taking liberties.

Beth reached up and pulled him back toward her, twining her fingers behind his neck and through his soft curls. "I do not find you ungentlemanly." She rested one hand lightly on his thigh and delighted at the excited shudder that coursed through him. She had nearly forgotten how incredible it felt to be the first person to touch someone that way. "Kiss me again," she said, slipping her hand further up his thigh.

Henry did not disappoint. Returning her embrace, he quickly tired of leaning to meet her and pulled her from her chair onto his lap, where he resumed the business at hand. Beth couldn't remember the last time someone had been so excited to be with her. She could feel him, even through her heavy skirts, hard as iron. And for her! It made her want to laugh and cry and fuck his brains out.

"God's teeth, you are beautiful," he said between kisses. "I wanted you the first I saw you."

"Really?" Beth asked, pausing. "But you thought I was a spy."

"A lovely spy," he countered breathlessly.

Beth laughed with delight. "Did you ever for a moment think this would happen?"

"Nay," he admitted, taking one of her hands to his mouth and flirtatiously kissing the tip of each finger. "I didn't dare hope."

She felt giddy and about a million years younger than she had that morning. "Silly as it is to say, I'm glad you had me kidnapped by masked men. But don't ever do that again." She leaned in for another kiss.

"Kidnapped?" he asked quizzically, drawing back and giving her a questioning look.

"Er," she faltered, "Taken against my will? Stolen?"

"Ah," he said, understanding. "I must profess, I find your Frisian speech most charming. And I shall never again have you—kidnapped. I would that next time you join me willingly." Henry gave the top of her bodice, which had been loosened in her earlier struggles, a firm tug downward, but the stiff busk the maid had forced into the front of her corset thwarted him. Nothing happened. They looked at each other and laughed.

"Here," Beth said, twisting away. "I think it has... hooks and laces in the back?"

She felt his touch as he smoothed her hair out of the way and fumbled for the start of the laces. "Ah," he said, pulling at something, gaining momentum as he went. "I think—I think you shall have to stand?"

Beth rose to her feet and it took them a few moments of detective work together to figure out how to slip the gown off over her head without the skilled hand of a maid. "Zounds," he remarked at seeing her corseted form buffeted by an array of petticoats, bustles, and other props. "The raiments of women art… less simple than those of men." He laid her gown neatly across the chair she'd been sitting in.

Beth stifled a grin at "zounds."

"Yes, 'tis well true," she agreed. "I cannot even dress myself without a maid's help, and then it still takes half of an hour. I think we're nearly there." She made quick work of the petticoats and the rest of her costume, tossing them carelessly aside.

He turned her again and began to pick at the back laces holding fast her corset. Underneath she wore only a thin smock, and the warmth of his hands combined with his delicate touch was unbearably exciting so close to her skin. The corset's death grip on her torso loosened incrementally as he worked, and with an exclamation of triumph, he finally pulled the last lace and freed her.

Beth turned and stood before him in her shift, suddenly self-conscious. She was *so* much older than he was.

"Have you… changed your mind?" he inquired, mistaking her expression.

"No! Have you?"

"Absolutely not," he said, and set his hands lightly on her waist, as if afraid she might shatter if he grasped her too hard.

"I won't break," Beth whispered.

"No," he agreed, his expression solemn as he sank back into the chair and pulled her close to him. She settled comfortably into his lap, unable to keep from smiling at the feel of his hardness beneath her. With only her thin chemise between them, his excitement was unmistakable. Confidence bolstered, she tugged flirtatiously at the bosom of her shift, pulling it down little by little until he lost patience and gave it a single jerk. Her breasts spilled out into his eager hands.

Beth laughed, gasping a little as he flicked his thumbs over her nipples, then bent his head and took one of them in his teeth. She inhaled sharply at the sensation and he pulled back, startled. "Did I hurt you?"

"No, it feels good," she said. "But where did you learn to do that, if you—if this is your first time?"

"Virgin I may be," he said, cupping her breasts in his palms, "but complete chastity is impossible in this court."

Beth laughed and nodded in agreement. She'd forgotten how much young men loved to play with tits, almost worshipfully. It felt amazing. She shifted a little in his lap, enjoying the slippery wetness between her legs as she moved. He groaned with pleasure, closing his eyes.

Beth did a few calculations, trying to decide how to steer the rest of their encounter. Deflowering people could be tricky if you didn't account for all the variables. If she fucked him right now and he came too fast, he might be embarrassed. She didn't want that—and she also didn't want to pass up her own turn. On the other hand, he was young enough that he'd recover swiftly.

"Henry," she began, slipping from his lap and placing her hands at the waist of his hose as she knelt before him. She couldn't recall now what she'd ever read about oral sex during the Tudor period. Obviously, it was a huge sin, but so was fornication and he was down with that. Maybe it was all just context…

"This is a Frisian custom, so don't be alarmed," she said, pulling the garment down as he watched her with excited interest. "Oh," she said in pleasant surprise as his eager cock sprang free. Height, it seemed, wasn't his only physical virtue. "*Very* nice," she told him, discarding the hose and taking him firmly in hand. He was uncircumcised, as were most men of the time. It wasn't something she'd ever minded, though.

Beth gave the head of his cock a preparatory swipe with her tongue, and he made a strangled sound, shifting against her, clutching her shoulder. She glanced up as she set about her task. His eyes were squeezed tightly shut and he couldn't seem to still his thighs beneath her as she reached to cup his testicles. He was breathing fast, in short inhalations, and as she dragged her tongue roughly up his long shaft he made a noise somewhere between a sob and a moan.

Yep. Beth was still the fucking queen of blow jobs.

She planted a tiny kiss on the head of his cock, smiling as he sighed with pleasure and strained against her. Seizing his shaft, she swirled her tongue around the head and parted her lips to take him in her mouth, grazing him with her teeth, just enough to make his breath ragged. "Oh, God," Henry groaned, unable to control his thrusting hips as she rasped her tongue along the underside of his cock. Beth felt another surge of arousal at his sounds of desperation, and moved her hips just enough to give herself a little friction as she took him deep inside her mouth.

It was only a little while before his balls contracted in her hand, signaling his imminent climax, and a moment later she finished him off neatly, swallowing. She was glad she hadn't taken him straight to bed. This way, he'd experienced something special and he'd also last a lot longer with her.

Beth reached for the cup he'd set aside earlier, washing away the taste with a long drink of wine, hyper-aware of the slickness between her thighs. Henry stared at her in stark amazement. "Did you like it?" she asked, rising from her knees.

"I shall have to make certain that England is ever on friendly terms with Frisia in the hereafter," he answered. "Although… what of your pleasure? I have heard that women may also enjoy the act, much as a man does. I would that you should take the selfsame joy as I have."

Beth looked at him, impressed. He might be more progressive than some of the twenty-first-century men she'd met. "You are a sweet man," she told him. "I would like that very much."

"What do we—" He left off, looking embarrassed. The endearing flush had crept back to his face.

"Just do what feels right," Beth said, shrugging out of her chemise and letting it drop to the floor at her feet. She stepped delicately out of it, showing him all of her. He studied her body, his eyes paying homage in all the right places, then reached for her, drawing her back in for a long, deep kiss. She reached down and took his cock again, delighting when it twitched and stiffened in her hand almost immediately.

Her insides turned to liquid desire as he cupped her breasts again, sending darts of passion rocketing through her body. He broke their kiss to move his attention to them, licking and nipping at her as if he'd understood the concept of foreplay all his life. Every inch of her skin was on fire, every nerve screaming at his touch.

Then he reached an uncertain hand between her legs. "Oh," Henry said in surprise when he felt her slick wetness on his fingers. His touch was like heaven and she had to concentrate not to lose her balance. "This is nice," he said.

"Yes… good," Beth managed, wondering how long she could keep standing at this rate.

The same must have occurred to him, because at that moment he stood and took her hand, leading her to the bed. In another moment he had removed his shirt and joined her.

"Do you find that a fog of the mind has come upon you?" he asked, situating himself next to her.

"Something like that," she said as she felt his gentle touch between her legs again.

"'Twas for me too. Then I must be doing it right," he said, sounding pleased with himself.

"Yes," she said weakly. "You are most definitely doing it right."

Henry explored her slippery folds slowly and with reverence, wearing an expression of frank delight when he slipped two fingers into her hot core and she lifted her hips to meet him. "Here," she said, showing him where to place his thumb. "Touch me here."

He did, marveling equal parts at her reaction and her anatomy. "It is like a tiny cock," he observed in an awestruck tone.

"Smart man," Beth said. "Treat it like one." He nodded, giving her a long, firm stroke with his thumb as he worked his fingers inside her. He seemed to sense exactly what she needed, matching his pace to the movement of her hips, flexing his strong fingers inside her in a rhythmic motion that drove her almost to the brink. Everything faded away then, except the perfect awareness of every single place he touched her, and the first tendrils of her release began to unwind somewhere deep inside.

With a desperate cry, Beth tumbled over the edge, clutching at the bedclothes, and reality went away. The only thing left was the tidal wave washing over her, carrying with it the worry that any part of this encounter wasn't right.

When it was over, she opened her eyes, still breathing heavily, feeling dazed. Henry was watching her, a rapturous expression lighting his face. "That was almost as good as mine own," he told her. "I have never seen the like of that."

Beth blinked, coming more fully out of her stupor. "We're not finished," she said. "You have not yet taken me yourself." She spread her legs in a slow, deliberate motion, leaving no room for doubt as to her intention.

"Are you sure?" he asked, looking as though he hated himself for saying something that might get the offer retracted.

It made Beth smile. "Very sure," she said, taking hold of his straining cock and giving it a firm squeeze.

He needed no further convincing. Beth helped him climb atop her, showing him how to hold himself so not to pin her with his full weight, positioning him between her legs. "Come here," she said, pulling his head down for a kiss and guiding him to her slippery cleft with her other hand.

He hesitated at the first feel of her, tight on the head of his cock. "Will it fit?" he asked doubtfully. "Does it hurt?"

"Not at all," she said. "It feels wonderful. You won't hurt me." She lifted her hips to him, urging on his welcome intrusion, and he nudged a little further in, still watching her intently for any signs of pain. "You won't hurt me," she said, "really." Beth wrapped one leg behind him, pulling him deeper, and he ducked his head and groaned with pleasure, stopping when he was fully sheathed.

He felt amazing inside her, thick and eager and pressing against her in all the right places.

She reached up and stroked his cheek, indescribably happy to be there with him in that beautiful moment.

"What?" he asked, moving his hips experimentally against hers.

"Nothing," she said, rocking against him. "Just... I like your wonderful hair," she told him, tousling her fingers through it. "And your wonderful eyes. And your wonderful... cock."

He smiled at the string of compliments. "I like all your wonderful things too."

Beth slipped her hand between her legs, stroking herself as he moved inside her. "Why don't you show me how much you like me?"

"Gladly," he said, and she felt the difference right away as he moved faster and deeper, giving her the powerful, hungry strokes of a virgin who hasn't yet learned to marshal his desire. Her hips crashed to meet his again and again, flesh pounding flesh, and Beth panted for air as the slow fade began anew.

Soon the wave took hold of her again and washed her over the edge into a soft realm of pure sensation, her tension set free. She felt herself clenching around him, and he reacted immediately, slamming straight into the center of her. Suddenly he tensed against her, his body rigid, crying out with his own release. Henry managed a few more strokes before collapsing into her arms with a sigh of contented exhaustion.

They lay there together for a few long moments as their breathing gradually stabilized and the world reasserted itself. Beth stroked his hair absently in her pleasant haze, staring up at the underside of the bed's canopy.

"Did you like it?" he asked after a while, twisting to look at her.

"You have to ask?" She smiled sleepily at him and moved to settle herself in the crook of his arm. "Yes. More than liked it. It was perfect." She traced a fond circle on his chest with one finger. "Are you *sure* you were a virgin and you weren't just making that up to get me in bed with you?" she teased.

"In sooth!" he said, squeezing her hand. He seemed pleased at her verdict.

I should go find Tawny, she thought as she drifted to sleep, head on his chest. *In a little while.*

BETH WOKE SOME TIME LATER, IN THE DEAD OF NIGHT, BLINKING THE sleep from her eyes. Henry stirred next to her, awakening quickly to perfect alertness in the manner of the very young. His closeness, paired with the memory of their recent encounter, brought her back to full consciousness with a renewed tingle of excitement between her legs.

"Good morrow," she whispered.

Henry propped himself up on one elbow and looked at her with an expression of vast satisfaction. "Never have I met a lady such as you," he said, reaching over and tracing the curve of Beth's breast with one finger. "Wit to match any man's, more radiant with loveliness than any maid who has ever lived, and bold as a lion. My little Frisian lioness."

Beth smiled and shimmied a little closer to him. He clasped her against his chest, stroking her hair fondly and kissing the top of her head. She slipped her arm around him, pulling herself closer. Another go might be nice. They were well past the awkward part, and he was young enough that it wouldn't matter a bit that he'd already come twice that night.

"I shall send word to Frisia first thing on the morrow," he said, just as she was about to reach down and take his cock in her hand.

Beth froze in his arms. "Wherefore?" she asked faintly.

"I must have your hand, of course. I will have the other marriage annulled on grounds of nonconsummation, and I will take you as wife immediately. Do not fret," he assured her, "I would never dishonor you by refusing you marriage after our night together, and I am not my lord father. I shall never set aside my beloved Elizabeth."

Oh, no. Beth hadn't counted on Henry FitzRoy being one of those men who falls in love with the first woman to come along and deflower him, especially considering his parentage. It was possible she had made a slight miscalculation.

"Nothing would make me happier, Henry, but I do not know if my father will give consent," she demurred.

"Unthinkable," he said gaily. "What father would refuse his daughter a chance to be Queen? At the worst, you will be my duchess and cherished love till the quit of our time on earth."

He was not to be deterred. Perhaps it was best to play along.

"I can already imagine our children at play," he told her. "A boy—we shall name him Arthur for my father's brother, and a girl—naturally, you should choose her name. She will be as glorious and sharp of wit as her mother, I have little doubt."

She nodded, hoping her smile didn't look as stiff as it felt, because it felt like one hell of a death rictus. What was she going to do now? Oh, why had she been so stupid? She'd given Tawny grief for coming here alone, but Beth herself had broken almost all the rules that night. She'd gotten drunk, for one, and she also hadn't made it clear to her quarry that they weren't going to be a thing. How would Tawny ever forgive her for the mess she had made of everything?

"If we are fortunate," he continued, "perhaps you are already with child. We shall easily convince Father to make me his heir if our union is thus proven fertile—oh, no, dearest, why do you weep?"

Beth wiped her eyes. "I'm feeling a little homesick," she said truthfully. "I'm—so far from there."

"We will bring some of your kin to dwell with you at court, love," Henry told her in a comforting voice. "And we shall visit the Low Countries. You need not yearn in vain for your home. Fear not on that account. I shall not be an unkind or unfaithful husband to you. And I shall never beat you," he added, "or give you cause to fear me."

She sniffled at this, wiping ineffectually at her eyes. Henry seemed to understand that no more words were in order, instead pulling her to him and rocking her gently while stroking her hair and murmuring soothing nothings, occasionally wiping a tear from her cheek with his thumb. He was a natural. Her own husband, a man she had actually married and had a child with, had never shown this sort of nurturing instinct. Tears had been an occasion for awkwardness, not tenderness. Part of her wanted nothing more than to stay here indefinitely, basking in the warmth of his unflappable affection. She must have been, Beth realized belatedly, rather starved for a little love.

The worst part was knowing he would be dead in a few months. She might be far too old for him, but she really, really liked Henry FitzRoy. He deserved better.

FOURTEEN

IN WHICH TAWNY REVEALS HERSELF TO BE A SPECIAL UNICORN

For Hell, it looked pretty luxurious. And underpopulated.

No ubiquitous bustle of servants, no looming guards—just her and this woman, who was almost certainly the Queen and who had just called Tawny a whore—"doxy" was one of the more popular insults they liked to sling around on *Henry's Women*. Not that Tawny objected to sex work like some ignorant prude, but still, she and the Queen obviously wouldn't be besties anytime soon.

"No, I—" Tawny was about to launch into the spiel she'd memorized from Beth, but something, perhaps exhaustion from the chase, or the frankness with which this woman had spoken to her, made her want to tell the damn truth. "That's precisely what I came here to do. I was here to fuck King Henry." She curtsied. "Your Majesty," she added.

"Well." The woman blinked her dark eyes rapidly. "That is not what I expected to hear."

"It was supposed to be this awesome thing. I'd been planning it for months."

The Queen's expression hardened. "I could ring a bell and have you killed, you know."

Shit. That would bring the goons a-runnin'. "You'd have to ring it pretty loud. This part of the palace is deserted, what with the King's huge banquet going on."

The woman continued in a light, pleasant tone, as if she hadn't just threatened Tawny with murder. "You're a pretty thing, if less than whelming in the bosom."

Like she had any room to talk.

"Why are you not in my husband's bed?"

Tawny shuddered. "When I saw him—I just couldn't do it. I didn't realize he'd be so gross and festering."

Anne Boleyn, Queen of England, for that was without a doubt who she was, threw back her head and laughed with abandon. "Ah, the fickleness of women!" She laughed a moment longer, then finally stopped, dabbing at her eyes with a lacy handkerchief. "But here, you're panting like a hound, did you run all the way from Marathon in that outlandish dress?"

They had marathons? Not that it mattered. She was about to keel over. "Oh, yeah. I, uh, just had to get out of that banquet. Way too warm. I think I have the vapors." Sudden truthiness impulses aside, it would be hard to explain what had happened just before she had burst in. She didn't quite understand it herself.

"It wouldn't do to have you die in my chambers when I've no one to do the washing-up. Here, let me help you out of that—thing." The Queen moved around her and fiddled with the elaborate laces in the back of the gown.

"You sure you know how?" Tawny had figured that any Tudor noblewoman would be as helpless as a flipped turtle without her maidservants.

"Hush. What in heaven's name is amiss with your stays?" Then the evil corset released her rib cage from its viselike grasp and Tawny drank in a huge gulp of air.

"Ohhhhh, thank you."

"You can thank me better by removing that hat and consigning it to a slag-heap."

"I thought no one was supposed to be bare-headed in the presence of royalty." Fuck all the haters. Tawny loved her hat and wasn't giving it up. Anne gave her quite the royal side-eye, but by way of response simply flicked her skirts and walked to a sideboard covered in decanters of various sizes.

"Wine?"

"Absolutely." Tawny had just gotten pleasantly tipsy by the end of dinner, but that had faded quickly, like always. It took forever for her to get drunk, and then she couldn't stay that way without plowing into full-on black-out territory.

Anne handed her a crystal goblet of white wine and Tawny sipped eagerly. Like the other drinks she'd had in 1536, this one dripped sweetness, which suited her fine. She'd always unapologetically adored syrupy white wines, well past the age when she should have been sniffing full-bodied reds with her fellow adults. She was holding the glass up, watching the candlelight play on the soft golden color of the wine, when it struck her that she'd just made yet another etiquette blunder.

"Uh, this isn't some kind of test as to my worthiness, right? Because I should totally have poured that for you."

Anne arched a dark, well-manicured brow. "Worthiness for what?"

"Not—getting flogged for impertinence?"

"You should sit down so you don't have to clutch at your clothes for decency," the Queen suggested. Tawny's gown had begun a slow slide off her right shoulder. She tugged it up with an undignified squeak and plopped gratefully onto a nearby ottoman.

"And as you observed earlier, my ladies are gone, no doubt being questioned. Or perhaps my lord husband simply wishes me to understand that I have nothing in this world unless he give it me. Either way, I am alone." She looked out the window into the darkness for a moment, then smiled ruefully. "Or not entirely so—you are here, and so I am happy to play cup-bearer for my honored guest."

Now that Tawny's brain could absorb oxygen again, she noticed some odd details. The room was luxurious, yes, but not as befit a Queen, and not compared to Henry's receiving hall. Nor was Anne dressed for her station. She wore her trademark "B" necklace and French hood, but her gown was simple, plain even. Then there was the absence of servants or even guards, whose presence Tawny would have expected, what with the impending trial and all.

Whatever. This had been quite an exciting adventure, but it was time to leave before shit got even more out of control. Tawny would finish her wine and then go looking for Beth. By now, she hoped, the masked men would have given up the hunt. Just how she would find her remained to be seen. She could always sing "Don't Stop Believing" at the top of her lungs and hope Beth could either find her or holla back.

"Clearly we are both women of the world," Anne's voice cut through her thoughts, "but who exactly are you?"

"I'm the Lady Tawny, of, of—Copenhagen." Copenhagen was her real last name—what was it about this woman that made her want to spill her guts? "Also of Frisia."

The Queen said something that sounded like complete gibberish until Tawny recognized something that sounded a little like "Where in Frisia?" in German.

Oh. Great. Anne was asking her in *actual Frisian*. Where was Google Translate when she needed it?

"Uh—*du weißt schon*," she faltered in modern German, trying to recall classes she'd taken a good ten years ago now, "*den östlichen Teil?*"

Smooth. *Uh, you know, the eastern part?* Worse, she'd used the familiar *du* with a goddamn queen, instead of the polite *Sie*. *Idiot*, she berated herself.

The Queen stared at her, confused, but recovered quickly. "A Germanic name, you have, and Germanic speech, yet unlike any of those which I know. You do have an echo of *de Nederlanden* in your voice." She furrowed her brow adorably. "Do you know that I waited upon Queen Claude when I was a girl?"

Ha! She was trying to catch Tawny in a lie, but at last *Henry's Women* would be of genuine use to her. Claude was, as she recalled vividly from the first season, the Queen of France, not of Germany. Though it was possible that the accuracy of *Henry's Women* might end there. It now seemed unlikely that Queen Claude had ever in real life been in a three-way with Anne's sister Mary and the Pope.

"You know, I haven't spent much time in France. A summer when I was nineteen," which happened to be true—she met the most amazing marine biologist there, with hands like a feisty squid and—

"I was referring to the time I spent with her in the Low Countries."

Tawny bit her lip and said nothing, trying to look disdainfully unconcerned, as though she knew what Anne was getting at but couldn't be bothered to reply.

Anne, however, was not deterred. "The Low Countries? Where Frisia is?"

"Yeah." Goddammit. "My family is minor nobility from a remote village. Like, really remote. The village is so small that there's no reason a royal entourage would have stopped there." Tawny realized suddenly that she had cribbed her story whole cloth from *Inglourious Basterds,* but somehow she suspected Her Majesty wasn't familiar with the works of the great Renaissance master, Tarantino.

The Queen locked eyes with her. Hers were so dark they were almost black, but somehow shone in an unearthly way. Luminous, that was the word. "You are clean, sweet-smelling, and educated," she mused. "And yet, you seem but a newborn babe in your understanding of the habits of the gentry. I shall puzzle you out, Tawny of Copenhagen." Something about the way she said it gave Tawny a thrilling shiver.

Why was she even bothering with her false identity? Anne was in deep disgrace with Henry and his court, and Tawny could say anything she wanted with no fear of being caught—who would believe the soon-to-be ex-Queen? Then it hit her. She was genuinely enjoying herself playing a game of wits with one of the most famous women in history.

But, she reminded herself, she needed to leave and go find Beth.

"You have the look about you of the North, tall and fair as you are. In sooth you resemble nothing so much as one of the Saxon she-devils who of old gathered the souls of the dead from the field of battle."

Tawny was briefly confused, then realized that the concept of Norse mythology as a harmless trivia night category probably hadn't caught on yet. In this century it was probably more of a pagan-witch-indicator. "A Valkyrie?"

"Aye, a shield-maiden of Woden."

She couldn't help but preen a little at the compliment. Wait—it was a compliment, right?

"Is it—dangerous for us to be talking about pagan stuff? I know you guys take witchcraft really seriously here."

Anne shrugged. "I am accused of high treason so that Henry can court that milksop Seymour girl. If anything, claims of trafficking with the devil might absolve me of guilt. Henry would love it if I played the penitent, unable to keep myself from temptation because of my weak woman's will."

"And you married him why, exactly? I don't mean to be a jerk, but you saw how he treated Queen Catherine. Why didn't you think he'd do the same to you?"

She shrugged again. "I was young and foolish, and I thought I could give him sons. And he was not always so—how did you say it?—gross and festering. Once upon a time, he was brave of countenance and nimble of wit, fit to rule because he embodied the best of mankind." She twirled the stem of her goblet, seeming to search for words.

"I do not know why I want to tell you this—not even my own sweet brother knows, though he suspects—but in sooth I did not want to marry the King. I had another love. At my family's behest, I led Henry on a merry chase. I refused to dishonor myself, but I dared not hazard his displeasure. And he hunted me, relentlessly, as a man would hunt a fox or a hind. Sir Thomas Wyatt, one of my truest friends, wrote a poem on it in which he called His Majesty 'Caesar,' and Henry took it for praise."

Tawny remembered the roiling disgust she'd felt when she'd seen the King up close. "Honestly, it was the absolute power thing that turned me off more than the festering. Or, as much as the festering, at least. It was like he had 'tyrant' stamped all over his face and I was actually scared of him for a minute."

"In the kingdom of the Rus' they have a saying: to be near Caesar is to be near death."

"Wow." How horrifyingly accurate. *Poor Anne*, Tawny thought.

"When I thought Henry wanted simply to make use of me the way he had my sister and Bessie Blount, it was easier by far to keep him at bay. Thinking myself clever, I told him I would submit to his longings only if we were wed, thinking to present him a task so impossible that he would give up the chase."

"But instead—"

"Instead I became his 'Great Matter.' For a time I found myself thinking I desired him as much as he did me. He could have had any number of fertile young things currying his favor, but he shone on me like the sun, and mine eyes were dazzled."

"I imagine it's hard not to be at least a little flattered when someone offers to literally change the world for you."

"Vanity is the most subtle of sins, 'tis true. Though I should have seen the iron hand beneath his velvet glove. I think some part of me knew even then that he would have his way, or there would be ruin for anyone who denied him aught. When it came to the separation with Catherine, the Pope denied him, and he imprisoned *the Pope*! What was *I* to do?"

"I don't know what else you could have done." Tawny fidgeted. What she wanted to say was that in a different time, Anne wouldn't have been forced into an all-or-nothing marriage with a tyrant. No real way to explain that, though.

"When he severed himself from Rome, Henry said he would usher in reforms that before had only been dreamt of. Now I think it an ill thing to have the same ruler in Earth and Heaven alike. This is a world in which I fear for my little girl."

"It's not a great place for big girls, either."

Anne laughed. The Queen had, Tawny observed, at least two kinds of laughs—one petite and obliging, a courtier's titter, and one full and rich, a woman's expression of delight. Tawny felt a burst of pride at having elicited the second laugh twice now.

"Big girls, aye. Would that I had the wisdom of old age. I might have found the way out of my snare." She gave another sad smile. "But all this you know. Else, you'd not be here."

Tawny felt awful. She wished she could take back everything she'd said earlier about her plans for the King. "Oh, yeah, that. Look, I don't want you to get the wrong idea about my intentions for Henry."

"You mean your intentions to fuck him?"

"It—uh—wasn't like the other ladies. I don't want to be a queen. I just wanted to understand what all the fuss was about."

"Ah, yes. I see." Anne nodded. "You are dedicated to understanding—a philosopher, then?"

"Well, yes—a natural philosopher, that is. In the tradition of—" she had to stop herself from name-dropping Isaac Newton or Robert Hooke, neither of whom would be born for another hundred years, "—Roger Bacon and Saint Thomas Aquinas."

"You mean to tell me you are a scion of the New Learning?" Now there was no trace of sarcasm in the Queen's voice.

This was a historical subject Tawny actually knew something about. As an undergrad, she was surprised to find her History of Physics class, while less than mathematically rigorous, still extremely engaging. "Yes. I perform"—what had they called it back in the day?—"experimental verification on hypotheses as to the mechanistic workings of the universe. Not to brag or anything."

Anne looked at her warily. "So you will have heard Johann Albrecht Widmannstetter's lectures on Copernicus' latest work, as yet unpublished, on the notion that the Earth moves around the Sun?"

The Queen of England wanted to talk to her about heliocentrism.

Jesus H. Christ, what else did Anne know? Was there some secret cult of science at work in Early Modern England? Had that hack motherfucker who wrote *The Michelangelo Cipher* actually been on to something?

Tawny's throat had gone dry. She swigged the rest of her wine in one gulp. In for a penny, in for a pound, she decided.

"Better than that—I've read the book. The first draft, anyway." *De revolutionibus orbium coelestium* wouldn't be published for nearly a decade, but "advance copies" had already made their way onto the European intellectual scene by this time.

"And?"

"Oh, he's totally right. And Philolaus was right. Sort of. The Earth is not remotely the center of the universe. We go around the Sun, and—here's a little something that may not make it into Copernicus—uh, his first book, that is—the Sun orbits the center of the *via lactae*, the Milky Way, and the Milky Way, along with billions of other galaxies like ours, orbits an axis that turns the universe."

Tawny felt a little guilty for telling future-science secrets, but it was unlikely that Anne would include theories on the *axis mundi* in her final confession, and the look on the Queen's face was just so, so happy. How could anyone deny her that?

"Then you must be from a noble family of some sort. How did you get away?" Anne asked, her eyes shining with eagerness.

"What?"

"Why were you not made to marry? Do you have a literary society? Or… a convent? I've met women philosophers before, you know."

Tawny wanted to tell her everything—her awkward childhood and adolescence, the endless party of undergrad studies, life as a scientist, her struggles with getting older. She had the feeling, call it woman's intuition, that Anne would "get" her. And that sad, longing look in her eyes—if it would give Anne a momentary window out of her oppressive life, Tawny would happily narrate her life story.

"Well, okay. I guess I started my work on—"

Anne waved her hands. "No, wait, let me guess the tale. You were—a prodigious child, and you studied at a convent with other like-minded girls."

Tawny smiled at the idea of her fellow Psi Phis as nuns-in-training. Though, she reflected, that wasn't so far off the mark. Did women's colleges even exist in this century?

"You could say that. I'm still loosely associated with my… convent."

"And yet you plotted and executed a pilgrimage to the shrine of Priapus." Anne grinned at her wickedly, then frowned again. "Are you in fact a spy? Or a lascivious noblewoman possessed by the devil?"

"Nope. Just a scientist."

"Is that what Frisians call natural philosophers?"

"In my convent, they do."

"It must be quite a convent. If I weren't confined here, I would wish to visit you." The Queen's expression turned dark. "Henry has refused my bed for months now, and my company for weeks. I expect that once this jape of a trial is concluded, I will be exiled somewhere cold and dreary and far from pleasing discourse like yours."

Wow, she ran hot and cold. Of course, Tawny might feel the same if it weren't for the fact that she could, at any minute, return to the twenty-first century and enjoy not being married, not having to bear children at the demands of her family, or be put on trial for failing to deliver a child of the right sex. Something about Tawny's scientific revelations seemed to have unlocked a fury in Anne, and now she stood and paced the room as she spoke.

"Even with the prying eyes of Thomas Cromwell's creatures placed amongst my maids, there was acknowledgment that I was here, that I was alive. That I was—human." Abruptly, she threw her goblet into the fireplace, where it shattered.

"This is how it was for Catherine. He wants me to be *grateful*. When the news of my banishment comes at last, he wants me to be so heartsick with privation and loneliness that I fall to my knees and thank him, kiss his hand, beg forgiveness for my sins." She balled her hands into fists, knuckles white. "He wants me, and all his subjects, to worship and adore him, even as he plays the tyrant."

Tawny knew the truth of it. Henry was stripping her of power so she couldn't fight back, even if he ordered her to die. The hunted woman had no one to turn to, nowhere to run. No wonder she threw goblets around.

She reached out and took Anne by the hand. "I can't tell you everything I know, but the Copernicus stuff—trust me—it's gonna be great. The world will get better."

Anne turned her face away, but didn't let go. "You are like me, I think," she said after a moment. "A Penelope awash in Odyssei, great bellowing men who insist on being the ruler of the house, despite their inferior understanding of the universe. Out of place, and not just because of that pink monstrosity you wear."

Tawny slid her hat down over her forehead and thrust outward with her head, neighing softly. "Because I'm a special unicorn." Anne looked at her blankly and Tawny shoved the hat off her head, embarrassed. "Sorry, that was super weird. I'm socially awkward and I don't always deal well with serious moments. Sorry."

And then Anne Boleyn kissed her.

FIFTEEN

IN WHICH TAWNY JOURNEYS TO
EXOTIC REALMS IN THE SOUTH

IT WAS A LONG KISS—AND A HUNGRY ONE. ANNE KISSED LIKE A SHE-
wolf, with little nips at Tawny's lower lip. Tawny closed her eyes
and leaned into it, her shock melting away in the sudden heat
of desire that had kindled in her. Heliocentrism could do that
to a girl.

This was one of the most powerful women on Earth. She had
changed the course of European history, and now her soft, warm
lips were sealed to Tawny's. Anne's hot, playful tongue was dancing against the tip of hers, twisting, flicking, teasing her.

She opened her eyes. Anne had leaned in to kiss her; now she
clasped both of Tawny's wrists, pulled her to her feet, and into an
embrace stronger than her slender stature would have suggested
was possible.

They devoured each other, falling into a kind of circular
breathing, little gasps of air sucked in through the sides of their
mouths so they didn't have to stop touching each other for even
a second. Anne caressed her back through the lacings of her par-
tially undone dress, her fingers leaving trails of fire in their wake.
Tawny wanted to run her hands through that long, dark, lus-
trous hair, and reached for Anne's headdress, to set it free.

"Ah, ah," and the Queen pulled away, wagging a finger at her. "Not yet. You must earn it."

"Okay. How. What?"

Anne smiled knowingly and gently traced Tawny's lower lip. "Just kiss me. Let your mouth play the wanton."

Their bodies pressed tightly together, Tawny's loose dress shifted against her, brushing against her bare nipples and her flushed, sensitive skin. A half-sigh, half-moan escaped her. Anne gazed up at her with those luminous eyes, a look that at once beckoned and challenged, then lingeringly kissed her way up Tawny's neck and found her lips again.

Her rational mind could catalogue all the symptoms of desire: reddened cheeks, dilated pupils, racing heart. But her rational mind was far away. She felt faint and feverish, wobbly-legged. She wanted Anne's touch so badly that she was swooning.

Anne bit Tawny's lower lip and ground her pelvis up against her. God, there were way too many clothes in between them. She could feel herself opening up inside, already aching and wet and ready for licking and playing and fucking. What was the word Anne had used? Wanton. Yes, she felt wanton. A fluttery rush coursed through her. If Anne Boleyn didn't fuck her, Tawny thought she might just die.

After a dark eternity of kisses, and more kisses, when Tawny was utterly intoxicated, Anne finally pulled back from her with a devilish smile, leaving Tawny literally gasping for more.

"Such a wicked girl you are. Will you make a tribade of me?"

"A what?"

Anne stared deeply into her eyes as she thrust her fingers up and under Tawny's skirts and inside her. Tawny gasped again. With her other hand, Anne reached up and pulled her close against her, stroking the back of her neck. She teased Tawny's soaking wet pussy open with an expert touch, and slid another finger inside, her thumb forcefully working in tight circular motions against the little nub of nerves at the top. Then she abruptly halted.

"Wha—don't stop." Tawny could feel her heart beating through her swollen clitoris.

"You want me to do that again?"

"Yes."

Anne pursed her lips, as if pondering something. "Very well, but when I bid you act, you must obey me. Will you do that?"

"Yes." Tawny had played submissive before, when the situation called for it, but she was amazed at her responsiveness to Anne's commands. In this moment, no matter what Anne asked, Tawny would make it happen for her.

"Then I want to see you as God made you," Anne whispered, and withdrew her fingers, leaving her full of yearning.

Tawny was more than ready to tear her clothes off. She slipped her unlaced dress off her shoulders.

"No. Slowly. Your corset first."

"It's, uh—actually a one-piece."

Anne's expression told her she was not to be denied. "Then unfold it from yourself—as a butterfly would its chrysalis."

It took all of her self-control not to just shuck the damn thing off, but she did as she was told, peeling off the dress centimeter by careful centimeter to reveal first the gentle line of her clavicle, and then her small, pert breasts.

Thank heavens she'd had her spray tan reapplied a few days ago.

"Slowly, I say," Anne told her as she moved to the mantle and picked up a candlestick, illuminating Tawny's naked upper half. "I would see you properly."

"There's nothing proper about me," Tawny replied saucily, giving her hair a coquettish toss. If Anne wanted a show, she'd happily give her one.

"No, indeed." Anne laughed her rich, full laugh again and began a circuit of the room, lighting all of its candles, one by one, until the chamber seemed ablaze with twinkling light. Who needed the Milky Way when they had their own galaxy here at their fingertips?

Tawny knew a thing or two about optics, and she posed herself to catch the light just so as she continued to slide the dress down, holding the fabric lightly with one hand. The soft, golden light shimmered off her taut stomach and long thighs. Tawny was a little vain about her abs, but she felt suddenly shy, remembering that in the past people generally preferred their women with more meat on their bones. Of course, Anne was unfashionably slender, too, and she seemed to appreciate Tawny for being like her. She closed her eyes to keep the self-consciousness at bay.

At last, Tawny let the dress slide fully off her legs. She was naked, except for the black, lacy, crotchless panties she'd worn (and hastily washed shortly before the banquet). She paused for a long moment, standing perfectly still so that Anne could see everything. Then she started pulling off the panties.

"That—that can stay for now."

Tawny picked her dress up with the edge of her foot, and kicked it to the side, the better to show off her slim ankles. She tilted her pelvis ever-so-slightly forward, trying to imitate the posture she'd seen on Renaissance-era paintings and sculptures.

"Very good. I shall summon you a clam shell and some cherubs forthwith." Tawny tried to keep her pouty model expression, but couldn't help laughing at this.

"Now." Anne's tone grew serious again, her voice like silk wrapped around iron. "I want you to touch yourself. Here, on your—your crest." She gestured between her legs.

Tawny shivered with anticipation. "Like this?" She reached down and spread her outer lips with two fingers, exposing her "crest"—a nice word for it—then drew her other hand up her thigh, and traced a line up the wet cleft.

Anne made a small noise of satisfaction. "Mm, like that. But do not dare arrive at your little death until I grant you leave."

It was a tall order, but Tawny thrilled at the command, found herself even hotter at the thought of having to surrender herself to Anne's will. She went to work, stroking herself slowly at first, then faster.

"Neglect not your duckies."

Tawny's brain was so befogged with lust it took her a minute to process what Anne had said.

"My—?"

Anne sighed dramatically. "Oh, you Frisian girls. I mean those beautiful breasts of yours."

Tawny slid one hand up her torso, trying not to go too fast. Anne would like that more. She ran her fingers across her chest, spiraling around one nipple. Locking eyes with Anne, she licked her fingertip and drew it across her lips.

Tawny felt the tension building under her fingertips, riding the knife's edge of pleasure until she couldn't stand it anymore. Anne watched avidly, candlelight glittering in her eyes.

"May I?" she begged, her breath coming rapidly.

"Not yet. I will do it. Come here." Anne walked a few steps toward her and held out one elegant hand. Tawny took it, her thighs shaking. The velvet of Anne's gown rubbed against her sensitive skin, making her feel even more naked, if that was possible.

With a sleek, catlike grace, Anne thrust her fingers under the black panties and into Tawny's wet, welcoming cunt. Tawny clenched around her, aching for more, but Anne withdrew and licked her long, delicate fingers. "Your cunny tastes as sweet as your tongue," she whispered.

Tawny could only whimper in response.

Anne trailed a finger down her chest, then under and around one breast, then the other, just skirting the edge of her straining, erect nipples.

"They are as impudent as you are."

Just as Tawny was about to beg for her touch, Anne took one pink nipple fully into her mouth, flicking her tongue in a circle. Tawny gasped at the sensation.

First one, then two fingers slid into her, then Tawny felt the hard pressure of Anne's thumb against her clit. She moaned, grinding her hips against her busy fingers. Anne massaged her, creating a sweet friction between her legs, then gave her nipple one last lick before kissing her way up her chest. She pulled back and began whispering a sinful litany, her breath hot on Tawny's neck.

"Like the ambrosia of the Olympians. Like the apple in the Garden of Eden. That is how sweet your sex is." Anne leaned up to nip at her ear, then her neck, then bit her, harder this time. *"Numquid, cum crisas, blandior esse potes?"*

Tawny didn't even try to understand her—she was too afire with longing. She slid her hand on top of Anne's and pressed down, her whole body begging for release.

"Give it to me now, Tawny."

The sound of her name from those lips pulled the trigger on her climax. There was an instant of perfect stillness, like an atomic blast before the shock wave breaks the sound barrier, then the waves of pleasure exploded outward from her core. She heard herself cry out as she rocked against Anne's hand, grinding herself like waves against a rock. After a moment, sanity returned. Tawny blinked and looked around.

Somehow, shockingly, she had managed to stay upright.

Anne stroked her cheek, a look of satisfaction on her lovely face. But Tawny knew she wasn't finished with her yet. Tawny wanted to make the first move this time.

"It seems rude of me not to offer something in return," she said.

Anne arched a dark eyebrow. "Well then, you should undress me to make amends."

With her heart still pounding from the brain-shattering climax, Tawny moved behind Anne to loosen, then undo her bodice. Touching Anne, but not *actually* touching Anne, was maddening. Tawny wanted to run her hands over the Queen's naked breasts and thighs and ass, but she dutifully worked to remove each layer of clothing: a corset, a smaller corset that covered the abdomen, an embroidered underskirt, and a farthingale. This was some serious Russian nesting doll shit.

Underneath it all, she wore a cream-colored chemise that seemed regal in its simplicity, and charmingly girlish at the same time. Tawny reached out and caressed her breasts through the fabric, wanting to give Anne a taste of her own medicine. Anne's eyes fluttered and she inhaled sharply.

"Off with it, then."

Tawny pulled the chemise over Anne's head.

She had stretch marks around her softly rounded belly, but in the flickering candlelight, it made her look exotic and wild. Anne posed, just as Tawny had, to reveal her small, firm breasts, tipped with adorable brown nipples—and a neatly manicured patch of dark hair invitingly perched on her *mons pubis*.

"I wear all the latest fashions from the Continent," she said coyly, smiling at Tawny's obvious surprise. No wonder she hadn't been shocked by Tawny's landing strip. Anne trailed her finger down the soft, triangular patch, beckoning.

Tawny reached for her, but Anne caught her hands and slid them up her lithe body, over her buttocks—for Anne, it was definitely buttocks—skimmed her breasts, the nape of her neck, and at long last, came to her elaborate French hood. Anne guided Tawny's fingers to the clips and combs that held the headdress in place, gently loosening them, until the spangled thing came free, and Anne's hair flowed down around her shoulders in a river of shining sable brown.

Anne gave Tawny a long moment to admire her, then stepped in and claimed her lips again. When she pulled back, there was hunger in her dark eyes.

"You will fuck me now, Tawny," she breathed.

"Didn't you—are you okay to—" Tawny's brain swam momentarily out of its haze of desire, and she recalled that Anne had recently suffered a miscarriage. Tawny didn't want to hurt her, but there wasn't a polite way to bring it up. Anne, however, solved the problem with her commanding instincts.

"You have lain with a woman before?"

"Yes."

"Then teach me of these new sciences—pleasure me with your mouth."

Tawny's pussy clenched with a surge of desire. "As my Queen commands."

She knelt as Anne gracefully sat down on a tall chair with gilded claws for legs. Looking up at her, Tawny knew she would carry this image with her for the rest of her life: Anne Boleyn, naked and enthroned in candlelight, awaiting her pleasure.

Tawny had slept with fewer women than she had men, but her female partners had told her on multiple occasions that she passed her oral exams with flying colors. She had another startling moment of clarity—of course Anne was an expert lover—she'd had to be, with her and her family's lives and livelihood depending on King Henry's lusts. No wonder she wanted to take command herself for a night. Well, Tawny decided, she deserved better than a lifetime spent giving and never receiving. She was going to make Anne come so hard she forgot her name.

She slid her hands up the back of Anne's calves, then caressed and spread her thighs, pressing little kisses on them to mark her passage. With one finger, she traced a line down her cleft, already wet for her. With exquisite care, she spread Anne's outer lips apart with her fingers, then proceeded to lick, nibble, and suck the delicate pink inner lips, making sure to tease and arouse every inch of her glistening sex before directing her attentions to the crown jewel.

"Yes, that, oh, prithee more there."

"Here?" Tawny grinned and licked the spot again, rolling her tongue softly at first, then harder against the yielding flesh.

"Yes, there." Anne tilted her hips up toward Tawny and reached down to run her fingers through her hair. Tawny laid down rhythmic strokes of her tongue as Anne began to rock beneath her like a stormy sea. With satisfaction, Tawny felt the Queen's clit hardening with desire under her tongue. She buried her face in royal pussy, savoring the salty richness of her, then ever so gently flicked her tongue inside.

Anne moaned, and Tawny knew she was close. She pressed harder with her tongue, then pulled back, teasing, then licking upwards.

"Oh, God, oh—oh, yes."

She felt Anne shudder and gave her one last kiss on her shining lips. At last she came undone on Tawny's tongue, her wetness drenching her mouth like a bite from a juicy peach.

Tawny wiped her lips and leaned back on her elbows. Anne slumped, languid, in her chair. They rested for a moment, sharing a breathless, secret smile. Then, as if they were of one mind, they each reached for the other and crashed together, Anne sliding off the chair on top of her as they fell onto the floor in a cartwheel of arms and legs.

Now Tawny could touch all of Anne, and she did, fondling, caressing, groping. Anne responded with equal force, her hungry mouth everywhere. They both went wild, grinding their pussies together in a spasm of passion, so wet and hot for each other that neither even noticed that they'd knocked the chair over. She felt Anne bucking wildly atop her, felt herself draw near climax again, and then everything became a blur of sensation until they tumbled over and came to rest against the base of a couch.

"Whoo!" Tawny said, panting.

"Amen," Anne replied.

EARLIER, TAWNY HAD BEEN ABSURDLY DISAPPOINTED FOR ONE FLEETING moment when she'd first seen that Anne did not in fact have six fingers on one hand. She was sure they would have found an excellent use for an extra finger.

That was the only disappointing thing about tonight. She was so, so glad she hadn't ended up sleeping with gross old Henry. She hadn't remotely planned on this encounter, but she wouldn't trade being here now for anything.

Anne opened the windows after they could stand again, and cool, sweet spring air wafted into the room. They lay on a couch together, in the early hours of the morning, nibbling on cheese and candied fruit—the height of neoclassical sapphic indulgence.

With the difference in their heights, Anne fit perfectly into Tawny's arms. She looked even more beautiful now than when Tawny first stumbled into her chamber. Being confined with nothing but the uncertain future for company wasn't good for anybody's complexion. Now, a rosy flush lit Anne's cheeks, and she looked relaxed, her limbs slack with pleasure.

They'd been silent for a while, basking in their postcoital glow, when Anne suddenly spoke. "When it became clear to me that Henry was in sooth going to divorce his wife, that I would have to marry him whether I willed it or no, I bestowed my carnal favors upon him. I knew I could never give him all, though, or he would tire of me." She looked into Tawny's eyes. "I always held some part of myself in reserve."

No one would ever accuse Tawny of being a genius regarding interpersonal skills, but she could parse the subtext and hear what Anne was really saying to her. Tawny felt a flutter of happiness.

She wanted to give Anne something precious, something that no one on Earth, not even other Kings and Queens, could have.

"Remember what I said about the planets orbiting the sun?"

"Yes."

"It's not entirely true."

"Copernicus is wrong? If you fed me a plate of lies to gain my favors—"

"Not wrong. He's mostly right. This is secret knowledge, something that won't be announced publicly for hundreds of years. Uh, probably, that is."

"Deep mysteries, indeed."

"So, it goes like this—everything in the universe exerts a force on everything else, a kind of pull." She tugged a little on Anne's fingertips to illustrate her point. "Even the smallest things. Because of that, the Earth, along with all the other celestial bodies in our solar system, moves around a point called a barycenter. Right now, it's just outside the surface of the sun, but it moves around."

"Even the smallest things, you say." Anne sighed, pulling herself to a sitting position. "If I were a man, I'd at the very least dabble in astronomy. In between commanding a terrible host on the field of battle, scratching myself whenever I pleased, and shouting at people, of course."

"If you were a man, you wouldn't be half as interesting."

"Flatterer."

Tawny had a sudden urge to tell Anne how famous she was, even almost five centuries in the future, how many times she'd been portrayed in books and on film—though then she'd have to explain moving pictures, too. It was just so unfair. This remarkable woman had lived in the shadow of men her whole life—and would soon die there as well.

Anne roused her from these meditations on the unfairness of the patriarchy by picking up the discarded pair of black, lacy panties and dangling them in front of Tawny's face on one dainty finger.

"What is this? I like it, whatever it is."

"Special Frisian undergarments," Tawny giggled.

"I have been away from the Continent for far too long."

Tawny resisted the urge to crack a joke about how it was better not to be in-continent. "Speaking of the Continent, that verse you quoted earlier, was that French?"

"Latin."

"Oh." Jesus, Anne was well read. "What does it mean?"

"*Numquid, cum crisas, blandior esse potes.* Could you be any prettier as you—you—" she trailed off, gesturing vaguely with one hand.

"Turning shy on me?"

"No, you wicked thing." Anne gave her a playful swat on the bottom. "The phrase doesn't translate well. It means—" She stood, thrusting her hips out and swiveling them in an unmistakably sexual—and sexy—way before resuming her spot next to Tawny.

"They had a word for that?"

"The Romans had a word for everything. And the answer is no. You could not possibly be any prettier." She twirled a strand of Tawny's hair around a finger. "You are a golden dream of a woman. In sooth, this has all been the sweetest of dreams. I half expect that, come the morrow, I will wake to find that all is well, that I am not in disgrace with my husband, and I will walk in the palace gardens with my ladies and my little Elizabeth beside me."

Elizabeth.

Oh. Fuck.

Beth.

She'd been having a royal tryst while her friend endured God knows what at the hands of God knows who.

"I have to go!" Tawny sat up and began frantically rooting around for her clothes, flinging cushions left and right.

"Have I given offense?"

"No, no, you're fine. Better than fine. I have to find Beth. My friend or—kinswoman, whatever. I don't know where she is, but I'm responsible for her. She can't go back to—uh, Frisia without me."

"Calm yourself." Anne rose unperturbed from the couch and slipped on a robe. "How was it that you lost her? I suppose I never asked what brought you to my chambers to begin with. You made mention of a banquet giving you the vapors, but then—?"

Anne's memory for detail was impressive. "We were heading back to the room Henry's people gave us, but we got ambushed by a bunch of guys in black masks and black guard uniforms. I knocked a tapestry down on them, and we ran, but I lost Beth somewhere along the way without noticing. I ducked in here to get away from those men."

She was near tears, wondering how on earth she would find Beth now, and how she could have been so irresponsible as to forget her.

Anne set a gentle handle on her forearm, stilling her.

"Describe them to me."

Tawny recounted their run-in with the masked goons as best she could, based on height, weight, and body type. Anne thought for a moment. "It sounds as though you and your friend ran foul of Henry's not-so-little bastard."

"FitzRoy?"

"Aye. He plays at being a statesman and contriver that his father might love him better." She gave a wry smile. "No doubt he saw it as his sworn duty to bring you to justice and sent some of his personal guards to collect you. Only a boy on the cusp of manhood would outfit his personal guards in costumes more suited for a masqued ball than an ambush."

"He was gunning for us from the minute I showed up at court, and he harassed Beth all night at the banquet. Oh, I hope she's okay."

"All shall be well, I have little doubt. Even if his men captured her, the boy has no heart for villainy. You're not like to find your friend strung up on the rack or rotting in an *oubliette*, so be at ease. I can tell you the way to his apartments."

"Can you say *oubliette* again?"

Anne gave her an appraising look. "You are more than passing strange, you know."

"I'm sorry, I just—like the way you talk." On Anne, the weird accent sounded charming.

"'Tis no bad thing, special unicorn." Anne smiled fondly at her and Tawny felt her heart swell with feeling—what kind of feeling, she wasn't sure.

She finished dressing and Anne helped her tie up the multiple lacings on her bodice. She was half tempted to leave her underwear with the Queen as a sexy memento, but the last thing she wanted to do was alter the course of history by allowing polyester mesh to be discovered five hundred years too soon.

Anne walked her to the chamber door, her expression unreadable.

As she stepped outside, Tawny couldn't help repeating herself. She so desperately wanted Anne to be all right, even though history was about to come crashing down on her. "All the stuff I said about things getting better? I meant that. I can't explain how I know, but I do. It's true. Your daughter will be okay. Better than okay."

"I believe you." Anne reached up and stroked her cheek. "Get ye gone, Tawny of Copenhagen. Find your friend and return to your convent of the New Learning. My soul rests easier knowing there are women like you out there, strong and free and forming this sinful earth into something better."

Tawny nodded eagerly. "Oh, brave new world, that has such motherfuckers in't!"

"What?"

"Never mind." *Dumbass,* she silently berated herself. That was Shakespeare, not—whoever wrote plays in Henry's time.

Tawny realized she was stalling. She wanted, more than anything, to be able to say she'd see the Queen again. But going back through time was one thing—getting it to stop was impossible.

"Off with you, now." Anne gave her a little nudge and a regal, dismissive wave.

Tawny allowed herself one last glance to take in her lovely dark eyes and delicate bone structure. "Okay. I—bye."

As the door closed behind her, she heard a soft murmur on the other side.

"Thank you."

SIXTEEN

IN WHICH BETH IS CHECKED
BY THE EXCHEQUER

There was a violent pounding at the door, and Beth jerked awake at the same time Henry did. He gave her a hasty kiss and sprang hurriedly from the bed, leaving her chilly in the absence of his warmth. She gathered the coverlet around her, shivering a little, wondering what was going on and whether she ought to be concerned. He picked up a dressing gown from a nearby chair and pulled it on.

"Richmond! The hour grows late, and I grow impatient!" a powerful voice thundered from outside. Henry gave her a slightly worried glance, then crossed to the door and threw open the bolt.

The Lord Chancellor of the Exchequer, Thomas Cromwell, looked just like his portraits. He strode into the room without acknowledging either of them and cast his ferocious gaze around with immense disapproval. Beth could see a handful of men-at-arms waiting outside for him.

"And who is this strumpet with whom you have apparently fouled your marriage bed?" he inquired sourly of Henry FitzRoy.

Beth wished she could make herself invisible. Cromwell was the King's most valued advisor, and probably the closest anyone in England came to being above the law. He basically *was* the law. She hesitated, trying to decide whether to speak up in Fitz-Roy's defense, but he chose that moment to settle on her with a particularly murderous look. Her heart skipped a panicked beat in the face of his rage. She closed her mouth.

"Christ's wounds, is that one of those damned Frisians?" he demanded, looking at her a second time.

"She is the daughter of a duke," Henry said coldly, drawing himself up to his full height, which was taller than Cromwell. "And I kindly request you not to impugn the lady. She is to be my wife."

Cromwell raised an eyebrow. "You already have a wife, *boy*, or did you forget that while you were sniffing round this one's skirts?"

"Interesting, methinks, that you should feel so at leave to comment on my conduct. It mattered not to you that my father was already married when you replaced his first Queen with another." Henry's voice was calm and collected. Beth watched from the bed, silently proud of him for standing up to Cromwell. "As you well know, Lord Chancellor, my legal marriage is a farce. I mean to have it annulled on the ground of nonconsummation."

"Oh? And what do you think your father and Lord Howard might have to say about that?"

"I care not. My father has chosen love over propriety once already, and is about to do so a second time. I hardly think he will deny me my domestic happiness."

"That might be well true," Cromwell allowed, "if the woman in question were anything near what she claimed. I very much doubt she is a lord's daughter. I have been to the Low Countries, and as I assured His Majesty this very morn, there is no duchy in Saterland. I question whether the creature is even Frisian."

A spark of fear darted through Beth as he glanced indifferently in her direction, and she clutched at the bedclothes, trying to cover her nakedness. Under his harsh gaze, she no longer felt like the beautiful siren she had been for Henry. She felt cheap and exposed. "That is not so, my lord," she protested. "I doubt not that you have visited the Low Countries, but Saterland is but a small area and my father's dukedom is a new one. We may be tiny and unimportant, but that does not diminish the truth of me."

She chanced a look at Henry. He was staring straight at Cromwell, his posture stiff.

"What is not true," Cromwell said, "is your pedigree, or anything else about you, I wager. Pass the woman her smock, Fitz-Roy, unless you wish your *bride*"—he spoke this word in a disdainful voice—"to be marched through the halls as she is now."

Henry bent and scooped up the garment, passing it to Beth without a word. She pulled it over her head, trying to let Cromwell see as little of her as possible.

"Madam," he told her, "you will accompany me, and we shall soon uncover the sooth of your person."

Henry turned to him. "I will not allow you to take her," he said, placing himself between Cromwell and where Beth knelt in her shift on the bed. "As my future wife, the lady is under my protection. I surrender her to no man."

Cromwell crossed to him in one stride and struck him hard across the face as Beth watched in horror. A trickle of blood began to flow from a small wound on Henry's brow, probably from the stone in the large ring Cromwell wore, but he stood straight and defiant, glaring.

"Mayhap you would like to rethink that position, boy."

"Henry," she said, sliding from the bed to the floor and moving to his side. "Are you all right?" He didn't answer, but slipped an arm about her, pulling her close to him. While she knew it was an illusion, she felt safer there with him towering over her.

"If you intend to commit further violence against my person or hers," Henry informed Cromwell, "I suggest you seek my father's counsel on the matter beforehand."

"Your father," Cromwell said, "is the man who requested me to attend to these unlikely Frisians after news arrived that they took leave of their ladies' maids last eve and escaped to commit God knows what mischief. He wished that his son should accompany me in this endeavor. Then, I come here and find you have passed the night rutting with one of the creatures. But, I ask, do you in troth think that the King cares to trouble himself with your childish transgressions when he is at once consumed with the crimes his Queen hath wrought?"

"My father is not in possession of the relevant facts," Henry countered. "As you can see, Lady Elizabeth passed the eve in my company, and no mischief was done. Of which fact, I would inform him myself, without the meddling of you, his *squire*."

Cromwell's expression at this grievous insult was one of wroth. "I shall ignore your claim of 'no mischief,' as much evidence of it is apparent. But of the other one? How hath *that* woman passed the eve? Have you lately clapped eyes on her?" Cromwell pretended to look about the room as if Tawny were hiding somewhere.

Henry said nothing, but pressed his lips tightly together, a resentful expression marring his handsome features.

Where *was* Tawny? It occurred to Beth with a little pang of fear that she ought to have been looking for Tawny instead of fooling around with Henry FitzRoy all night. What kind of trouble might she have gotten herself into without Beth to steer her clear of major gaffes? And how would Beth get back if she let Tawny get captured by Thomas Cromwell?

"No answer, I see," Cromwell observed. "Your father shall hear of this impudence, mark my words, as well as your coarse choice of bedmates. I would sooner counsel His Majesty to put a woman on the throne, than to make you his heir. You will never be King, I promise you this!"

"Your ugly countenance, sir, however evil, doth not scare me," Henry replied.

This had gone on long enough. She might be frightened of Cromwell, but Beth couldn't let Henry continue to insult him like this. The man was his father's most trusted advisor, and she didn't want to be the one responsible for souring the King against his son, or otherwise interfering with the course of history. If she let Henry defend her any further there was no telling what might happen. Either way, she couldn't stay here.

Anyway, she might be able to escape Cromwell somehow. Or Tawny might find her, failing that. And if Tawny was caught, they'd still be able to get back as long as they were together. Their only provable crime was the (alleged) impersonation of nobles, which was a huge no-no, but they wouldn't be summarily put to death for that. As long as nobody could affirmatively prove they were spies, she might be able to convince someone that it was cruel to separate two kinswomen from each other, considering their ill treatment in this foreign country, blah, blah, blah. As soon as she could get Tawny alone they'd be home free.

"Henry," she said softly. "I will go with him."

"No," he argued. "I know something of the man and his methods of inquiry. I would not consign a lowly hound to his care, even less the lady I would to wife."

"He will not let me remain with you."

Cromwell stood glaring at the two of them as Henry wordlessly tightened his arms about her, crushing her to his chest. Tears sprang to her eyes, and she moved to wipe them away. Beth knew better than to think it was love, but it was hard not to be moved by the strength of his affection. It felt like a long time since anyone had cared so much what happened to her.

"I shall go to my father forthwith," he said, loosening his embrace enough to look down at her. His eyes shone with fierce emotion. "I will repair all of this. And I will find your kinswoman."

"It's all right," Beth whispered, blinking her tears away. His hand brushed the top of her head, smoothing her rumpled hair in a timeless gesture of tenderness, and then he released her into the custody of the Lord Chancellor.

Cromwell had just taken her by the elbow, preparing to lead her from the room, when Beth heard a commotion in the hall outside. Someone was arguing with the guards.

Then she saw the shocking splash of pink and heard Tawny's raised voice as she shouted, "Out of my way, you scoundrelly shits!"

So she hadn't been caught!

Beth wrested herself free of Cromwell's grasp and ran to Tawny, who had fought her way through the crush of puzzled soldiers into FitzRoy's chamber. "Tawny," she cried, dizzy with relief. "Let's—"

Tawny clasped Beth's hand and without hesitation, tapped the thumb and forefinger of her other hand together, just as she had described.

Only, Tawny blinked instantly out of existence, and Beth did not. She stared in shock at the place where her friend had been moments ago, and then registered the appalled horror on the faces of everyone who had just seen a woman disappear into thin air.

Beth hadn't expected Tawny to do that right in front of everyone.

She saw one of the guards make the sign of the cross in her peripheral vision, and Cromwell himself looked rather stunned for a moment.

"Never until now," the Lord Chancellor said in a cold voice, "can I claim to have truly believed the church's tedious stories of witches. However, I can scarce deny that which I have witnessed with mine own eye. Seize the enchantress!"

His men shrank away, reluctant to have anything to do with the woman who had worked such magic.

"Cowards," he said contemptuously to all of them. "I shall convey the creature away myself."

Beth tried to catch Henry's eye, but he was looking studiously at the floor, a troubled expression on his face. So she could expect no succor there.

CROMWELL DID NOT PERMIT HER TIME TO DRESS BEFORE MARCHING HER away through the palace corridors, and she suspected this was calculated on his part, rather than evidence that he was in a hurry. She was almost naked by the standards of the time, and she felt every bit of it. He no doubt knew how vulnerable and powerless she must feel without even enough clothing to protect her modesty.

It was hard not to wonder what he might do now that he believed her to be a witch on top of whatever else he had suspected, but she forced herself to keep silent. He was already furious from his altercation with FitzRoy, and there was little she could add in her defense after what he had seen. Her best hope now was that Tawny would find some way to come back and find her.

Thinking of Tawny sent another tremor of fear through her. They had barely discussed how the device worked. She didn't even know if it was possible for Tawny to return to a time she'd already visited. Even if she could and did, would Beth still have a job to go back to? Tawny might fire her once she realized just how irresponsible she had been. Where would she and Jules go when that happened? A thick lump rose in her throat just thinking about it, so she pushed it away and forced herself to pay careful attention to her surroundings.

It didn't help much. The palace, as palaces are wont to be, was huge and meandering and she had little idea where she was. It also didn't help that she'd been unconscious when taken to FitzRoy's chambers and that she didn't even know what part of the palace they'd started in. The hallways were mostly deserted, save for a few servants who hurried by with lowered eyes as the Lord Chancellor passed with his prisoner in tow.

After they had walked for what seemed like miles, her bare feet chilly on the stone floors, Cromwell took a torch from its sconce on the wall and motioned for her to follow him down a small, dim passage. *Does Greenwich have dungeons?* Beth wondered anxiously, trying to decide how fast he could run. Maybe she could escape before he locked her up.

It was a half-hearted thought at most. She was impossibly lost and it would just make things worse when he caught her. Besides, there was no one to whom she might appeal for help. Anybody she encountered would turn her over to Cromwell. Nobody would want to risk the anger of someone so powerful.

They hadn't gone far down the dark hall before he stopped and threw a small door open. Beth hesitated a moment, peering fearfully into the tiny, meager room, and he took her roughly by the arm and shoved her inside.

"The King will have the truth of your Satanical plot against him, I assure you," Cromwell told her.

"Prithee, my lord," Beth pleaded, "There is no plot. I have no desire in this world but for His Majesty's continued good health and fortune."

"I much doubt that, witch," he said. "I doubt whether any man has seen a clearer or more demonstrable case of witchcraft in all the history of Christendom. I shall dispense with the proceedings in this case, as I think your trial requires not the usual body of evidence. We shall have your secrets and then we shall quit you from your sad life."

Beth felt a terrified chill at his words.

"I am no witch!" she argued, trying to hold back her tears of panic and barely succeeding.

"His Majesty is not like to believe the words of the Jezebel who hath stolen his son's innocence," Cromwell said. "Mayhap the stories of the Queen's witchcraft are truer than I imagined. It seems you share her propension for adulterous dalliances. Mayhap you are in league with her… the boy was thoroughly enchanted by your wile."

"Henry FitzRoy is no boy! He is a lion among men!" she blurted, surprised to realize she meant it. It couldn't have been easy to face down the Lord Chancellor Thomas Cromwell, especially after getting a wallop in the head. "Whereas you, sir, are nothing but a dogsbody and a bully!"

Cromwell laughed aloud at her outburst. "I think I can assume that 'dogsbody' is a fearsome sling, indeed. You have made a pretty speech, madam, but save it for these stone walls. I think you will find them more moved to pity than I."

She was afraid to ask, but she did anyway. "What happens now?"

"You will wait here, at the pleasure—or displeasure, more likely—of the Crown. Use this time to pray," he suggested. "Perhaps God will attend to your cause and speed along the end of your black heart's dolorous time on earth."

And with that he exited, closing the door behind him. Beth heard the sound of a key turning in the lock, and his footsteps fading in the distance, and then nothing.

She turned around, taking in the room in which she was imprisoned. It was cramped, maybe seven feet at its widest dimension, and drably furnished with a rough chair and a small bed. It had a slit of a window up high on one wall, through which the morning sun streamed, but no other source of light. If they kept her here until sundown, she'd be alone in the dark.

Beth sank to the bed, trying to calm herself, but it was difficult when she'd been closed up in some remote corner of the palace with no idea how she might get home, and naught but a cracked chamber pot for company. How would Tawny even find her? Her resolve didn't last long before she began to cry in great, choking sobs, gulping air and surrendering for a little while to her despair.

Finally she got herself under control. Tawny might still have a way to come back for her, she reminded herself, and even if she were angry with Beth, she would never just leave her here to face the crude justice that women could expect from the sixteenth century. This was what she told herself as she fought to calm her hammering heart and slow her panicked breathing.

Eventually, her tears were spent. Beth slept.

SEVENTEEN

IN WHICH DISGORGED WOMBS ARE THREATENED TO THE GENERAL DISMAY OF ALL

BETH WOKE TO A QUIET SCRATCHING SOUND. STILL DUMB WITH SLEEP, she sat up and listened, growing tense with fear as she awakened more completely. Had Cromwell returned for her?

Only a little light graced the room now, for the sun no longer filtered through the tiny window to her chamber. Hours must have passed since she had been shut up in here.

Stealthily she crept to the door, listening. Someone was tinkering with the lock on the other side. It didn't sound like they had a key. So, not Cromwell. Who, then? She could think of no one who might have taken pity on the woman whose apparent witchcraft was observed by multiple witnesses.

"Who's there?" she whispered.

"Elizabeth?" She heard Henry's voice outside. The heavy door made him sound far away, but it was him, sure enough.

"I'm here!" she said, scarcely able to believe he was there.

"Oh, thank God," he said with evident relief. "I think I'm almost in." He left off speaking, the scratching sound continuing as he kept at work on the lock. After a near eternity she heard a click and backed away from the door as it swung open into the room.

Henry caught her in a fierce embrace and held her there for a long moment before giving her a quick buss on the top of her head. "You must come with me immediately," he told her. "We cannot risk being found here. I do not pretend to know what hideous miscarriage of justice the Lord Chancellor hath in mind for you, but I will not suffer you to take part in it."

"Why did you come find me?" Beth asked, her voice tight with relieved gratitude. "What if it causes trouble with your father?"

"I could not in sooth consider myself a man had I taken any other course," he said, holding out a folded piece of cloth. "And here. This should serve to conceal you for a time. Anyone in Cromwell's employ will be searching for a woman in naught but her shift."

It was a robe, richly decorated enough to pass for a dress, at first glance at least. Beth wrapped it around herself, grateful that she wouldn't have to face the peers of the realm with her tits hanging out. Henry took her hand. "Quickly, now!"

He led her through a maze of corridors, much as Cromwell had done, Beth hurrying to keep up with his long strides. At one point he stopped, listening intently, and pulled her into an alcove with him, where they waited in strained silence for a long moment while a crowd of ladies and their maids passed by. When they were gone, Beth whispered, "Where are you taking me?"

"To safety," he said in a low voice. "I have made an accord with Queen Anne against our mutual adversary, Cromwell. We shall conceal you in her rooms until eventide and hence steal you away from the palace under cover of dark."

Beth's eyes widened, but she had no time to ask anything else as he again seized her hand and rushed with her from their hiding place.

SHE WAS GRATEFUL FOR HIS INTIMATE FAMILIARITY WITH THE PALACE. Their route required a dizzying number of twists and turns that she never could have navigated on her own. They had a few close calls, ducking into empty rooms or behind doors while unwitting courtiers passed by, but reached their destination without further incident.

"Where is everyone? Is the palace always this empty?" Beth asked as Henry knocked softly on the Queen's chamber door.

"No, it is our good fortune that near all my father's court is celebrating the first of May in good cheer."

"Won't they notice you're missing?"

He shrugged. "I care not."

"But Henry—" she began, and then the door opened and she stopped to stare in startled amazement at her first sight of Anne Boleyn.

The Queen gestured them both inside, then turned to Fitz-Roy as he closed the door behind them and threw the bolt. "So this is the lady who hath inspired such boldness and loyalty," she said, her gaze sweeping over Beth with mild curiosity.

"Your Majesty," Beth said, dropping into a low curtsy, "I cannot express my gratitude for your kind help."

Anne made a dismissive little gesture. "I find I am fond of Frisians. Your friend Lady Tawny made a most favorable impression last eve. And I am ever a supporter of lady philosophers, as it were. Are you also a student of natural philosophy?"

So Tawny had been here. "Lady Philosopher" about covered it for both of them, she supposed.

"Something like that," Beth allowed.

Anne held her eyes for a long, inscrutable moment, then looked away. "You will want your privacy, of course," she said to the two of them. "I shall retire to the other room."

"I am most grievously sorry," Henry said as they watched Anne leave.

Beth stared at him in surprise. "But, for what? You have done nothing wrong."

"It was all day before I found you. I cannot imagine how you must have anguished as his prisoner. Would that I could undo it all."

Beth's eyes flooded with tears. "You have nothing to be sorry for," she told him. "I didn't think anybody at all would come to help me, besides Tawny. Aren't you afraid that I'm a witch?"

"No," he said, pulling her to him. "I have seen the truth of your heart, and discovered no evil therein. I may not understand who or what you are, and I can sooner reckon the man in the moon than I can what I witnessed this morn. But I can see well enough that you are not a witch. An elf queen from the kingdom of faerie, perhaps." He said this last part with a wry little smile that made her think it was possible things might still work out all right.

"Henry," Beth sniffled, "you might just be the nicest person I have ever met."

"Excellent tidings," he said. "I have finally prevailed in love against that notorious charmer of women, the Lord Chancellor of the Exchequer. Tell me, how hath that gentleman fared in your esteem?"

The joke made her giggle through her tears, and he smiled at her for a moment before his expression grew serious. "Japery aside—you are not from Frisia, are you?"

"No," she said, afraid to meet his eyes. "I'm not."

"And you are also not the daughter of a duke."

"No." She hung her head. "I'm not high-born."

"I care not about that," he said. "But—you are not at liberty to take me to husband, are you? I would still have you, did you will it."

"I… no," she said. "I still hope Tawny—my kinswoman—might return for me. That she might take me back to our own… place."

"I thought as much," he said. "Of course you must go back to the ethereal realm whence you came. More the sadder for me, I admit."

"Henry," she began, then stopped. "Even if I remained, we couldn't be together. Your father would never allow it. I would ruin any chance you had of making a life here." *Plus, you'll be dead in three months.* The thought brought fresh tears to her eyes.

"For you," he remarked, "I might well quit England and remove us to the Continent to live out our lives in peace. I would renounce my claim to the throne and be the richer for the trade, methinks."

"You really would have made an awfully good husband," Beth said. The thought had just occurred to her that in sixteenth-century terms, eighteen was about on par with the thirty of the twenty-first century. Perhaps they were not so mismatched after all. Still, there was nothing to be done about it. "I wish I had met you under different circumstances," she said. *I wish you were my husband instead of the shithead I did marry.*

"It is kind of you to say."

"It is the truth."

"Still, a kind truth. You are a marvelous creature, Elizabeth."

"You can call me Beth," she said. "If—if it please you."

"My mother's name is Elizabeth," he said, "and she likes to be called Bess. It would please me greatly to use your nurse-name… Beth."

Henry tipped her chin up and gave her a gentle kiss on the lips. It was a kiss of love, of longing, and, she realized sadly, also a goodbye kiss.

"I want to tell you," he said as he broke away, "that I enjoyed the… congress we shared." He kept his expression carefully straight as he spoke, but Beth saw the red flush spread over his face. "I shall treasure its memory for all my life."

"And I," she said. "You might not understand what our night together meant to me. But it gave me back something I thought I had lost forever. So, know that you have changed my life's course."

He smiled. "As you have mine." He extended his hand, palm up, and Beth took it in hers. "As you promised," he said, "we are become the best of friends. But we need not say our final farewell yet. Will you take some wine?"

Beth's stomach growled loudly, reminding her that she hadn't eaten in almost a day now. FitzRoy laughed. "I take this as affirmative. And, you must be near starved." He moved to the table and poured wine into two cups, handing one to her and pulling out a chair for her. She sank into it and took a long, grateful drink, watching as he took bread and cheese from a little covered plate, slicing off a generous portion of each. "A crude repast, mayhap, but nourishing nonetheless for it."

Suddenly there was a terrible clatter outside. Beth sprang to her feet, nearly spilling her wine. "What was that?" she breathed, setting the cup hastily on the table.

He motioned her to be quiet. Anne reappeared at once, her expression wary.

Someone pounded on the door with a heavy object. "Anne Boleyn!" roared Thomas Cromwell on the other side of the door. "You have perverted the cause of holy justice for the last time!"

"Quickly, in here." Anne threw open the doors to her wardrobe. Beth and Henry scrambled inside, and she closed it up behind them.

"I know not your meaning, Chancellor," Anne called. "If any perversion hath been wrought, surely it is of your making."

"Let me pass! Or so help me, I shall tear this very door down! I know it was you and FitzRoy who loosed that creature!"

Beth heard footsteps, and then the sound of the bolt being thrown open. Henry squeezed her hand.

"Where is the witch?" Cromwell demanded.

"I do not know of any witch," Anne retorted. "You well know that I have been confined here for nigh a fortnight by your order."

"You lie!" Cromwell raged. "I have it from your maid's own lips that you and FitzRoy plotted to remove the witch from her jail. What was the aim of this treason against His Majesty, I wonder? Perhaps you thought to bring his demise with the help of this sorceress. Blame me not when Hell's fury descends upon you as payment!"

"I have not seen FitzRoy or any other person," Anne said coolly. "I think you are well aware of how little faith can be placed in the word of ladies' maids... not that I have any of those left."

"If you speak in whole sooth," Cromwell said, his voice moving closer to the wardrobe, "then you will not object to a search of your quarters."

There was no answer.

Beth heard footsteps as the Lord Chancellor moved across the room. "And I suppose you claim to be alone?"

"You know that I am," came the reply.

"Odd," Cromwell mused, "that a lady supping alone should require two cups."

Shit! She'd left her wine out on the table. How could she have been so stupid? Beth's heart pounded in her chest.

"Who were you entertaining?" he asked. "Mayhap you are hiding FitzRoy and his little plaything? Or perhaps you think to conceal from me another of your adulterous ventures."

Anne remained silent.

"Now where"—Beth heard his voice moving again—"might a fallen Queen hide her co-conspirators?"

Beth closed her eyes, trying to control her terror. She'd heard something of the torturous interrogation techniques used against witches in the sixteenth century. Many didn't even survive long enough to be executed, which of course was the presumed outcome of any witch trial. No innocent woman could be accused of witchcraft.

Thomas Cromwell threw open the door to the wardrobe then and bestowed a coldly triumphant smile upon Beth as he seized her by the hair and dragged her savagely into the light. She yelped in pain as he pulled her to her feet. "A fine den of vipers we have here," he observed.

Anne withdrew to one side, her dark eyes wide and alert.

Henry made a vain effort to rush to Beth's aid, but the room filled with guards. He dispatched the first with a hard sock to the jaw, then turned and caught another guard's fist in mid-air and gave him a rough shove backward into the sideboard, sending the Queen's wine carafe and glasses flying in shards to the floor.

Beth's breath caught in her throat as she saw a third guard advance behind him, blade in hand. "Henry!" she screamed, and he whirled, stopping short at the point of the man's sword. Unarmed, he had little choice but to put his reluctant hands up in surrender.

It was over, Beth realized with sudden clarity. It had been hours and hours, and Tawny still hadn't returned. A time traveler ought to be able to come back any time she pleased, if she could return at all. So it must be that it wasn't possible.

Beth would die here, in the sixteenth century, probably painfully, and there would be no one in her own time to say for sure what had happened.

It gave her a sick pang to think of Jules growing up without a mother. Without *her*.

She hoped Tawny would take care of things so her daughter wouldn't have to go live with Dan. She should have had legal paperwork drawn up about it—it was just that she'd always thought there would be more time for things like that.

Beth choked back a sob and elbowed Thomas Cromwell as hard as she could. If she was to be killed for treason, or witchcraft, or whatever, she might as well go out fighting. Nothing she did now could make her situation worse.

Cromwell repaid her for her trouble with a hard slap in the face that set her ears ringing and made her eyes water. With an angry exclamation, she raised her free hand and slapped him right back.

"Bitch," he spat, smacking the back of his hand across her cheek. She would have fallen but for his firm grip on her other arm.

"Whoreson!" she replied, raking her fingernails over his face.

Cromwell sputtered with anger and moved to slap her a third time, but Beth lunged forward and caught his hand in her teeth, champing down with all her strength. He roared in pain and attempted to jerk his bloodied hand away, but she held tight until he took her again by the hair and gave it a hard yank that fairly rattled her teeth in her skull. With a cry of pain, she lost her grip on his hand.

Henry struggled against the guards holding him, yelling something at Cromwell that sounded like a threat of disembowelment.

There was a crackling sound then and a heavy sensation in the air. From the corner of her eye, Beth saw Anne turn her head in apparent surprise, as Tawny materialized just outside the doorway.

"Oh, weird," Tawny said as she cut through the press of guards, who shrank away to let her pass. "Nothing is where I left it. Including the room. What time is it, anyway?"

"Er, ha' past six," one of the men-at-arms volunteered hesitantly.

"Silence, fool!" Cromwell thundered. "Do not speak to the witch!"

Tawny turned and looked at him, a strange, smirking expression on her face. "Indeed," she declared. "*These ladies* are no scholars of the dark arts,"—Tawny gestured at Beth and Anne—"but yes, you may call *me* witch! Satan's mistress, I am! Release you now that innocent woman, lest I disgorge my womb and send it to plague thee!"

Beth thought she saw Anne stifle a laugh, but several of the armed men shrank back in horror at this threat despite the Lord Chancellor's dark scowl. It was understandable. Tawny was taller than most of them, and the ghastliness of her disgorged womb could not be over-imagined.

"She speaks the truth," one of them said. "I have seen it before."

"That's right, bitches!" Tawny crowed, then turned. "Beth! I went back-slash-ahead to where we, uh, normally live and gave you… the thing! You've got the power! It's in your hands!"

What the hell was she talking about? Tawny was probably trying to avoid saying "time travel" in front of the denizens of the sixteenth century, but otherwise she was talking eighties-cartoon-sounding nonsense. Beth almost laughed at the absurdity, except that she was still being held by her hair, and she couldn't yet see how they planned to get out of this. Henry caught her eye and raised a questioning eyebrow. She shrugged helplessly.

"Cravens!" Cromwell accused his men, forgetting to hang on to Beth's hair in his fury. She moved away from him, her scalp stinging viciously. "Take the creature, fools! She is yet but a woman!"

No one moved.

"My lord," someone objected weakly, "she may curse us." There was a general murmur of agreement from the other men.

"*I* will curse you," he raged, throwing his hat to the floor and stamping angrily upon it. "Must I do everything myself?"

Henry FitzRoy laughed outright. Cromwell shot him a dark look and strode toward Tawny. "Quick, Beth!" Tawny cried. "Use the clicker!"

Beth stared at her in shock. *This* was the plan? "I haven't got one!" she said.

"Yes, you have! I went back to a week before you found the shower and surgically implanted it while you were asleep! It's how I tracked you here. Left hand! Click your thumb and index finger together!"

"What?"

"Think *Back to the Future*! *Bill and Ted*! The TARDIS! Come on! You're smarter than this!"

The light bulb flashed. Of course.

Cromwell took Tawny roughly by the shoulders. "Avaunt thou, douche-paladin!" she declared, and was gone. He stumbled, thrown off balance by her sudden disappearance, and crashed heavily to the floor, bellowing like an aurochs.

"Beth!" Henry FitzRoy cried, shrugging off the stunned men-at-arms and running to her. She turned to him, still dazed, staring at her hand. "Whence do you truly hail?" he asked.

She hesitated. It couldn't hurt anything now, she supposed. "America. The New World."

Cromwell was getting to his feet.

"I have to go," she said, snapping her thumb and fingers together twice.

"Will I see you again?" His eyes met hers, hope and something else she couldn't identify warring in their blue depths.

"I hope so," she said, then snapped her fingers once more.

EIGHTEEN

IN WHICH THE WORLD IS SET ARIGHT AFTER AN APPROPRIATE AMOUNT OF DRAMATIC TENSION

THE MINUTE SHE ARRIVED BACK IN THE FUTURE WITH NO BETH (THE FIRST time), Tawny had jumped out of the shower, reset the machine to a week in the past, and hopped back in. She successfully implanted the controls in Beth's hand without alerting anyone, including her past self. Then, of course, she had to rig up a tracking device that would allow the machine to send her straight to Beth's location so she could fight off Cromwell's goons and tell Beth that she had a clicker of her own.

Building something with electronic components meant she needed the lab with no chance of interruption. To do this she had waited until Other Tawny and Beth were both outside, then snuck into her bedroom, put on an outfit nearly identical to that which Other Tawny was wearing that day (white T-shirt, distressed skinny jeans, strappy sandals) and found Jules in her castle.

"Hey Jules, how's it going?"

"Great! The ponies are helping me build a pyramid."

"Awesome. You know how sometimes you want to go see a movie but your mom doesn't want to?"

"Yeah."

"I kind of have a similar issue, but I don't want to bug your mom about it. I was thinking, if you asked too, she might go with us?"

"What movie do you want to see?"

"Well, *Toy Tales 5*, of course." She knew that Jules desperately wanted to see the latest installment of Spiff Sprocket and Woodrow the Cowboy's adventures, and that Beth had been dragging her feet about it due to Jules's insistence that they watch *Toy Tales 4* approximately seven million times over the course of the last month.

"Yesssss!"

"And remember, no telling your mom that we're scamming her." Even if she did, Beth would most likely attribute it to Jules trying to con Tawny into taking her to *Toy Tales*, not the other way around.

"It's our secret." Jules twiddled her fingers malevolently, the way she'd seen cartoon villains do. At least, Tawny hoped that was where she'd learned it.

They shared a fat parrots wing bump, and Tawny crept off to hide in the attic.

Fifteen minutes later, she watched from an upstairs window as the three of them got into Tawny's car and headed out. Jules was the perfect co-conspirator.

Everything went well—in retrospect, too well. She changed back into her awesome dress and hat combo, uploaded Beth's coordinates into the machine, and headed off to the boss fight after looking up a few choice phrases in Early Modern English so she'd have plenty of snappy patter for Cromwell. After helping to free Beth, watching her realize that she had an implant, and relishing the Lord Chancellor's impotent rage at their imminent escape, Tawny was flush with the satisfaction of a job well done. She confidently snapped her fingers to return... only to find herself back in the lab, a full week before she'd left for 1536 the first time.

Fuuuuuuuuuuuuck.

She couldn't jump forward into the future—she didn't think that was even possible—and since she'd foolishly gone back to 1536 *before* her original trip, the machine had returned her to her "current" time. Which meant she had to wait an entire week for Other Tawny to leave for the initial voyage to Henry's court. Well, six days, twenty-three hours and fifty-five minutes.

So it was back to sharing her time between the attic and the drop-ceiling of her lab, sneaking out at night for food (she was absurdly grateful to find an abandoned box of Leia Bars left over from her failed attempt to go vegan) and some of Jules's colored chalk, so she could write out calculations on the floor. She filched a washcloth and some bottled water, which she split between drinking and whore's baths. Sometime around day four she realized that her current—past?—time travel difficulties were an updated version of that song about the old lady who swallowed a fly. By day five it was playing on a constant loop through her head.

Thankfully, she hadn't yet installed the security system she'd been considering, so she could move undetected around the house and the lab. At the end of the longest week she had ever spent, she watched from the ventilation shaft as Other Tawny tinkered with the machine settings, turned on the shower, stepped in, and disappeared. A couple of minutes later, Beth followed.

Tawny sighed with relief. Now that there weren't two of her in the same place any longer, the timelines would merge and everything would be okay. At least, that's what her calculations suggested. She had no idea what would really happen, which was why she'd brought the baseball bat and the plastic tarp. She desperately hoped it would be Beth and not Other Tawny who emerged from the shower. She didn't *want* to bludgeon her past self to death, but if it came down to that versus undoing reality… Tawny choked up on her bat.

She waited for what felt like a terrifying eternity—in reality, less than ninety seconds—before Beth popped back into existence.

"Um," Beth said, looking at the bat. Tawny tossed it aside.

"Uh," Tawny said, trying to figure out how to begin all the apologies this situation so urgently required.

But Beth just said, "I have to go get Jules," and dashed out of the lab, apparently forgetting that she was still wearing a bejeweled sixteenth-century robe and no shoes. Tawny made herself scarce the minute Beth was out the door, secluding herself in the lab to run a battery of tests confirming some basic facts and to make sure they were still living in the same universe.

She had extracted both herself and Beth from the jaws of death and back to the safety of the twenty-first century, with no apparent harm done—except, of course, to their friendship and all of Tawny's hopes and dreams. She had screwed shit up royally. Not in the "you changed the course of history and now everyone is a David-Icke-lizard-person" kind of way. That would almost have been better. At least she and Beth might have been lizard-friends. They could hang out together on the same rock, flick their tongues derisively at basic lizard bitches, and parthenogenically hatch a few more lizard-Juleses. Instead, she had to deal with all the good, old-fashioned uncomfortable weirdsies that seemed to naturally result from the complete emotional upheaval of any human relationship.

After that, she'd kept to herself, doing her best to stay away from Beth. The palpable silence between them made Tawny feel even worse, but she didn't know how to fix things. And she couldn't bring herself to begin the conversation that would no doubt lead to Beth quitting because Tawny had so irresponsibly endangered both her and her daughter. How could she face her friend after almost getting her burned at the stake? Or whatever the English did to witches back then.

Jules didn't seem to notice anything unusual, chattering about her school adventures and constantly asking Tawny when she'd have time to eat dinner with them again—which made the situation even more strained. It was an Ouroborosian nightmare of awkwardness.

FINALLY, THREE DAYS AFTER THEY'D RETURNED, TAWNY SNEAKED DOWN to the kitchen in the middle of the night. Beth had no doubt made something delicious, but Tawny felt guilty at even the thought of eating her (probably former) friend's good cooking. She didn't deserve it. Also, the sound of the microwave might give her position away. So PB and J it was.

Suddenly she stepped on something hard and pointy, which threw her off balance, and her ankle gave way under her weight. She toppled over with a yelp and rolled into the legs of an end table, knocking it over and breaking a lamp, which fell on her.

Lights switched on unbelievably fast. Oh, God. Tawny tried to scuttle away, but something had bound her feet together like a bola. Now that the lights were on, she could see it was two somethings, brightly colored and tied up with string.

"Damn you, ponies!" Tawny cursed, just as Beth ran into the living room, trailed by a wide-eyed Jules. Beth took one look at the chaos and sighed, running her hand backward through her hair.

"God, Jules, what have I told you about leaving your toys out? Tawny might be seriously hurt!"

"No, I'm fine." Tawny protested, trying and failing to wriggle into an upright sitting position. She'd somehow gotten herself tangled up in the lamp cord. "Really, I am. I know I've got a pair of scissors around here somewhere."

Beth knelt next to Tawny and, without looking her in the eye, began fussing at the string tying the ponies together around her ankles while Tawny cringed with embarrassment. After a moment, Beth sat back, rubbing her hands.

"I can't get this string undone. Jules, did you weave fishing line in with the yarn?"

"You guys should just go back to bed." This had officially reached DEFCON-one-caliber humiliation. "If I can't find the scissors I can free myself by rubbing the string against something sharp." Why wouldn't they just leave her to her misery?

Jules came up to them, squeezing past her mother. "I'll help you, Tawny." She knelt down and deftly picked the knots apart, releasing Tawny's feet from the bonds of pony slavery. Beth shook her head.

"Okay, Jules, time to go back to bed, sweetie. We'll talk about this thing with your toys in the morning."

Jules blinked solemnly at her mother, turned to leave, then turned back and did her kakapo run to Tawny. She flapped her arms and reached out an elbow.

"Fat parrots forever?"

Tawny blinked back her tears and stuck out her own elbow, bumping Jules's gently. "Fat parrots forever."

Jules straightened up and gave them both a long look. "Quit being silly, you guys." Then she trotted back to her room.

"Wow." Tawny got to her feet and brushed herself off, marveling in awe at the genius of five-year-olds. "I think she Parent-Trapped us." Beth looked like she was trying to work up the courage to say something, so Tawny attempted an ice-breaker. "Or, should I say… Parrot-Trapped us?"

Beth made several half-laugh, half-uncomfortable-throat-clearing sounds, then drew herself up straight and took a deep breath. Shit. It was time for the "I'm leaving forever because you almost got me killed and you're far too weird to be actual friends with" speech. Tawny swallowed the lump in her throat. She should have stuck to making robot companions. At least robots wouldn't break her heart after she alienated them out of utter stupidity.

She stared dully at the bits of shattered lamp scattered across the floor, waiting for the news.

"Are you going to fire me?" Beth asked after a moment. "I respect the fact that you don't want to talk about what happened, but if you're firing me I need to know. I have to make plans for where Jules and I will go, and—"

Tawny was stunned. "Are you kidding? Me, fire *you*?" She stood there, staring for a moment until she realized Beth was serious. "After all that shit that went down with Cromwell? I almost got you killed, and all because I didn't think to put a 'Do Not Disturb' sign on the lab door. It was so thoughtless of me. And then, when you showed up, I should've just taken us home like you wanted, before the banquet. We would have figured out the issue with the machine then, I'd have given you an implant before we had an emergency on our hands, and there would have been no threat to anyone's life."

"Yeah, well, if I hadn't shown up, none of the stuff with Cromwell would have even happened. That's all my fault for—" She broke off, and Tawny noticed that she was actually blushing.

"For what? Getting caught up in my stupid plans to recreate my sorority glory days?"

Beth stared at her feet. "I... deflowered Henry FitzRoy."

"Uh... whoa. Is... was... he legal?"

"Yeah, it turned out his date of birth was fudged for political reasons. He was legal even by our standards."

"So I guess he wasn't such an asshole after all?"

"After his guards took me back to his chambers, I thought I could seduce him to get away, but he turned out to be sweet. The snarky persona was just an act to impress his father."

"That's what Anne said, too. Well, in that case—get it, girl!" Tawny held up a hand for a high five, only to be disappointed as Beth continued to stare miserably at the floor. She awkwardly lowered her hand.

"I'm the reason everything went so badly. It must have taken hours for you to find me. I—" She glanced up at Tawny. "I was so caught up I didn't even think once about how worried you must be. And all just for some sex."

"Don't feel bad about that. I got side-tracked, too. Was it at least *good* sex?"

Beth didn't answer for a moment. "It was... wonderful. Maybe because—maybe because I needed so badly to feel like I could still matter to someone in that way. It was like he gave me back something I didn't realize I'd lost. I mean, I'm sure he only felt that way about me because he's so young and he was also a virgin, but he made me feel beautiful. And... loved. Or something."

Tawny felt a rush of sympathy for her friend. "It wasn't because he was a virgin who didn't know any better. He—he was the one who tried to save you, right? From Cromwell?"

Beth nodded.

"You know what? I think the fact of Dan forgetting what an awesome bitch you are made *you* forget what an awesome bitch you are. Henry FitzRoy saw who you were right away. He didn't do anything except show you where to look for something that was never gone in the first place."

"Well, I'm glad you think I'm an awesome bitch. I... I hope you're right." Beth looked at Tawny with a serious expression. "What happened to you, by the way? How did you get side-tracked?"

"I—well, it wasn't like your thing with Henry." Tawny wanted to tell Beth about her encounter, to share with someone else how much it had mattered, but something stopped her. Maybe it was that she'd never had sex with anyone on the eve of their imprisonment and execution. Or maybe she just felt like Anne was famous enough already and deserved a little privacy. "Long story short, I ended up hanging out with Anne Boleyn for several hours, talking about science and feminism. God, she was so smart—I told her about our run-in with the guards and she was the one who figured out it was FitzRoy's people and helped me her find the way to his chambers to look for you. She's an amazing person."

Beth shook her head. "I just can't let go of this idea that we've done some irreparable damage to the fabric of space and time and it's all going to come unraveled at any minute."

"I've spent the last couple of days dredging up every resource I could find about the history of that day to make sure we didn't change the past. I even called an acquaintance at Oxford and got her to dig around in their archives and all she can find is records of Anne and some of her ladies being charged with witchcraft, but apparently modern historians believe that was just a discrediting tactic by Anne's detractors."

"Wow. I haven't been able to bring myself to even look at a history book. I've been too sick over it. We disappeared right in front of them. Twice."

"It seems like anything we did got swept up in all the chaos and excitement surrounding Anne's removal to the Tower, the arrests of several men connected to her, and her eventual trial. Which syncs up with my theories on time travel… I think the past is 'stretchy' enough to accommodate some changes, as long as it's nothing major. Nobody died or didn't die when they weren't supposed to. The events we took part in fit with what was already happening—there were visitors to the palace, and an overnight kerfuffle that coincided with the Queen's trial preparations."

"That makes sense," Beth said. "In fact, I bet Cromwell would have wanted to cover up the evidence that he had failed. It's funny how the historical record doesn't reflect what a colossal jerk he was."

"Yeah, he was a dickhole," Tawny agreed. "I found a reference to a letter of Cromwell's that described an 'incident of female lewdness and witchcraft most foul,' but apparently the letter itself was lost. That may have something to do with observed versus non-observed realities, which is why I implanted the controls in your hand while you were sleeping. I didn't want to change your behavior in what was technically our past."

"Wow. That's brilliant."

"Aw, well." Tawny shrugged, pleased.

"So we're off the hook?" Beth asked. "You're sure we haven't created some kind of parallel universe… or collapsed a bunch of wave functions?"

"What?"

"You've been reading up on history, well, I've been reading up on time travel."

Tawny tried to conceal her amusement. "As far as I can tell, we're in the clear."

"We got lucky," Beth said.

"Yeah, we did!"

Beth groaned and rolled her eyes.

Well—now was as good a time as any to discuss things. "So," Tawny segued, "now that you have the implant for the machine, want to try it out again sometime?"

She winced as the words came out. God, she was so bad at dealing with people. She couldn't even talk to her only friend in the entire world without sounding like a cheesy pickup artist.

But how else did one propose time traveling sex shenanigans?

"I can't," Beth said. "I want to—but—I just don't think I can."

"Why?"

Beth looked miserable. "I'm not responsible enough."

"I don't understand. You're more responsible than I am, by a long shot."

"You don't get it—how many of the rules I broke. I got drunk. I let Henry fall practically in love with me because I wasn't honest with him. And I let my thing with him take priority over trying to find you. And—" There seemed to be more, but Beth choked up.

"What?" Tawny asked, lamely putting her hand on Beth's shoulder. "What is it?"

Beth immediately hugged her around the middle, crying for real now. "I'm scared it's my fault he died," she mumbled. "Jules had a fever last week, remember? I think I gave him my future microbes and that's what made him sick."

"I don't think that's possible," Tawny said. "That's how it happened before we ever went back, right?"

"Well, yeah," she sniffled. "But… paradoxes. Or something. Would we even know if we had accidentally changed things?"

"I don't think it works like that. When you travel, you're briefly on the outside of time, so you'd at least have a moment of remembering the original timeline. Henry wasn't your fault." Just the same, Tawny felt a sudden chill of doubt. What if it was the fracas in Anne's apartments that had sealed the Queen's fate? Would Tawny know the difference if what she remembered now wasn't what had happened originally? Her equations said she would, but…

"He deserved better. I just—he deserved more, that's all." Beth pulled away, wiping her eyes. "I can't believe how much crying I've done over this the last few days."

"Was... Henry the only thing bothering you about doing this again?"

"Well, I mean, I have Jules to worry about too. I just... don't think I should." Beth looked at the floor.

Tawny struggled to hide her disappointment, keeping her expression carefully neutral. "Sure, I get that, but... you don't ever want to date again?"

"Of course I want to date again. I've been so sexually deprived for the last two years that I half-considered dragging some poor delivery boy into the foyer the other day to have my way with him. I don't want a relationship, not now, anyway. I just keep thinking about how many crappy people there are in the world, and it only takes exposure to one scuzzy boyfriend to do serious damage to a kid. I have to put her needs before my wants."

"You wouldn't pick someone scummy."

"No, but they never start off that way, do they? I picked Dan, and he ran away with the divorced lady down the street. Last I knew they were living on her alimony because if he worked he'd have to pay me child support." Beth wiped her eyes. "Oh, and remember how cute I thought Lance was? Yeah. So he's gay. He's bringing his partner with him on Saturday."

"He is?" Tawny asked in surprise. "Huh. Well... I may be overstepping my bounds here, but you've got to stop punishing yourself over how things worked out with Dan. At least half his DNA didn't suck."

Beth didn't answer.

"And Jules—kids don't care what you're doing when you're off having 'grown-up' time. Like you said, it's scuzzy guys hanging around that would be a bad example for her, not a girls' night out. So here's the thing. I think you should say yes—we'll follow the rules now, and the five minute thing means that unlike a night out, Jules will never even know you were gone. She would want you to be happy. You deserve it."

"You really believe that?"

Tawny looked straight into Beth's eyes and did her best Luigi impression. "Daisy. I wanna be witchoo."

Beth's eyes welled up again.

"Oh, God, I'm sorry, I was trying to both lighten the mood and communicate how much you mean to me by referencing a fun moment that we shared with only each other and a phone psychic, and that was wrong, I swear I didn't mean to be flippant."

"It's not you, it's just—I can't believe I'm being offered this chance to get to 'have it all'—spending my days with a job I enjoy, getting to use my education, and being able to spend all the time with Jules that I need to. Getting to have an actual, fully realized adult life and still be there for her. I keep feeling like it's too good to be true, like it's all just going to slip away from me and I'll have to go back to the way we were living before. Jules is so happy here and I thought I'd ruined everything with you and me."

Tawny swallowed her fear, reached out, and hugged her. "All this time since we got back, I was convinced you were going to quit because I was such a dumbass and didn't tell you about my secret time travel experiments. I didn't know what I would do if I had to live with having screwed all this up. Curl up and die, maybe."

Beth smiled through her tears and returned the hug with a little choking sound. "I was so sure you were going to fire me. I'm sorry. For everything. For not talking to you about this sooner."

Tawny felt tears pricking the back of her eyes and broke away. "Jesus, this is some serious 'Gift of the Magi' shit." She took a deep breath. "I'm sorry, too. And you didn't screw up—you were the one who rescued me from Henry's court, remember? I couldn't believe how quick you were on your toes."

"Yeah, well, okay. But when you threatened Cromwell and his guards with your demonic uterus? That was *ah-mazing*. They believed you! Well, the guards did, anyway. I think Anne knew better."

Tawny felt the lump of sadness in her throat melt away. "Thanks. In undergrad, I had this History of Physics class, which at first made the ancient world seem surprisingly sophisticated with their understanding of advanced concepts, until our teacher told us about the persistence of the wandering womb theory, to make sure we understood that Plato didn't get *everything* right. People believed that dumb shit up through the 1800s."

Beth giggled.

"Anyway, I'm glad we didn't have sex with Henry," Tawny said, trying to lighten the mood. "I wish nobody ever had to sleep with him ever again. In the past when he was alive, I mean."

"Agreed. There are so many other monarchs I'd much rather get it on with." Beth wiped her eyes. "Hell, English monarchs, even. I've had a crush on Richard the Third since high school."

Tawny's breath caught. "Does that mean—"

Beth looked up and met her eyes briefly before looking away again. "I don't know. I'm still a little worried I'm not cut out for this—but I also can hardly remember the last time I felt so alive. I was almost at a point where I thought I had to give up that part of my life. I mean, not that I thought I'd never have sex again, but I didn't think I'd get to have sex like we used to."

"So…"

Beth took a shaky breath. "So—okay. Yes. I'll do this with you. And you have a point about what's really best for Jules. Fucking famous people in the past isn't without risk, but it's not likely to ruin my daughter's childhood or give her a bad example of adult relationships. And—it was so much fun. Besides, the buddy system is a rule for a reason. I shouldn't let you go alone."

Tawny couldn't keep the huge grin off her face. "Come to think of it, we should develop some new Field Protocols to deal with all of these time travel issues."

"Like what, taking extra precautions not to change major events?"

"Sure, some of it is pretty obvious. But in addition to medical prophylaxis for us, we should monitor our general health and the state of our microflora to keep the chances of disease transmission as low as possible."

"Good idea." Beth nodded. "I think I'll finally get that IUD I've been considering. I don't want to even imagine what kind of havoc a time travel baby would cause. Also, can you imagine having another Jules around? We can't let there be as many of them as there are of us."

"Though… it might be neat to at least collect samples and sequence people's genomes."

"Ugh, I vote no on that one. But we will need to update our record-keeping system to reflect the dates of our research encounters—and what if we end up researching somebody at multiple points in their lives?"

"Oh man, I hadn't even thought of that. Think of the graphs we could plot!" Tawny rubbed her hands together in anticipation. She thought for a moment. "You know," she said, "I've always been curious not only if all the fuss about Einstein is true, but whether he made some huge leap forward, sexually speaking, after he published his theory of general relativity."

"What, was he supposed to be a secret sex god or something?"

"Nothing secret about it. While he was working on that he was getting more ass than a port-a-potty at a music festival."

Beth laughed, hard, before her expression grew serious. "Wait—before we go any further—promise me you don't have a Southern belle fetish or anything like that? I don't think I can pretend like plantation life was morally okay. I mean, I know it's just a fantasy and those people aren't actually condoning slavery… but for me, I'd feel gross."

"Ugh, yeah. Hard pass. Abolitionists only."

"Oh, good, me too." Beth looked relieved. "I mean, if I'm banging anyone in the antebellum or—bellum—era, I'd rather be double-teamed by John Brown and Frederick Douglass."

"That's fine. Leaves more Joshua Lawrence Chamberlain for me."

Beth raised an eyebrow.

"What? I saw that Ken Burns documentary."

"Well, if we're talking 1800s, then I want to visit John Humphrey Noyes and the Oneida community."

"Oh, God, Rosalind Franklin."

"Who's that?"

"Basically she discovered DNA."

"Oh. Wow. And what about Mansa Musa?"

"The king dude who made the pilgrimage to Mecca and left a trail of gold in his wake? Geez, we should write this down." Tawny crossed to the counter, grabbed one of the many notebooks she had scattered throughout the house in case of random ideas, and quickly scribbled the names. "Okay, what next?"

Beth thought for a second. "Flavius Josephus."

Tawny added it to the page. "You can tell me later who that is. And I'm putting down Mary Read and Anne Bonny."

"God, yes. And Hot Young Joseph Stalin."

"Was that a thing?"

"You bet your ass it was. He was way hotter than Trotsky. Oh, Trotsky, though—write him down. And Lord Byron."

"How about Helen Keller?"

"Ann Sullivan would be better. Besides, we'd have to learn to finger spell first or something."

"Oh, trust me, I already know all about finger… spelling."

"Gross, Tawny. Gross. Add Emma Goldman. She's my favorite anarcho-syndicalist."

Tawny jotted down the names. "Oh my God, I'm so glad you agreed to do this with me. I'm not sure I've ever been happier than in this moment. Oh, Ching Shih. I want to know if she really was the pirate queen of a whole fleet that was bigger than the Spanish Armada."

"That's three pirates you've named."

"What?" Tawny shrugged. "Maybe I have a thing for pirates. Anyway, what else?"

Beth laughed. "The Marquis de Sade. Although, that's a little on the nose. Never mind. I'm not into sadism anyway."

"What about the Borgias?"

"Which ones?"

"Dunno. Dealer's choice?"

When they ran out of steam an hour later—they'd been too convulsed with laughter to continue after Beth suggested they should spy on Caligula to find out if he was really the pervert history claimed he was—Tawny had recorded over two hundred names, including (jokingly) the name of Caligula's horse Incitatus, who had been made a Roman senator at the decree of his master.

"Holy shit, look at this," Beth said. "This is going to be just like our old project, except better because we're no longer restricted to the twenty-first century. Although, there's fully a third of this list I wouldn't even touch. I mean, King Herod? Why did you write him down?"

Tawny brightened. "Apparently he died from complications related to genital gangrene. Maggots were involved. Anyway, some of the names I listed are more curiosity than sexual interest. The entirety of the space-time continuum is within our reach, so we might as well write down anyone who sounds interesting. We can be anywhere, visit anyone, at any time. We might as well be open-minded about our genital research."

Beth snorted. "Genital research? You make it sound so appealing."

They grinned at each other like dweebs.

Tawny looked down at the pages they'd filled. "One thing's for sure."

"What's that?"

"We're gonna need a bigger book."

ABOUT THE AUTHORS

IVERY KIRK lives in Kansas City, where she still practices her first profession of financial workflow optimization. She accepts the general lack of enthusiasm that most people have for her first passion, but holds out hope that adventure stories about time traveling sexcapades will prove more interesting to the general public.

LUNA TEAGUE lives in the Midwest and is a Ph.D. candidate in the biosciences, which takes up most of her life. However, she finds time to write her sexy adventures when in the grip of a condition she calls "Ambien madness." TimeBangers is her first novel-length published work.